POWER & GLORY

LAURA DOWERS

Blue Laurel
Press

ISBN: 978-1-912968-25-1

ALSO AVAILABLE BY LAURA DOWERS

THE TUDOR COURT

The Queen's Favourite

The Queen's Rebel

The Queen's Spymaster

The Queen's Rival: A Short Story

Master Wolsey

THE RISE OF ROME

The Last King of Rome

The Eagle in the Dovecote

STANDALONE NOVELS

When the Siren Sings

POWER & GLORY

CHAPTER ONE

1515

Charles Brandon was telling a bawdy tale.

The duke had commandeered the attention of the entire top table, flapping his massive hands at the diners to listen, assuring them they'd like what he had to say. There was no ignoring Brandon once he'd started talking, and so he had an attentive audience.

His tale concerned a French lady-in-waiting of dubious morals, and he swore it was a true story. He had heard about it, he said, when he went to France to bring Mary back to England after the death of her husband, the king. At times, he was barely able to get the words out, he was sniggering so much. The anecdote was typical Brandon, boisterous and ribald, and Thomas Wolsey looked along the table at his fellow listeners to see if they did indeed find his story as amusing as the duke had promised.

His wife, the Mary in the story whom the duke had fetched from France, was sitting by his side, petite, pretty, a willing listener. She smiled knowingly as her husband talked, as if she had heard the story many times before and delighted in letting him tell it.

Her brother, Henry, was leaning forward, peeking around Mary to catch Brandon's every word. His handsome face was flushed pink and his small mouth pinched old-maidishly, twitching at words he knew he shouldn't condone but couldn't help but attend to. Once or twice, he glanced at his wife sitting on his other side, checking to see whether Katherine found Brandon's words offensive. If she did, he would silence his friend.

But Henry need not concern himself. Katherine had long ago learnt to ignore Brandon when he became garrulous and vulgar. She sat almost painfully erect, her nose tilted up – whether out of disdain, or because raising it was the only way to ensure her heavy gable hood stayed in place, it was difficult to tell. Her eyes were determinedly fixed on the trestle tables that lined the Great Hall of York Place. A little too determinedly, one might say, as if she was trying to show she was above such rude comedy. Katherine had no great liking for her husband's best friend, but as his loyal wife she tolerated Brandon. Despite Henry's care for her sensibilities, it would never occur to her to ask Henry to tell his friend to moderate his language.

The obscene ending of the story delivered, Brandon gave his bull roar of a laugh, provoking the guests seated at the lower tables into turning their heads in his direction. It was only Brandon, they quickly concluded, and returned to their own conversations.

Thomas beamed as Brandon sought the eyes of each of his listeners to make sure they had got the joke, not because he had considered the story amusing, merely to be polite. The duke of Suffolk was nothing to him, just a recently ennobled young man with rather too much arrogance for comfort, but Brandon was important to Henry, and that was reason enough for Thomas to be civil.

And to be fair to Brandon, he had been of some use in the last month or so in distracting Henry from the goings on in Italy. Back in September, the Council had learnt that the new king of France was planning a military expedition into Italy to take back lands lost decades, if not centuries, before. Almost all the Council had agreed that this plan, if true, was doomed to failure as King Francis had no great experience in leading a military campaign. Henry had been even more sceptical, declaring Francis wouldn't dare invade Italy because he was scared of what England would do if he did. The counsellors had looked at one another beneath lowered lids at this quite ridiculous remark. If the Council was sure of anything, it was that England was perceived as a threat to no one, least of all the king of France, but none dared say so to Henry. Instead, they all agreed that King Francis would suffer an ignominious defeat in Italy and scuttle back to France with his tail between his legs.

But that hadn't happened, and the Council had

read with horror and disbelief the reports of a French victory at the town of Marignano. The pope was deeply worried that this battle would prove to be the first of many such victories for the young French king.

When Thomas had told Henry of the French victory, he had raged up and down his privy chamber, cursing everyone who had told him France could not possibly prevail, forgetting it had been he who had prophesied disaster for the French. He demanded to know how Francis had managed such a victory, and Thomas had consulted his notes with trembling hands. The Venetians had aided the French, he told Henry, and this had made Henry halt. 'The blasted Venetians,' Henry said, shaking his head at Thomas as if to say, 'What could anyone expect?' The Venetians, an independent republic, were always causing problems, delighting in any endeavour that would antagonise the pope.

But Thomas had discerned that what made Henry truly angry was less the French victory and more learning that the pope was paying court to King Francis. Pope Leo evidently believed France was a force to be reckoned with and therefore worth cultivating as an ally, and Henry's vanity was offended. Pope Leo had never bothered to court Henry. In an effort to soothe his affronted heart, Thomas had urged Brandon to convince Henry the pope was just hedging his bets in befriending Francis. Brandon's assurances had taken Henry's mind off the young French king, whom he had come to think of as a rival.

And yet, though Henry might have put France to

the back of his mind, Thomas had not. In many respects, he thought Henry right to consider Francis a rival, and he sensed an opportunity. It occurred to Thomas that all the other powers in Europe would be just as unhappy as Henry about the French victory, and that it would take only a little nudge to persuade them to enter into an alliance against France. When Thomas suggested this, Henry was delighted, if a little dubious.

'We've made alliances before, Thomas,' he said, 'and been taken advantage of.'

Thomas knew Henry was remembering a previous alliance against the French with his father-in-law, King Ferdinand of Spain, when he said this. That alliance had ended in humiliation for Henry when it became clear Ferdinand had no intention of keeping to his side of the bargain. But Thomas assured Henry he didn't mean an alliance with King Ferdinand but with the Emperor Maximilian.

'But Maximilian is as slippery as Ferdinand,' Henry had cried, and Thomas had smiled and agreed, admitting they would need to be very careful. And so Richard Pace, Henry's secretary, had been dispatched to meet with the Emperor Maximilian to broach the idea of an anti-French alliance. He may even have arrived at the emperor's palace already, Thomas reasoned, and wondered if there was any news from the king's secretary.

Thomas let his gaze wander around the hall as he sipped at his wine. His guests seemed to be enjoying themselves, and so they should, for he set a magnificent table. There had been dishes of boar and venison, and peacocks cooked and fitted back inside their skins to display their full plumage. The wine came from Burgundy, and the desserts were flavoured with spices from India. He doubted whether these courtiers stuffing their faces with his food and drink had ever eaten or drank as well anywhere else.

The feast had been going on for almost four hours and was very nearly over. He could see his servers hovering at the entrance to the hall, waiting for the signal from the steward that they could begin to clear away. The head steward would be waiting for his own signal from Thomas, and Thomas gave it when, out of the corner of his eye, he saw Henry slump back in his chair with an exhausted puff, a sign he had finished eating.

The steward signalled, and the servers swarmed into the hall and began to clear the tables. The half-empty dishes would be taken back to the kitchen and the leavings scraped into a large wooden bowl to give to the people waiting at the gates as broken meats. There would be an especially large crowd this evening, for all of London knew this had been a special day for Thomas, the day he had been made a cardinal.

It was strange how long ago the ceremony already seemed. Had it really been only a few hours since he had left Westminster Abbey and embarked on a stately procession to York Place to show the people their new cardinal? His own personal entourage of bodyguards and servants had gone before him, blowing trumpets and holding up banners bearing his coat of arms. Following Thomas had been the king and queen, all the nobles and a collection of arch-bishops and bishops. All these important people had walked behind him, the butcher's son from Ipswich!

The banging of the trestle tables as they were dismantled and taken into the corridor returned Thomas to the present. The courtiers had been shooed to the sides of the hall and now mingled freely, finishing conversations, beginning others. Thomas knew Henry would want to dance and looked up towards the minstrels' gallery. The musicians were there, fiddling with their instruments. They had been given their instructions and knew they were to begin playing when the tables had been cleared away. As the first notes of music wafted over the gallery and down into the hall below, the courtiers smiled at one another, their eyes already picking out their partners for the dancing.

Henry chuckled and turned to Thomas. He jerked his head at the gallery. 'One of mine, Thomas?'

'Indeed, Your Grace,' Thomas said. *What else would I have played? I know how to please you.*

'What's that?' Brandon asked. 'This tune's written by you, Hal?'

Katherine patted Henry's hand with her left while her right hand caressed the swell of her pregnant belly. ''Tis one of my favourites. My lord claims he wrote it for me.'

'I don't claim, Kate, I did write it for you,' Henry sighed, shaking his head in mock exasperation.

Ever the gallant knight, Thomas thought, his foot tapping to the music. There would be no dancing for him; clergymen did not dance. He wasn't sorry for it. Had he attempted to dance, he would have made a fool of himself for he had never been taught such an accomplishment, dancing never being required of a secretary or a priest.

Henry rose and extended his hand to Katherine. She smiled and took it, and he led her to the centre of the hall, calling for the musicians to play a pavane tune. Brandon and Mary fell in behind them, and other courtiers hurried to do the same.

Thomas moved away, heading for the wooden arches behind which he knew at least one of his secretaries would be waiting to update him on what had been happening in his office during the day. He smiled as he went, accepting the congratulations of courtiers eager to be acknowledged by the new cardinal.

He passed through an arch and Brian Tuke, his chief secretary, greeted him.

'My congratulations, sir,' he said. 'I understand everything passed off well.'

'Everything passed off extremely well, Brian, thank you,' Thomas said. 'Anything important I should know about?' There was always something that had to be dealt with, but he trusted Tuke not to bother him with routine matters today.

Tuke shook his head. 'Nothing of any importance.'

'What about Pace? Have we heard anything from him yet?' Thomas asked hopefully.

'Not yet, but there is a letter from your sister,' Tuke said, holding up a piece of paper. 'I brought it in case you would like to read it now?'

Thomas considered the letter for a moment, staring at Elizabeth's scratchy writing, then said, 'Later. Put it in my chamber and I shall read it when I go to bed.'

'Very good.' Tuke made to go, then halted. 'If I may just ask, should I call you "Your Eminence" now?'

Thomas's chest swelled at the new title. 'Yes, Brian. "Your Eminence" from this moment on. Give instruction to all the staff that it be so.'

'Of course, Your Eminence.' Tuke bowed and left to return to the office he shared with six other secretaries and a dozen clerks.

Your Eminence, Thomas mentally repeated as he returned to the hall to watch the dancing. *Of course, Your Eminence. At once, Your Eminence.* How good that title sounded.

~

The bells had chimed the second hour by the time his guests had either left for their own London homes or taken advantage of the rooms Thomas had offered to those without private London residences and retired.

It had been a very long day, thoroughly enjoyable, yes, but long, and Thomas climbed the wooden stairs to his bedchamber with leaden legs. He disrobed in the antechamber, his body servant taking the scarlet cardinal robes with reverence and laying them neatly in a trunk. The cardinal's hat with its broad brim and long tassels had its own silk-lined box to rest in.

Clad in his nightgown, Thomas took the candle the man held out to him and bid him goodnight. He opened the bedchamber door quietly, wincing as it squealed on its hinges. As he stepped inside, he looked towards the bed and saw the shape beneath the covers move.

'Tom, is that you?' a voice mumbled.

'Yes, it's me,' he replied, closing the door. 'I didn't mean to wake you.'

He set his candle down on the bedside table and it cast a weak glow over the woman pushing herself up onto her elbow. Joan Larke's nightcap sat lopsided on her head and tendrils of dark yellow hair clung to her cheeks. She wore the slightly confused expression of someone who wasn't sure whether she was awake or not.

'I told you to wake me,' Joan scolded, reaching for the cup of beer on the table beside her. She took a mouthful. 'Has everyone gone?'

'All gone or retired for the night,' he said.

Joan folded back the bed covers on his side and patted the goose-feather mattress. 'Brian told me the ceremony at the abbey went well. And the feast? How was the feast?'

Thomas climbed into the bed and sank back against the soft pillows with a grateful sigh. He pulled the covers up to his chest. 'Excellent, too. The king enjoyed himself, that's the main thing.'

'I heard the music. I wanted to come down and watch the dancing, but I thought you wouldn't like that.'

'Just as well you did not, my dear. It wouldn't have done if you had been seen.'

'No, I suppose not,' she said, putting her hand on his. He heard the sad note in her voice but decided not to comment on it. It was too late and he was too tired for that old conversation. And besides, Joan knew he was right, knew her place was not in plain sight but behind closed doors. 'Tell me, did you feel God with you when you were made cardinal?'

Thomas considered. 'I believe I did, Joan, when the cardinal's hat was put on my head.' He gave a little laugh. 'It's all such a blur, though, I may have imagined it.'

'He was there, Tom,' Joan said. 'How could He not be when you have moved so much closer to him?'

'Huh,' Thomas snorted, 'you wouldn't think I've moved closer to God if you had heard John Colet speak today.'

'Who is John Colet?'

'Colet is the dean of St Paul's,' he said, his voice turning angry as the memory of Colet returned. 'Colet took it upon himself to remind me in his sermon of the duties of a churchman. He said the scarlet robes of a cardinal are a symbol of love that must be bestowed upon everyone, rich and poor alike, and that a cardinal does not exist to be served but to serve others. Who does Colet think he is that he can lecture me so?'

'Oh, never mind him. Read your letter.' Joan nodded at his side table and he saw he had put his candle down upon the letter from Elizabeth. He slid it out and broke the seal. His tired eyes skimmed over Elizabeth's words. To his surprise, she was not after a favour but was instead offering her congratulations. It was a kind letter and Thomas was touched.

'There, you see,' Joan said when he had read it to her as she asked. 'She does love you.'

'I suppose she does,' Thomas conceded and was about to shift down the bed and close his eyes when Joan asked him to tell her about the feast.

'I'm tired, Joan,' he protested.

'Oh, please, Tom. You won't have time to tell me tomorrow and you will forget all the details.'

Thomas sighed and told her of the king and queen, of Brandon and Mary, and of the dancing and music. He did his best to satisfy her curiosity about the dresses the women wore and the jewels that glinted in the men's caps.

'Now, that's enough,' he said eventually, patting her thigh beneath the covers. 'I am very tired and I have an early start.'

'You always have an early start,' she grumbled as he lay down. 'You should delegate more of your work now you are a cardinal.'

'And if I do that, and the work is not done as it should be, what then? Do I say to the king, "Forgive me, Your Grace, but I could not be bothered to attend to it myself?"'

Joan tutted. 'The king would not complain at the odd mistake.'

'Perhaps not the odd one, no,' Thomas agreed, 'but he would if I made a habit of them.'

'Plenty of people around the king make mistakes. Look how he forgave the duke of Suffolk for marrying his sister against his express command.'

'And there you have it. The *duke* of Suffolk! I'm not a duke, Joan, nor an earl, I'm not even a knight. I have no noble blood to protect me, no family to rally round and defend me. Everything I have, everything I am, I owe to the king. If I displease him, and he sought to punish me by taking away my office, I would have nothing but my Church titles and benefices.'

'Would that be so terrible, Tom? You already have so many Church titles and benefices, far more than any man needs. You make it sound as if the king's favour is all.'

'It is all,' Thomas insisted. 'Without it, I am nothing.'

'You were made cardinal today,' Joan said angrily. 'Does that count for nothing?'

'I will never make you understand, will I, my dear?'

'Understand what, Tom?'

'That serving God is not enough for me, it never has been. I need to be doing good in this world and in ways that will make a difference. A simple priest can

13

serve his parish and be happy in his duty, but to the wide world, he is nothing.'

'Fame and glory. Is that what you want?'

Thomas shook his head. 'Fame and glory are one and the same thing. But power and glory,' he reached up and pinched her cheek, 'now those are things worth trying for.'

CHAPTER TWO

His Imperial Majesty, Emperor Maximilian, took his
doctor's arm and dropped by painful degrees into his
cushioned chair, cursing the doctor, cursing the horse
that had caused his riding accident all those years ago,
and cursing God for making him endure such
torment. When his leg ached as much as this, he
almost wished he could have it cut off. He looked out
of the window and cursed the weather too for good
measure. Rain always made his leg worse, and it had
been raining for days. Maximilian wished fervently it
would stop.

'You should put your leg up when it starts to
swell,' the doctor said, peering at Maximilian's puffy
ankle, the mottled flesh almost folding down over his
shoe. 'How many times must I tell you?'

'I should have you imprisoned for impertinence,'
Maximilian said and waved him away.

The doctor, unimpressed by the threat, shuffled

away, muttering under his breath about stubborn patients who wouldn't follow their doctor's advice.

Maximilian made a face as the door closed upon him. He knew his doctor was right, but he hated the idea of his subjects seeing him with his foot up on a cushion like an old man with the gout. He *was* an old man, but at least he didn't have gout.

The door opened and his chief minister, Bishop Gurk, entered. 'You've upset your doctor again, I see.'

'I pay him a very good salary just so I can upset him. What do you want?'

'An emissary has arrived from England. A Master Richard Pace, sent by the king to discuss the situation with France.'

Maximilian frowned up at him. 'Do we have a situation with France?'

'We don't, but it seems England would like us to.'

'What has got young King Henry worked up now?' Maximilian said, wincing as a burning streak of pain shot up his leg.

'I suspect he is jealous of King Francis's success,' Gurk said, moving a chair towards Maximilian and sitting down. He and his master had long since moved beyond protocol and were as easy in each other's company as if they were two labourers sharing a jug of beer in a tavern.

Maximilian smirked. 'The foolish boy. Must I bother with this Master Pace he has sent to us?'

'It cannot hurt to hear what Henry wants. Pace is just outside. I'll call him in.' Gurk didn't wait for Maximilian to agree and left the room. He reappeared a moment later with a slim, dark-haired man in his early thirties. 'This is Master Pace, Your Imperial Majesty,' Gurk said, using Maximilian's title now they had company.

Pace made the necessary obeisance, but Maximilian could tell the young man was keen to get down to business. Maximilian, who had a lifetime's experience of summing men up in moments, read the impatience behind Pace's eyes. *He thinks this is a waste of time and I daresay he is right.*

'Master Pace, my minister here tells me you have something to say on the matter of France.'

'That is correct, Your Imperial Majesty,' Pace said. 'King Henry would like to know your mind regarding entering into an alliance with England to counter the French aggression currently taking place in Italy.'

He's succinct, at least. That is a mercy. 'Yes, King Francis has been rather more successful than anyone thought possible,' Maximilian agreed, glancing up at Gurk. 'What would such an alliance involve?'

'King Henry suggests an army is raised to fight the French,' Pace said.

'An army to fight the French, eh?' Maximilian laughed. 'Well, someone needs to stop them, don't they, Gurk?'

'Indeed, Your Imperial Majesty,' Gurk nodded and turned to the young secretary. 'But armies are expensive.'

'And alas, Master Pace, my money is tied up elsewhere.' Maximilian made an apologetic gesture even he appreciated lacked sincerity.

'King Henry would not expect you to bear the full cost of mustering an army,' Pace explained impatiently.

Maximilian perked up. He always liked to talk about money, especially if there was a chance of it coming his way. 'How much is he willing to pay?'

'We would require at least twelve thousand marks,' Gurk added before Pace gave his answer.

Pace shifted from one foot to the other, uncomfortable at being put on the spot. 'Forgive me, gentlemen, but actual sums are not what I've come here to discuss. I have come to obtain your approval for such an enterprise only.'

'That's not good enough, Master Pace,' Gurk said, shaking his head. 'We would need to know an exact sum before we agreed, or indeed disagreed, to anything. We like to know what we are getting into before we actually get into it, you see. Perhaps you should have worked out a sum before coming.'

Pace, his cheeks reddening at this suggestion of incompetency, said, 'I will write to Cardinal Wolsey and obtain that information for you.'

'Then, until that matter is known, there is nothing further to discuss. Do not let us keep you, Master Pace,' Gurk said, opening the door and holding it open.

Pace hesitated, but Gurk had not given him any choice but to leave. He bowed to Maximilian and Gurk and exited.

Gurk closed the door behind him. 'He's a clever

one, that Master Pace. And not at all happy about being sent here, if you ask me.'

Maximilian shrugged. 'Young King Henry gets these silly ideas and his servants must hurry to humour him.'

'I doubt that this was Henry's idea,' Gurk said, moving to the window and peering out into the darkness.

'But I thought you said that man is Henry's secretary.'

'He is, but I'll wager my soul that his coming here is Wolsey's idea.'

Maximilian considered this. 'I'm not sure I agree with you, Gurk. It's not like Thomas Wolsey to be precipitate. He wouldn't have sent this man on a speculative mission. He would have written first, I think.'

'Perhaps you are right,' Gurk conceded with a one-shoulder shrug, 'and it does come from the king. I expect Wolsey has a lot on his mind at present. The Church in England is in trouble, I hear. The English people are complaining about its power and all the high clergy are having to defend it, without a great deal of success. Pope Leo is insisting the clergy take a stand and defend it to the utmost.' Gurk sat down and tapped his lips with his forefinger. 'I do not believe we should dismiss this idea of an alliance against France without due consideration. It just may be worth the effort of discussing it with England. If King Henry is willing to pay us to muster an army…'

Maximilian caught his meaning. 'Take the money and see what we can do with it, you mean?'

'Why not?' Gurk shrugged. 'I can always find a use for money.'

'You're right, of course, and yet, now you have made me think on it, I feel that I would quite like to fight against the French,' Maximilian said. 'You know how much I detest them.'

'Then let us, by all means, take the Tudor's money and fight the French. But,' Gurk held up a forefinger, 'only as long as it suits us.'

'Agreed.' Maximilian nodded, then gestured impatiently at his back.

Gurk rose with a sigh and stuffed a cushion behind his master's back.

~

To his disgust, Richard Pace had not been given a bed in the emperor's palace but had had to take a room in the tavern located just outside the gates. *This is a bloody waste of time*, he thought as he hurried through the rain to the tavern. *Everyone knows Maximilian can't be trusted.*

He shouted an order for beer and cheese to the pot-boy as he threw open the tavern door and crossed the straw-strewn floor to the stairs. He felt the eyes of all the patrons upon him as he took the stairs two at a time, each judging the stranger from England, wondering what he was doing there. He mentally told them to mind their own business.

Pace was relieved to see that the man he was forced to share a bed with was not in the room. He threw his soaking wet cap on the windowsill and shook the rain out of his hair. There was a rat-tat-tat on the door and the pot-boy entered warily with a tray. Pace pointed to the bed and the boy set the tray down. He pressed a mark into the boy's hand and closed the door behind him, listening for the boy's footsteps as he retreated down the stairs.

Pace took a deep breath and told himself to calm down. There was no point being angry about his first interview with the emperor coming to nothing. He had expected that. It was the way he had been put down that rankled for he had come away looking like a fool. He imagined what the cardinal would say if he told him what he felt. 'That's your role in this, Richard,' Wolsey would say. 'Swallow your resentment down and bear it, as all men of our station must.' It was all very well for the great Cardinal Thomas Wolsey to say so; no one would dare make a fool of him the way the emperor and Gurk had of lowly Master Secretary Richard Pace.

Pace dragged out the stool from beneath the rickety table by the window and took out his secretarial supplies – bottled ink, quills and paper – from his satchel hung over the bedpost. He sat down to write but his quill hovered over the page.

What should he write? He had no doubt the innkeeper was in Gurk's pay and would pass on any letter Pace gave him to dispatch to the bishop before sending it on to England. Pace was used to being diplomatic in his correspondence, but he didn't feel inclined to be so. Gurk and the emperor had treated him with contempt and he was feeling irked. *Oh, to hell with them*, he decided. *Let them read what I have to say about their treatment of me. With any luck, my words will shame them.*

He looked down at the paper and saw that ink had dripped from the nib and blotted the page. The blot added to his annoyance and he tried to mop it with a cloth but to little avail. Paper being too precious to waste, Pace began to write.

Your Eminence,

I have this day met with the Emperor Maximilian and informed him of the king's desire to move against the French. The emperor has expressed an interest in such a venture but has stipulated that he must know the sum King Henry intends to supply before he agrees officially. The minimum Bishop Gurk claims would be required for the emperor's agreement is twelve thousand marks.

I feel I must point out the concerns I have regarding this matter. Firstly, I was treated most shamefully during my audience with the emperor, with no respect for my position as the king's secretary and envoy being shown, and, I feel, the reason for my visit not being considered with the seriousness it deserves. Secondly, as is well known throughout Europe, the Emperor Maximilian is notoriously unreliable and rarely enters into any agreement that does not benefit him a great deal more than it does his ally.

I must be blunt, Your Eminence. The Emperor Maximilian is not to be trusted. It is my belief that, if the money is sent, it may not be used for its intended purpose, that of opposing the French.

I will remain here and await further instructions.

Yours, and the king's, most obedient servant,
Richard Pace

There, that was short and to the point, and if the emperor did read it before it reached Wolsey, it might make him blush, although Pace doubted it. He blew on the ink to dry it, then folded and sealed his letter. Clattering back down the stairs, he handed it to the innkeeper and instructed him to dispatch it at once. He returned to his room and prepared himself for a long, uncomfortable wait.

CHAPTER THREE

Thomas stifled a sigh and glanced over his desk at all the work he wasn't being allowed to get on with because of his newly arrived visitors.

Archbishop William Warham and Bishop Fox had turned up at York Place that morning without an appointment and demanding to see him. Tuke had done his best to inform them Thomas already had a very full morning – petitioners had been arriving since five o'clock and the Great Hall was very nearly full – but he knew he could not turn away two such estimable churchmen and ask them to arrange a more convenient time, however busy his master was.

And so he had shown them through to Thomas's office and asked if Thomas would see the two churchmen. Thomas had hesitated a moment, a moment too long, for Warham, impatient, had pushed past Tuke and announced himself. Bishop Fox had followed, an apologetic expression upon his face. Trying to hide his annoyance, Thomas had nodded to Tuke that he could go and invited both of his guests to take a seat.

Warham hadn't wasted any time on pleasantries but began on the reason for their visit, namely, the debate over the Church's long-held right to try malefactors in their own courts.

'As cardinal,' Warham said, his hangdog face growing red at the title, 'it is your duty to speak to the king about this matter and make it clear to him what the Church's position is and the rightness of that position. As cardinal, you are the pope's voice in England.'

Thomas didn't need Warham to remind him of his new status, but he wasn't such a fool as to believe that being cardinal gave him any real power. As cardinal, he was able to vote in papal elections, have complete control over all the friaries and monasteries in England, and be a suitably high-ranking representative for visiting heads of state. But as cardinal, he was, as Warham had pointed out, merely the pope's voice in England. As archbishop of Canterbury, it was Warham who had the power to actually change things, and Thomas envied him for it.

'We do need you to speak to the king about this, Thomas,' Fox said, a little less forcefully. 'This matter will not be resolved without some action on our part.'

'But that's the pity of it,' Thomas cried, irritated beyond tactfulness. 'What started all this strife was so trivial a matter.'

'Trivial to you, perhaps,' Fox said stiffly. 'Not to Richard Hunne.'

Oh, yes, Hunne, Hunne, Hunne. Thomas had heard his name a thousand times over the last few years. The man who refused to pay a rector for burying his son and had ended up challenging the right of the Church to have its own law courts. In Thomas's opinion, it was the Church's own fault that matters had come to this sorry pass. The Church had been harsh and vindictive in its treatment of Richard Hunne. Hunne had pursued the Church in the law courts several times and never once won against them. They could have been satisfied with their victories and left him alone, but they had preferred to rub salt into his wound and persecute not only the man but his soul. The Church had excommunicated Hunne. When he had tried to worship in his local church, the rector pronounced him an accursed man and refused to perform the service until he had left. On top of all this, the Church had then imprisoned Hunne, hoping to silence him for good.

Hunne had been silenced, but not in the way the Church had hoped. His prison cell was opened one morning to find him dangling from a beam in the ceiling. At the inquest that followed, the jury decided the prison gaolers had murdered Hunne, almost certainly on the orders of the Church. Though this was vehemently denied, the rumours of murder would not die and a great deal of anger had been roused against the Church.

Hunne's plight had aroused sympathy in others. One of the most prominent of these sympathisers was Dr Henry Standish, a warden of Greyfriars and one of the king's favourite preachers. Standish began to talk publicly about the Church's abuses. The Church was outraged and decided an example had to be made of Standish and summoned the warden to attend a tribunal to answer for his outspokenness. With some justification, Thomas felt, Standish feared the Church's prejudice and had asked for the king to be present when the tribunal took place. Henry had asked his Council's opinion on whether he should take part and both Warham and Fox had declared that he should not.

But privately, to Thomas, Henry had expressed concern. He was very fond of Henry Standish and, in acting against Standish, he felt the Church had gone too far. Henry was minded to do as the warden wanted and appear at the tribunal. Seeing how deeply troubled Henry was, Thomas had agreed.

When Warham and Fox had found out that the king intended to attend, they were furious. At least, Warham was furious. Fox, always the more reasonable of the two, understood Thomas's position better than his friend and could not blame him for giving the king what he wanted.

Despite wanting to keep Henry happy, Thomas knew he would have to agree to speak for the Church. He sighed. 'What is the Church's position, exactly?'

'That we must be allowed to try those who commit criminal acts against the Church in our own courts,' Warham said. 'That right cannot be taken away from us. The king must agree with the Church.'

'How do you know he will not?' Thomas asked,

wondering if Warham had had conversations with the king of which he was not aware.

But that didn't seem to be the case. Warham leant forward and said in a sly tone, which Thomas found very provoking, 'We don't know, do we? That's the point.'

'Thomas,' Fox intervened, casting a disapproving glance at Warham, 'if you were to speak to the king directly at Standish's tribunal... if you stated our case, the king would listen to you.'

'You must be vigorous in the Church's defence,' Warham said. 'You must tell the king that it would be better if he take no part in the judgement upon Standish and that he must refer the matter to the pope.'

'I must tell the king?' Thomas said, raising an eyebrow at Warham.

'Yes,' Warham said, 'you must tell him.'

'My lord archbishop,' Thomas said bemusedly, 'I cannot tell the king what he can and cannot say.'

Warham frowned. 'You are his adviser, are you not?' he demanded. 'You are there to advise him?'

'To advise him, yes, not to instruct him.'

Warham sniffed and drew himself up. 'His father would always listen to the words of his advisers.'

'But we are not dealing with his father, Your Grace,' Thomas pointed out.

'Aye, more's the pity.'

'William,' Fox breathed warningly.

Warham gave him a reproachful look but nodded, an agreement, Thomas supposed, that he would be more guarded in his comments about the king. He certainly needed to be. If Henry heard how Warham spoke of him, he could be mightily offended.

'I will state the Church's case,' Thomas said, spreading his hands wide as if to admit capitulation when in truth he just wanted the conversation to end. 'But that is all I can do.'

'All you are willing to do, you mean,' Warham snapped.

'Archbishop, you surely must realise that it would not serve our cause if I were to appear too prejudiced against Standish?'

Warham slammed his palm down on the arm of the chair. 'The sanctity and authority of the Church must be maintained.'

Thomas tried again. 'Do you not think Hunne and Standish may have a point? That the Church does abuse its position?'

'Are you quite serious?' Warham said incredulously. 'The Church is being questioned enough without our own clergy questioning it as well.'

'But perhaps that is why the Church is being challenged, because it has become corrupt.' Thomas reached to the edge of his desk and retrieved a paper. 'Parliament summed it up very succinctly. Here, they say, "It is a matter of record that clergymen decline to bury their parishioners unless they are rewarded by the most precious jewel, suit of clothes, or other possession of the deceased person." And they go further. "It is prayed that every incumbent should be compelled to bury the dead or administer the sacrament to the sick upon penalty of forty pound." It's clear there is a need for reform in this country, even Parliament says so. And as you are so very fond of Parliament, archbishop, I would have thought you would have welcomed their words.'

Warham drew himself up at Thomas's sarcasm. 'Parliament is a necessary instrument for the governance of a country. Without Parliament, a king has no restraint upon his power, and no one would wish that, not even you.'

'The point I am trying to make,' Thomas said patiently, 'is that if the Church doesn't reform itself, then it might be reformed by others less sympathetic to the Church, and then we will have no influence or power at all.'

Thomas felt Fox's eyes upon him as he said these last words. Was Fox reading his mind and realising Thomas thought Parliament a great nuisance and would willingly have done without them? As it was, Thomas had every intention of persuading Henry to dissolve Parliament and not allow it to meet again for some time.

'I will not listen to such talk,' Warham declared. 'It is not for the people to decide how the Church should be or how it should act. That is a matter for Rome. I am shocked to hear a cardinal speak so of the body that has made him. It is the most ungrateful account I have ever heard.' He got up a little unsteadily and Fox held out his hands to offer support. Warham waved them away. 'Think on what we have said, Thomas.'

He moved to the door and yanked it open, shuffling out without another word. Fox rose and shrugged at Thomas, then followed after his friend.

Thomas stared unhappily at the closed door, irritated with himself for not having convinced Warham that he was right and Warham was wrong. Warham could rail all he liked but Thomas had no intention of doing as he bid and instructing the king as to what he should feel and say. He would say nothing that might earn him the displeasure of Henry.

~

Thomas curled his fingers around the large gold cross that hung from his neck and pulled to make the chain dig into his skin. He needed the discomfort to keep him awake. The tribunal had already lasted for more than two hours, with the clergy offering the king every piece of evidence supporting their rights that they could find, and Thomas knew they had plenty more. His backside had grown numb from sitting in the same position for so long. He squeezed his buttock muscles, hoping the action would force some feeling back. He really needed to get up and walk around, get his blood moving, but he would have to wait his turn to speak.

Another hour passed and Thomas turned his attention to Henry. He saw the young man's irritation start to grow. Henry's leg jiggled, his fingers tapped out a tune on the pommel of his chair and he leant towards Katherine to say a word or two to her every now and then. Thomas knew the king's patience was not infinite and he decided it was time to bring the matter to a conclusion. He interrupted the clergyman making the latest interminable argument and rose, forcing the man to return to his seat.

Thomas felt an uncomfortable tingling in his calves as he moved to stand before Henry and Katherine. He knelt, feeling the cold stone of the floor against his knees.

'Your Grace,' he said, looking up at Henry and then around the hall, 'and my brother churchmen. We have listened long and attentively to the arguments both for and against Church authority. It seems clear to me that to allow the people to dictate to the Church would be contrary to the law of God and the liberties of the Holy Church, which it is our duty as churchmen, bound as we are by our oaths of service, to maintain. And yet, as Dr Standish has attempted to prove before us here today, it is also true that the laity may have just grievances against the Church and that reparation to those souls should be made where it can be made.' Thomas paused for a long moment before continuing. 'However, I fear this question will never be resolved fairly in England unless King Henry refers the matter to His Holiness the pope in Rome and allows him to decide the matter.' He looked expectantly at Henry.

Thomas felt he had done right by the Church. He also felt confident that, as a good Catholic and ardent supporter of the Church, Henry would agree with him and refer the matter to Rome.

Henry stared at Thomas and rubbed his chin.

Then he shook his head and Thomas's stomach lurched. Something was wrong. Henry wasn't going to give him the ready assurance he expected.

'It seems to me, Your Eminence,' Henry said, 'that the clergy has made its case, as has Dr Standish, but your suggestion the pope should have the ultimate say in how my subjects should be tried, whether in secular or Church courts, is not worthy of my consideration. By the ordinance and sufferance of God, we are king of England, and kings of England in time past have never had any superior but God alone. Therefore, we will maintain the right of our crown and of our temporal jurisdiction in this matter, as in all others.'

He gestured for Thomas to rise and Thomas got hurriedly to his feet, remembering to pull his long scarlet robes away to avoid treading on them.

Henry continued. 'I hereby pardon Dr Henry Standish and forbid the Church from mounting any prosecution against him. This is my command. This tribunal is at an end.'

Henry rose, holding his hand out to Katherine. Thomas looked to her, and it seemed to him that she hadn't cared for her husband's words. She was devout in her Catholic faith and Thomas knew she thought the pope's authority to be above that of a king's. Katherine stared at Henry's hand for a moment and Thomas guessed she was battling with herself over whether to ask him to reconsider his judgement. But she was a loyal wife. Katherine took Henry's hand and walked with him out of the hall.

Everyone in the hall had risen when Henry rose

and now they left their seats and moved to talk with one another. Fox and Warham hurried over to Thomas.

'Nothing has been resolved,' Warham said. 'This assembly was supposed to settle the Church's authority once and for all. But we're no further along than we were before.'

'What else could I do?' Thomas asked desperately, still reeling a little from his failure. 'I made our appeal as you asked and the king refused us.'

'Your argument was weak,' Warham scoffed. 'You should have prepared your words more carefully if you knew he was going to declare his own authority as a king of England.'

'You should have tried harder, Thomas,' Fox agreed.

'I didn't know the king would do that,' Thomas protested.

'I don't know what the world is coming to,' Warham said, shaking his head. 'The old king would never have dared question the pope's right to expect obedience from the people of England, nor his right to guide the king in how he rules.'

'Times have changed, archbishop,' Thomas said wearily, rubbing his forehead where it had begun to ache.

'Aye, and not for the better. This young king of yours, Thomas, will have his way and no other, it seems. You should be careful.'

Thomas frowned. 'Careful of what?'

'Careful of the king's will. As this debacle has

shown, the king will make up his own mind about matters and not listen to his ministers. You may find there will come a day when even you will be unable to check him. And God help us all then.' Warham tapped Fox on the arm. 'Come, Richard. Let us return to Lambeth and some semblance of sanity.'

Neither man bothered to bid Thomas farewell and he watched them leave the Great Hall, feeling more than a little aggrieved at both their words and their manner with him. Warham resented his rise, he knew that, while Fox, though his friend, had always thought Thomas lacked humility. But Warham's warning bothered him in a way he could not put his finger on. Could the old man possibly be right about Henry?

Thomas left the Great Hall and told his attendant that he would not be processing formally back to York Place as he usually did, that he would return without showing off his red cardinal robes or hat. He had nothing to be proud of. He had failed his Church and possibly angered his king. He wasn't sure which offence was worse.

Tuke looked up as Thomas entered the office. There was a smudge of ink upon his nose where he had scratched it with inky fingers. 'Your Eminence,' he said, getting to his feet. 'I didn't expect you back so soon. I thought you would be dining with the archbishop after the tribunal.'

Thomas had thought so too. 'It seems the archbishop did not desire my company.'

'Is something wrong, Your Eminence?' Tuke asked. 'You seem a little dispirited.'

Thomas fell into his chair and, resting his elbows on the desk, put his head into his hands. 'Oh, Brian, I made a mistake today. I assumed I knew the king better than I do and he proved to everyone in that hall at Baynard's Castle that I do not. The matter has not been resolved to anyone's satisfaction, Warham and Fox are furious with me and… oh, I don't know what else.'

'A bad day, Your Eminence,' Tuke commented wryly.

Thomas nodded. He suddenly wanted Joan. She would make him feel better. Joan would take him into her arms and press him against her breasts and tell him not to worry, that he had done what he could, that those old men had no idea of how hard he worked, and on, and on. All platitudes, of course, but they often managed to soothe him.

'So, what did Archbishop Warham say?' Tuke asked. 'Was he very rude?'

Thomas knew Tuke didn't care much for Warham. He found him pompous and dismissive. 'Actually, no, not for him. He just spluttered and complained that I had not spoken strongly enough in defence of the Church. I tell you, he won't be letting this matter lie.'

'But what can he do? The tribunal has been held, the king has heard it. Is it not now a matter for the courts?'

'There will be more delays. And I expect Warham

will rally Parliament to support him and insist Rome is involved. And if he does do that, the king will not be at all pleased.'

'But he will not be surprised, either,' Tuke said. 'I mean, from what you have always told me, and from what I have witnessed for myself, the archbishop is constantly opposing the king in Council.'

It was true, Thomas reflected. Warham was an annoying voice of opposition.

'What are you thinking, Your Eminence?' Tuke asked when Thomas didn't speak.

'I'm thinking,' Thomas said slowly, trying the words out in his head before giving them voice, 'that it would please the king greatly if I were to rid him of this troublesome archbishop.'

Tuke stared at him in horror. Thomas had used the words deliberately, knowing Tuke would recognise their resemblance to those allegedly spoken by King Henry II about Thomas Becket.

'Do you mean to get rid of the archbishop?' Tuke asked.

Thomas smiled impishly, pleased by his little joke, and shook his head. 'I will have no sword-wielding knights take off his head, Brian,' he assured him. 'Never that. But I do believe it may be time for William Warham, Lord Chancellor of England, to retire.'

~

Thomas's fears that he had upset Henry were soon dispelled. Henry invited him to dinner the day following the tribunal at Baynard's Castle. Thomas was worried that he had only been invited to be reprimanded, but Henry greeted him with a smile and not a word was said about the matter until they had both filled their stomachs.

'Was I right yesterday, Thomas?' Henry asked as the remnants of the dinner were cleared away.

'I believe you were, Your Grace,' Thomas said, anxious to please. 'Although we look to Rome, and should continue to do so for spiritual guidance, your sovereignty must be absolute.'

Henry smiled. 'I'm glad you're with me on that, Thomas. I appreciate how difficult it must be for you to take a side.'

'Not at all, Your Grace. You are my king.'

Henry liked that. 'If only your brethren thought the same. From the look on the archbishop's face, he was not of your mind.'

'No, but that is not unusual. Archbishop Warham and I often disagree.'

Henry's expression suggested he understood. 'Enough of yesterday. What I really want to know is whether you have had any news from my secretary.'

Thomas hesitated. There had been a letter from Pace waiting on his desk when he arrived back at York Place but its contents had only worsened his mood, for Pace's letter had been full of misgivings about the Emperor Maximilian. Thomas trusted the king's secretary. If Pace could foresee trouble ahead should

England enter into a treaty with Maximilian, then it would be wise to heed those misgivings. Maximilian's reputation for contrariness was well known and it wasn't with any pleasure that Thomas would pursue such an alliance, but he didn't really see that he, or more rightly Henry, had any choice. France was showing herself to be powerful and, if she wasn't checked, then England could fall far behind and, to the Continental powers, become the insignificant island over the Narrow Sea she had been when Henry's father had come to the throne.

'I received a letter from Master Pace yesterday. He has had an audience with the Emperor Maximilian and has secured his agreement to fight against the French in principle.'

'That's excellent,' Henry cried happily.

Thomas put his head to one side. 'In principle, Your Grace. The emperor insists on knowing how much money we are prepared to send for the hiring of Swiss mercenaries before he will agree officially.'

'And I thought all we rulers were gentlemen,' Henry said sourly. He banged his fist on the table. 'The French need to be stopped, Thomas, what with that coward Pope Leo begging Francis for help now.'

Thomas nodded understandingly.

'Do we have enough money in the treasury for this war?' Henry asked.

Again, Thomas hesitated. Money, he knew, could always be found if necessary, but the truth was the Exchequer was severely depleted. Not only had a great deal of money been spent in the last three years, not least of it on a rather pointless war in France, but only half of the monies Parliament voted to the Exchequer for the defence of the realm had ever been collected. It would be difficult to persuade Parliament to vote the king more money to spend in yet another, possibly fruitless, war.

But Thomas knew Henry needed this war with France for his self-esteem. Henry had been feeling a little battered of late, what with his father-in-law betraying him and no babies to show for all his wife's pregnancies. King Francis's success had made Henry feel inferior. Thomas couldn't have Henry feeling second-rate.

'We can finance the troops,' he assured Henry.

'Excellent. Send the money to Maximilian. And God help him if he deceives us.'

Thomas reached for his cup and drained it. In truth, there was little either Henry or he could do if Maximilian did play them false. It was a little unsettling to realise that the success of this war against France would rest on hope alone.

CHAPTER FOUR

Thomas had been sent for. The queen, still pregnant despite most courtiers' doubts as to her ability to carry a child to full term, was to enter her confinement, and Thomas was required to bless her and her unborn child.

Katherine and Henry were together when Thomas arrived in the privy apartments. Henry held his wife's hand, almost spilling out of his chair as he leaned forward to talk to her. Thomas hadn't seen Henry so happy for months. His face was aglow with expectation, and Thomas didn't blame him. There had been too many babies lost in Katherine's womb, and that the queen had carried this latest child so far was more than encouraging. For the first time in years, Henry had hope that he would be a father.

Henry turned as Thomas entered. 'Does my lady not look well, Thomas?'

To Thomas's eyes, Katherine looked old and exhausted. The pregnancy had caused not only her belly to swell but the flesh of her neck and, if the slippered feet poking out from beneath her skirts were anything to go by, her ankles, too.

'The very picture of womanhood,' he agreed, smiling down upon Katherine.

She tried to smile back, but it appeared beyond her. Thomas saw her clutch Henry's hand. Was it out of love or fear, he wondered?

'Come, Thomas,' Henry waved him closer and bid him perform the blessing.

Katherine prayed as Thomas blessed her and her child, and he heard the sibilance of Henry's whispered responses. When he had finished, one of Katherine's ladies came into the room and said they were ready to go. Katherine took a deep breath that strained her bodice, then her manner changed to one of resignation, and she rose.

'My dear,' Henry said, her hand still in his. He bent over her – she was so much smaller than he – and put his lips to her fingers.

Thomas saw her eyes brim with tears as she stared at the top of Henry's head. *It is fear she feels*, he thought, *fear that this may be the last time she ever sees her husband.*

'I hope I may give you a son,' she said in a voice barely above a whisper.

'I hope so, too,' Henry said.

Katherine turned away, her hand sliding reluctantly from his. 'Take good care of my lord, Your Eminence,' she bid Thomas.

'I will, madam,' he promised.

Katherine took the arm of her lady. They left the room and Thomas heard their footsteps retreating down the corridor. The queen would enter a suite of rooms in a secluded area of the palace where all the windows would be covered to prevent light entering and from which all men would be kept away. He didn't envy Katherine her confinement, but it was the custom for queens. When Thomas had told Joan of what Katherine must endure even before the birth of her child, Joan had shaken her head and said if ever there was a moment when she was glad to be a commoner, it was this. She couldn't imagine anything more deadening to the spirit than to be shut away in a darkened room, with silence all around and nothing to focus the mind upon except the impending labour. Nothing to do, she said with a sorrowful shake of her head, except wonder if she would come out of it alive.

Henry gave a loud sigh and clapped his hands with finality. 'May God give me a son, Thomas. He knows how much I need a son.'

'I have been praying that she carries a male child ever since the queen's pregnancy was announced,' Thomas said. 'The queen has my best wishes for the safe delivery of a boy. And her good health following,' he added.

Henry nodded grimly. 'But she is strong, Thomas, and she will have the best care.'

And if she does die, Thomas mused, *then there will be the opportunity for Henry to marry a younger woman, one who could provide him with son after son. A young widow with a child or two already would be best, so he would know she was fertile.* Having seen Katherine looking so weary, Thomas doubted that she had many childbearing years left to her.

Henry resumed his seat and looked up at Thomas expectantly. 'Was there anything else, Thomas?'

I'll never get a better moment to approach him about Warham, Thomas thought and gestured at the chair Katherine had vacated. Henry nodded and Thomas gathered his robes and settled them over his knees as he sat, mindful of how easily they creased.

'I would like to suggest that you dissolve Parliament, Your Grace. I have discovered that members of the House have been canvassed not to vote any subsidies for the war with France, and, while we are not reliant upon them for funding, their refusal does not help our cause.'

'Who has canvassed the members?' Henry asked, his face darkening as Thomas had hoped it would.

'Archbishop Warham,' he said after a pause, hoping the delay signified a reluctance to name names.

Henry growled. 'Will that old man never stop opposing me?'

'He is rather a thorn in your side,' Thomas agreed ruefully.

'And has been ever since I became king. But I won't be thwarted in this way, not by him or anyone.'

'Then you will dissolve Parliament as I suggest?'

Henry nodded. 'As you say, Thomas. But what can I do about Warham? Kate likes the old man and defends him whenever I complain, but she has a kind heart and knows not what problems he causes me.'

Yet another reason to diminish Warham if Katherine is his supporter, Thomas thought. 'There is nothing you can do to him in regard to his Church appointments,' he said. 'That leaves his secular appointments.'

'He is Lord Chancellor of England and a member of my Council. What are you suggesting?'

Say it, Thomas urged himself. *Say it, see what Henry thinks of it.* He took a deep breath. 'You could appoint a new Lord Chancellor.'

Henry studied him for a long moment, then his face broke into a grin. 'You, Thomas?'

Thomas didn't speak. He didn't want to risk saying anything that would sound self-serving and provoke Henry into considering other candidates.

'A sound notion,' Henry nodded. 'At least I know you will not be encouraging Parliament to vote against me.' He laughed and smacked Thomas's arm.

'I would prefer to do without Parliament altogether,' Thomas laughed, playing along.

'Ah, if only, Thomas, eh? So, the archbishop must be made to resign. Do I just tell him he is to go?'

Thomas winced. He could just imagine how Henry would do that. *You're old, archbishop, it's time you went and stopped bothering me.* Maybe Henry wouldn't be so callous as that, but he wouldn't be far from it, Thomas felt sure. 'You could leave it to me to tell him,' he suggested. 'Let him know it is your wish. He cannot refuse. You appointed him Lord Chancellor. It is your prerogative to take that position away if you so wish. The handing over of the Great Seal must be done in your presence, however.'

Henry nodded. 'I'll leave the telling to you. It's probably best coming from you, you being old friends.'

We were never friends, Thomas mentally contradicted him, but he nodded and left Henry alone to read his book. As he walked away down the corridor, it seemed to him that Katherine had already passed quite out of Henry's mind.

~

It had been a few months since Thomas had last visited Lambeth Palace. He could have asked the archbishop to come to him at York Place, but Thomas felt that he couldn't, in all conscience, ask the man to come to him only to rob him of his position. That would be too cruel.

Thomas walked into the hall at the palace and, almost immediately, a page appeared before him. Thomas knew he was difficult to miss when dressed in his cardinal's robes. He asked the page to take him to the archbishop, and the page hesitated, looking around the hall at all the people waiting.

'I don't expect to have to wait,' Thomas said, seeing the page's doubt. Time was when Thomas had been only a royal almoner and he would have been prepared to wait days to see the archbishop if he had to. Those days were gone. Thomas waited on nobody's pleasure now.

The page quickly made up his mind to obey and gestured Thomas towards the small door in the side of the hall he knew was a corridor that led to Warham's private study. In the corridor loitered more petitioners, those who had made it past the first hurdle of the wait in the Great Hall, and he noted with pleasure that he had far more waiting for him back at York Place. They bowed as Thomas passed by.

When he entered the archbishop's office, Thomas found Warham sitting by the fire with a blanket over his legs. Warham turned his head but didn't smile.

'I didn't realise we had an appointment, Your Eminence.'

He can't say my title without wincing, Thomas thought as he nodded at the page to close the door behind him. 'We didn't,' he said, pointing at the chair opposite Warham. Warham nodded and Thomas sat down.

'Then to what do I owe the pleasure?'

'The king wanted me to have a word with you,' Thomas began. He had tried a dozen different conversation openings in his head on the way over to Lambeth Palace and none of them had sounded well. How do you tell a man like Warham he is being put out of his place? Directly, Thomas decided, and took a deep breath. 'He is concerned you are being overworked. You are, after all, the Primate of All England, Lord Chancellor and a privy counsellor. It is, he fears, a great burden for someone of your advanced years.'

Warham stared at him from beneath furrowed brows. 'Have I displeased the king?'

'Not at all,' Thomas said, shaking his head vigorously. 'As I said, he is mindful of your health.'

'There's nothing wrong with my health,' Warham croaked. 'You can tell the king I am perfectly capable of doing all he asks of me.'

Thomas took a moment to consider this comment. He studied his hands as they lay in his lap, feeling the archbishop's eyes upon him. 'All that the king asks of you?' he repeated quietly. He glanced up, curious to see if Warham realised he had made a mistake. There was confusion in the old man's eyes, not realisation. 'Then understand that the king is asking you to resign,' Thomas said, and waited.

Warham's lips tightened and thinned. 'The king is asking this? Or you are?'

'This comes from the king,' Thomas lied. 'It is his wish.' He saw Warham's hands ball into fists on the arms of his chair.

'I have served two kings, Thomas, and I think I do not flatter myself when I say I have served them well. I had hoped to serve this king until the end of my days.'

'And you will continue to serve him, as a privy counsellor.'

'What good does that do me? The Council meets but rarely, you have seen to that.'

Thomas sighed. He had no desire to discuss the infrequency of the Council's meetings. 'Will you resign?'

'You've managed it very cleverly, I will own that,' Warham continued, ignoring his question. 'The king will hear no voice but yours, eh? That's your intention, is it not?'

'I will have your answer,' Thomas declared. 'Will you resign the Lord Chancellorship or no?'

'You can have it,' Warham said. 'What choice do I have? None, you've made that very clear.'

'It is the king's wish,' Thomas repeated, his jaw tightening in annoyance.

'Save your breath, Your Eminence,' Warham said, turning his gaze away to stare into the fire. 'You will not convince me of your innocence in this matter.'

There was no point in talking further. Thomas rose. 'I shall tell the king of your decision.' A spark of viciousness rose in him. 'You will come to York Place at ten o'clock tomorrow,' he said with satisfaction. Aye, let the old man make the journey. Thomas had planned to tell Warham he and the king would come to Lambeth, but after the way Warham had spoken, Thomas thought to make him pay. 'You will bring the Great Seal with you and we shall perform the resignation in my office.'

There was a certain set about the old man's mouth that seemed to presage a refusal, but Warham nodded and sunk his grizzled chin deeper into his fur collar.

'Till tomorrow, then,' Thomas said, heading for the door. His hand on the handle, he hesitated and looked back. Now that he had achieved his objective, he felt as if he should apologise for enforcing the resignation. Warham had, after all, been instrumental in his rise, and there was some remnant of gratitude for all he had done in Thomas's heart. *If Warham looks at me, I shall apologise*, Thomas decided, and gave the old man precious seconds. But Warham didn't turn his head and Thomas's moment passed.

'Good day, Your Grace,' Thomas said. He yanked the door open and strode out, slamming the door behind him.

～

The slamming of the door made Warham shudder, and he pulled his cloak tighter about him. Thomas's visit had left a chill in the room that he feared would never leave it.

Warham knew this day had been coming. Hadn't he said so not long before to Fox, who had shaken his head and said Thomas would never be so callous as to strip him of his position? Huh, what did Fox truly know of his former protégé? Thomas had moved far beyond them all now. He wouldn't stop until he had swallowed up everything he wanted. And why should he stop when the king allowed, nay, even encouraged him to act so?

Warham knew King Henry thought him a nuisance. God forgive him, there had been times when he had even enjoyed being a nuisance, enjoyed seeing the look of frustration on the young man's face when he had disagreed with him over such-and-such or reminded him he couldn't do something he desperately wanted to do. Well, he shrugged as he recollected, so what if he had been outspoken? It was his duty to be so. The young king needed reminding that there were limits to his power. England was no place for tyrants.

Try telling that to His High and Mighty Eminence, Cardinal Thomas Wolsey, he thought. If Thomas had his way, the king would be allowed to do whatever he wanted, so long as Thomas was standing by his side.

Another thought occurred to him, and this one made his fingers curl in anger. What if Thomas wanted to rob him of everything? What if Thomas wanted the archbishopric of Canterbury to add to his ever-increasing list of Church titles? Fox would no doubt dismiss this too, he knew. He would shake his head and wave his hand and say Thomas Wolsey was Lord Cardinal of England, there was no higher title Thomas could wish for.

But Fox would be wrong.

Thomas was England's only cardinal, it was true, but this was an appointment that benefited the pope more than Thomas. As archbishop of Canterbury, it was Warham who had power over the English clergy. Thomas didn't, and oh, yes, that must irk him. Once Thomas had secured the Lord Chancellorship, he would be coming after him for Canterbury too, Warham was sure.

'Over my dead body,' Warham muttered aloud and dragged the blanket from his legs.

Thomas had to be stopped, or at least fettered a little. King Henry must be made aware of the kind of man he was favouring and bestowing ever greater power upon.

Warham pushed himself up from his chair, wincing as his bones cracked and sent needle-like pains down the back of his legs. He shuffled over to his desk and fell heavily into the seat. Picking up his quill and placing a clean sheet of paper before him, he began to write to his friend, Bishop Fox.

~

Warham made sure he arrived at York Place at least half an hour before he was due to meet with the king and Thomas. As he expected, the Great Hall was packed with petitioners, and he was grateful for the chair one of them relinquished to him in deference to his age and position. He sat down, his eyes scanning the hall for Fox.

It was another five minutes before his friend arrived. Warham lifted his arm as Fox stood in the hall's archway, peering over heads to try to find him, and called out, 'Richard.'

Fox lifted his hand in acknowledgement and made his way through the crowd. 'There you are. So many people, eh?'

'Sit down, Richard,' Warham said and appealed to another of the petitioners if the bishop might have his stool. The petitioner's face suggested the bishop might go and hang for all he cared for his comfort, but he handed it over.

Fox thanked him and set it beside Warham. 'What

did you want to see me about, William? Your letter didn't say.'

Warham looked around before answering. Thomas probably had spies planted amongst the petitioners, ready to inform him of anything they weren't prepared to tell him face to face. 'I'm here to resign the Lord Chancellorship.'

'Oh,' Fox said, the smile vanishing from his face to be swiftly replaced by an expression of pity. 'Well, we are none of us getting any younger, I suppose.'

'It has nothing to do with my age,' Warham snapped. 'The king has asked for me to resign.'

'But... why?'

'Wolsey.'

'Thomas?' Fox asked doubtfully.

Warham nodded. 'Aye. He said it came from the king, but I know the truth.'

'Thomas would not deliberately put you out of office, William.'

Warham patted Fox's arm. 'You're a good man, Richard. I know Wolsey is a friend of yours and you are loath to think ill of him, but he has grown so grand, he remembers not his place.'

'And what is his place, William?' Fox said a little archly. 'Thomas is of common stock, is that it? Well, so am I. Do you also find fault with me?'

Warham had no desire to quarrel with his old friend, and he held up his hand to stop Fox. 'You are different, Richard. I speak not of your origins, nor even of Wolsey's. It doesn't bother me that he is of such low birth and has managed to raise himself.

What bothers me is that he has grown so great that he forgets his origins. That is something you have never done.'

'I wish I knew what you are talking about, William,' Fox said sadly. 'Why exactly have you brought me here?'

'To resign, I must see the king and hand over the Great Seal,' Warham explained. 'I want you with me to speak privately with the king once that is done.'

'Speak about what?'

'To warn him about Wolsey. Let me have my say, Richard,' he said, as Fox made to interrupt. 'You were my friend before you were his and I call on that friendship now.'

Fox sighed. 'Very well, William. You may trust me to speak with you. And, I must admit, there is some truth in what you say. Thomas has become very grand indeed. Not that his rise is not well deserved, though,' he added, pointing a finger at Warham. 'But, for his own sake, it would be wise to alert the king to the fact that he must restrain Thomas's desire to make changes. Not all change is for the better, and he may act in a way that the king comes to dislike. A king's anger is a terrible thing and I would do all I can to prevent Thomas facing that.'

It didn't matter to Warham what reason Fox had to speak with him to the king; it was enough that he would do so. Warham would need his support. If he spoke alone, Henry might think he did so out of resentment at losing the chancellorship. With Fox beside him, adding his voice to Warham's, there was a good chance Henry would heed their words.

The minutes passed, and he and Fox fell into easy talk until ten o'clock when a page wearing Thomas's cardinal badge upon his sleeve manoeuvred through the crowd and told the archbishop he was to come with him. The page had not had instructions regarding Bishop Fox, but he did not quibble the archbishop's insistence that the bishop accompany them.

Warham and Fox followed the page along several corridors before reaching Thomas's private apartments. When they entered the room, the king was seated at a table where a candle burned beneath a ladle of molten red wax, and five seal moulds were set out in a row. Behind him, standing by the window looking out, was Charles Brandon, and to Henry's side, standing with his hands over his belly, the gold cross hanging from his neck catching the light with every breath in and out, stood Thomas.

Warham and Fox bowed to Henry, who drummed his fingers upon the table almost impatiently. *He can't wait to get this over with*, Warham mused and looked up at Thomas. *You can take that supercilious smile off your face or I will make this difficult for you.*

Thomas must have read his mind for the smirk disappeared and, breaking eye contact, he nodded a greeting to Fox.

'Shall we get on with it?' Henry asked, looking up at Thomas.

'Would you mind, archbishop?' Thomas asked, gesturing Warham to step closer to the table.

So, there were going to be no pleasantries, no assurances from Henry that Warham had served him well, no pretence that he was sorry to see him resign. Warham shuffled forward and untied the small white leather bag that hung from his belt. The bag had five lengths of twine dangling from the opening, each finished with a red wax disc. He held it out to Henry.

Henry took the bag and opened it. His big freckled hand delved inside and pulled out the Great Seal, a wooden handle with a metal disc several inches across at its end. Henry studied the disc, examining the design.

'Such a beautiful thing,' he murmured, running his finger over the carved image of himself seated upon his throne.

''Tis but a piece of metal, Hal,' Brandon said. 'Stop dallying, for God's sake.'

'Have a little patience, Charles.' Henry dropped the seal back into the bag. He laid the white bag on the table and snapped each of the wax discs from the cords. They broke easily, splintering over the table surface.

Warham bit his lip as the symbols of his office broke. There was no going back now. *Did you think there would be? Did you think Henry would relent and say you could keep the Lord Chancellorship?* he chided himself. But even if Henry had thought of such a thing, he would have mentioned it to Thomas, Warham realised, and Thomas would have quickly talked him out of it.

Why, even now, Thomas was bending over the table and clearing the debris away.

Henry spread the cords out on a sheet of parchment Thomas slid into place. Thomas positioned a shallow pewter cup beneath each one, then picked up the ladle with the molten wax and handed it to Henry. Henry poured the wax into each cup, ensuring the cord lying across each was coated. He handed the ladle back to Thomas, then held out his hand for Thomas's seal.

Warham watched as Thomas handed Henry, almost reverently, his brand-new seal. Thomas passed it with the end towards him, and Warham saw the two figures with the tasselled hat of the cardinal beneath it carved into the metal. Henry pressed it into the cooling red wax in each disc.

'There, all done,' Henry said. He took up the bag, the metal cups clinking against each other, and handed it to Thomas. 'My new Lord Chancellor.'

'Thank you, Your Grace,' Thomas said, accepting the bag with a bow. He moved quickly to a table by the window and began prising the hardened wax from the cups.

'At last,' Brandon muttered and pushed himself away from the window jamb in expectation of leaving. Henry clapped his hands on his thighs and rose.

'Before we part, Your Grace,' Warham said quickly, holding out both his hands, 'would it be possible for Bishop Fox and I to have a word with you?'

Henry's shoulders slumped. 'About what?' he sighed.

Warham ignored his reluctance. 'A *private* word, Your Grace, if you please.'

'Very well,' Henry nodded. 'Charles, Thomas, leave us.'

'Don't be too long, Hal,' Brandon said, opening the door. 'Ladies are waiting.'

'Yes, yes.' Henry waved him away, his cheeks colouring a little.

Brandon stomped past and out of the door. Thomas looked from Warham to Fox and back again, his brow creasing, but, when he saw Henry watching him, he hurried from the room, closing the door quietly.

'Now, what is it?' Henry said.

Warham took a deep breath. 'We wish to offer Your Grace some advice,' he began and saw Henry stiffen. *Go on, you old fool. Be brave.* 'We wish to urge you not to suffer any servant to be greater than his master.'

'Of whom do you speak?' Henry asked, perplexed.

'We speak of Thomas Wolsey, Your Grace,' Fox said.

Henry looked at the two of them, then laughed. 'Of Thomas?'

'Thomas has risen so fast,' Warham carried on, undeterred. 'It is not ten years hence that he was merely an almoner.'

'Thomas knows his place,' Henry said. 'I need have no fear of him.'

Warham nudged Fox in the ribs to make him talk.

'Not at present,' Fox said, and Warham heard the reluctance in his voice, 'for he owes you a great deal. But there may come a time soon when he may forget to whom he owes most allegiance. It was the pope who made him a cardinal, remember, Your Grace. And now you have made him Lord Chancellor. He is becoming extremely rich and powerful on your benevolence.'

Henry's face changed. The boyish grin was gone, replaced by a stony shrewdness. 'I appreciate your concern. It is true, Thomas has risen fast as much as he has risen high. That could go to a man's head, I suppose, especially one of Thomas's station.'

'That is our worry, Your Grace,' Fox said.

'Then I shall take care to ensure any servant of mine is obedient to me and me alone. There, does that satisfy you?'

Fox glanced at Warham. 'William?'

'I am reassured, Your Grace.' Warham nodded.

'Then we are done here, I think,' Henry said, his face open and cheerful once more. 'If you will excuse me, gentlemen. Charles will be dragging me out of here if I do not leave this very minute.'

Warham and Fox smiled and stepped aside for him to pass. Fox closed the door behind him.

'There, it is done.'

'Aye, it is done, but was it enough?' Warham

wondered. 'The king did not seem unduly concerned by our words. He will take no action.'

'What did you expect him to say?' Fox asked, a little testily. 'He's just made Thomas his chancellor. Would he unmake him a moment later because of what we said? We have expressed our opinions. We can do no more, and,' he pointed his finger at Warham, 'to do more would be to do an injustice to Thomas. We have no reason to believe Thomas will not serve the king well, as we did the king's father and have continued to do unto the son. For all we know, Thomas may be exactly what the king needs.'

'Or what Thomas tells the king he needs,' Warham said fiercely. 'A king should make all the decisions, Richard. What decision has this king made that has not come originally from Thomas, tell me?'

Fox stared at him. 'I like Thomas, William. I do not see him as our enemy, merely a little presumptuous and puffed up with pride. I think you see him differently and inaccurately.'

'You think I am jealous of him,' Warham said with sudden understanding.

'Aren't you?'

'Of course not,' Warham said, but his assurance sounded doubtful even to himself. *Is that it? Am I jealous of Thomas's success?*

Fox sighed and put his hand on Warham's shoulder. 'Come, old friend. Let us go back to Lambeth and have a good dinner and chat about happier times.'

Warham nodded. 'I should like that.'

Fox opened the door, and they both stepped outside. Before they took more than two paces, Thomas was upon them.

'Was that anything I should know about, gentlemen?' he asked.

'If it was, you would have been included, Your Eminence,' Warham said. 'Good day to you.'

He began to walk away down the corridor and had gone several yards before he realised Fox wasn't with him. He didn't dare look back. To look back would be to admit he needed Fox by his side. He guessed Fox was speaking with Thomas, no doubt apologising for his rudeness, perhaps even congratulating him on his appointment to Lord Chancellor. Fox had been a friend to him for a great many years but, Warham realised ruefully, Thomas Wolsey was a man on the rise and he had the king's ear. Put simply, Wolsey's friendship could offer a great deal more than Warham's.

CHAPTER FIVE

1516

It was cold in the Council chamber at Baynard's Castle. All the privy counsellors wore their furred robes turned up about their ears, and, when they spoke, their breath came out smoky. It would be better, Thomas thought, if he could persuade the king that Council meetings should take place at York Place where there were fires and wine, things that warmed the blood and stopped men wondering how soon they could leave.

There had been news from Richard Pace, and it was bad. Thomas had sent the money Gurk insisted upon and Pace's fears had been borne out. Maximilian had begun well enough. He had mustered troops and marched them against the French. With the Swiss mercenaries Pace had hired in King Henry's name, the alliance had enjoyed some minor successes, helped in no small part by the onset of winter, for no army wanted to march in the winter when food was scarce and the ground hard. The French had

continued to move deeper inside Italy and, as a consequence of the encroaching winter, had suffered small
reversals of fortune. For a short while, Pace wrote, he
had had hopes of Maximilian keeping his word. But
then the secretary learnt that Maximilian's troops had
reached Milan and come to a halt. They had just
stopped and refused to march on. Whatever successes
Maximilian and Henry had enjoyed were quickly
undone, and now, it seemed to Pace, there was no
point in continuing. What shocked and infuriated all
who sat around the Council table was Pace's revela-
tion that Maximilian had met with the French on
terms of seeming amity. There were, Pace wrote,
rumours that the French had paid Maximilian to halt
his troops.

Implicit in the secretary's letter, Thomas felt, was
the accusation that Pace had told Thomas this would
happen. The counsellors had all looked at Thomas
when the clerk of the Council had finished reading
aloud Pace's letter, and he felt as if they were almost
accusing him of treachery. He watched the king out
of the corner of his eye, wondering what Henry was
thinking.

Henry, who had been sitting with his chin in his
hand, sighed and met Thomas's glance. 'Well, we
knew this might happen, didn't we, Thomas?'

Thomas breathed a silent sigh of relief. Henry did
not blame him for this debacle. 'You did express
doubts about the fidelity of the emperor, Your Grace,
and how wise those sentiments have proved to be. It is
very regrettable that it has turned out thus. I shall tell

Master Pace to conclude his business and return home with all haste.'

He nodded to the clerk sitting at a small table near the window to write the letter, thankful the matter had been concluded with so little comment from Henry. There was an end to it, for the moment, at least. With winter fast approaching, Francis would ensure his territorial gains in Italy were secure then take his army back to France. Then, he would either wait for the spring and return to Italy, or, as Thomas hoped he would, decide he had achieved enough and that Italy could wait for the moment.

'Moving on to the next item on the agenda,' he said, sliding a paper to the top of his pile. 'The death of King Ferdinand.'

The dispatch from the English ambassador in Spain announcing the death of King Ferdinand had arrived a few days earlier. Vigorous to the very end, Ferdinand had spent the last day of his life hunting, then had gone to his bed, fallen asleep and not awoken. No one around the Council table expressed any sympathy. In fact, most of their opinions were summed up by Sir Thomas Lovell's response. 'About time he died,' he said.

This comment was rather too tactless for Bishop Fox's liking. He leaned close to Lovell and murmured in his ear, reminding him King Ferdinand was Henry's father-in-law. Lovell's cheeks reddened, and he muttered, 'Forgive me,' in a voice so low the words were barely audible and began looking through his papers in earnest.

Thomas read aloud the letter from their ambassador. '"King Ferdinand claimed he made Spain more powerful than she had been for seven hundred years, and yet he died with no manner of treasure and wilfully shortened the days of his life, always in fair weather or foul labouring in hawking and hunting, following more the counsel of his falconers than of his physicians." Well, we knew that of him. He was never wont to stint himself.' He handed the letter to his neighbour to pass around the table. 'What the death of King Ferdinand means for Europe should be our primary concern.'

Fox agreed. 'His successor is Charles of Hapsburg. A very young man, only recently turned sixteen, I believe, and yet already governing the Netherlands. Quite successfully, I understand.'

That won't endear him to Henry, Thomas mused and was going to continue when he saw the king open his mouth to speak. He paused.

'The queen should not be told of King Ferdinand's death,' Henry said.

'Why not, Your Grace?' Warham asked, confused.

Henry made a noise of impatience. 'The queen is in her confinement, archbishop. I would not have her troubled with news of this sort. God only knows what it might do to her. I will have nothing threaten the health and safety of the child she carries.'

'But to keep the death of her father from her,' Warham persisted. 'She will want to pray for him.'

'She prays for him every day,' Henry snapped.

'Ferdinand has never been far from her thoughts, not even when he betrayed me.'

There was bitterness in his words, Thomas noted, and he willed Warham to shut up. There was no gain to be had in making Henry angry. 'I think it a wise decision to keep the news from her for the time being, Your Grace, and one that shows great consideration for the queen, if I may say so.'

'You may say so, Your Eminence,' Henry acknowledged gravely, glowering at Warham. 'Write to Charles and express our condolences at the loss of his grandfather. Also, give our congratulations on his accession.'

'And assure him of our continuing friendship with Spain, Your Grace?' Thomas reminded him.

Henry gritted his teeth. 'Yes, I suppose we must. The queen would wish it.' He clapped his hands together. 'If that is all, gentlemen.' He left the Council chamber before anyone could say aye or nay.

'Meeting over, gentlemen,' Thomas said to the others, gathering up his papers. There was a general shuffling and murmuring as the counsellors trooped out.

'Will we continue friendship with the Spanish, Thomas?' Fox asked, closing the door behind the last of them.

Thomas looked up in surprise. He hadn't realised Fox had lingered. 'I see no reason not to. The king did make friendly overtures to Ferdinand towards the end of last year, you remember, bishop.'

'At the queen's behest, I believe. Henry did not do so willingly.'

'No,' Thomas admitted, 'the betrayal by Ferdinand some years hence still rankles with him, and well it might. Ferdinand did him considerable wrong in not taking action against the French as he had promised. But the queen, as you say, persuaded him to extend an olive branch.'

'I'd have thought you would have tried to persuade him otherwise,' Fox said wryly. 'We all know you prefer to do business with the French.'

'I do,' Thomas said defiantly, feeling he had nothing to apologise for in his preference for the French.

'Why not forget the Spanish altogether, then?' Fox shrugged. 'Surely, this is the moment to do so if ever there was one.'

'The queen would not allow it,' Thomas said with a sigh.

'Ah, I see,' Fox nodded. 'She still has a great deal of influence over the king.'

'Her influence has lessened,' Thomas said.

'Oh, you mean since you had her friar put out of office,' Fox smiled. 'That was clever of you, Thomas.'

'The man was a fornicator, bishop,' Thomas said. 'His own actions prompted his dismissal. I merely facilitated it. But,' he admitted with a sly smile, 'it certainly helped me, diplomatically speaking, you understand. Now, all I need to do is stop ambassadors requesting audiences with the queen herself, and I could put a halt to any unofficial persuasion of the king altogether.'

'Is that to be wished for?'

'Of course it is. Foreign affairs cannot be well managed if the queen merely has to whisper in the king's ear and get him to undo months of diplomatic negotiations. 'Tis much better if all his information and advice comes from men who know what they are doing.'

'Or man, indeed,' Fox said, pointing at Thomas.

Thomas drew himself up. 'If it makes the king content to hear me before his other counsellors, then it contents me also, bishop. And that should be good enough for any man. Now, I must say good day to you. I have much work to do.'

～

It was February, and Katherine had had her baby. Richard Pace, only recently returned to England from the Continent, had dashed off a letter to Thomas to give him the less than joyful news. The queen, Thomas read with dismay, had been delivered of a baby girl, and Pace begged the cardinal to come.

Thomas told Tuke to cancel all his appointments for the next few hours and hurried out of York Place to cross the river to Greenwich. Fortunately, the tide was with him and he reached the palace in excellent time.

When he entered the privy apartments, Thomas saw three of the king's friends, Sir Francis Bryan,

William Compton and Thomas Coffin, idling in the antechamber, playing at cards. They turned in his direction at his approach, but not one of them rose to show any deference.

'Where is the king?' he asked, irked by their lack of respect.

'He's gone to the chapel to pray,' Compton answered lazily, not even glancing up from his cards.

Thomas should have realised where Henry would be. 'How is he?'

Bryan looked up at him. 'How do you think he is? The brat's a girl.'

'The girl is a princess, Sir Francis,' Thomas said testily, 'and you would do well to show some respect.'

Bryan snorted and looked back to his cards. None of the men seemed inclined to talk with Thomas further, and, for his part, he had no desire to remain in their company. He turned on his heel and left the room, making his way to the chapel.

When he reached the large double doors, he opened the left-hand door quietly and peered around it. Henry was sitting alone in the front pew. It was odd to see him so unattended – Henry was almost always surrounded by courtiers – and Thomas had a moment of doubt as to whether he would be welcome. It was Pace who had sent for him, not Henry. It was Pace who thought that the king, being very upset, needed Thomas's counsel. Perhaps Henry did need Thomas to talk to, but would he admit to such frailty?

Taking a deep breath, Thomas stepped inside the

chapel, feeling its cold air settle upon his face, the cold of the flagstones penetrating his satin shoes. His breath smoked as he walked up the aisle.

'Your Grace?' he murmured.

Henry started and jerked his head around. 'Oh, Thomas,' he said with relief, 'I did not hear you.'

'Master Pace wrote to tell me of the queen's delivery. May I sit with you, Your Grace?' Thomas asked, indicating the pew where Henry sat.

Henry nodded and Thomas walked past him to take a seat alongside. He settled himself, smoothing his robes over his knees, wondering how to begin.

'It was a girl, Thomas,' Henry said before he could decide. 'A girl.' He buried his face in his hands. 'Oh, God, why?'

'Only God knows why, Your Grace,' he said, wishing he could offer a better reason.

'Why does he deny me a son, Thomas? A son is all I ask for, all I beg him for. A son to make my father's line secure on the throne.'

'You may yet have a son, Your Grace,' Thomas said kindly. 'The queen is well?' He knew Katherine would need to have come through the birth without internal damage if she were to have an opportunity to give Henry the son he craved.

'What? Oh, yes, she's well, so they tell me. I haven't seen her.'

Thomas was surprised Henry had not visited Katherine. Was his disappointment only at the arrival of a girl, or was it with Katherine too? 'But you have seen the child? It is healthy?'

Henry snorted. 'She's a lusty child, Thomas. If she had been a boy, she would be perfect.'

He suddenly began to sob into his hands, and Thomas instinctively reached out his arm and placed it around the king. As his hand touched Henry's shoulder, he had a sudden and startling memory return of a time when he had comforted Henry over the death of his mother. How long ago was that now? More than ten years, it must be. How time had flown. And yet Henry still seemed a boy, despite all the growing up he had done.

He held his breath, half expecting a rebuke for daring to touch him, but Henry said nothing. Instead, he bent lower, hugging himself, and Thomas let his hand remain on his shoulder. It was only a small touch, but perhaps it was enough to give comfort.

'This is not the end, Your Grace,' he said. 'There will be more babes. The queen is in good health—'

'Kate is not young, Thomas.' Henry straightened and Thomas drew back his hand. 'There are six years between us.'

'Yes, but women older than she have gone on to have many children,' Thomas persisted, though he could not think of any such woman to provide an example.

'I suppose so,' Henry agreed reluctantly as he looked up at the image of Christ on the cross. 'I can but hope and pray.'

'Would you like me to bless the child, Your Grace?' Thomas asked after a moment. Henry nodded and Thomas rose. 'Then, with your leave, I shall do so at once.'

He bowed to Henry and moved past him, back into the aisle and towards the door. He heard Henry sniffing as he stepped out into the corridor and closed the door behind him. Henry, he felt, was right to be disappointed and worried that he would not have a son. A six-year age difference hadn't seemed a great deal when Henry had first married Katherine, but it was making a difference now. Katherine had grown very plump and had already lost her youthful prettiness. There was little left of the young woman Henry had fallen in love with.

Thomas made his way to the suite of rooms where Katherine had spent the last month. The guards let him through, but when he tried to enter the inner chamber, Katherine's closest friend, Maria de Salinas, Lady Willoughby, blocked his way.

'The queen cannot be disturbed, Your Eminence,' she said, planting herself between him and the door.

'I do not wish to disturb her,' he said a little testily. 'The king wishes me to bless the child.'

Maria looked abashed. 'Forgive me, I did not mean to be rude. 'Tis just that the queen is not – well, she is not happy.'

'No, I do not expect she is. But still, her child is healthy, I am told, and that is something to give praise for, is it not?'

'It is,' Maria said earnestly. ''Tis such a pretty babe. We took it out of the room so the queen could sleep.' She pointed behind Thomas to a door in the corner of the room. 'Come.'

She led Thomas through to an even smaller room, where a large wooden crib covered in velvet and silk had been stuffed in. Inside, a small, red and rather ugly creature lay fast asleep. Thomas made his blessing quietly, not wishing to wake the child. When he had finished, Maria led him back into the antechamber.

'Have you seen the king, Your Eminence?'

'I have, Lady Willoughby.'

Maria's face grew anxious. 'The queen fears she has disappointed him.'

'I cannot deny the king *is* disappointed, my lady.'

'He wanted a son. Oh, all men want sons. But what is wrong with a daughter, Your Eminence?'

'Daughters cannot rule, Lady Willoughby, as well you know.'

'I do not know,' she said, her Spanish accent growing stronger in her indignation. 'The queen's mother ruled in Spain.'

'But England is not Spain, my dear lady. And while we are on the subject of Spain, now the child is in no danger, I think it right the queen is told of her father's death.'

Maria's mouth fell open, a little shocked. 'Your Eminence, I do not know if she is strong enough for such a shock as that.'

Thomas shrugged. 'I shall leave it to you to decide the best moment, Lady Willoughby, but tell her you must.' He made to leave but Maria halted him.

'Will the king be coming to visit the queen? Only she has asked for him.'

'I cannot say. He is most distressed.'

'*He* is distressed?' she cried loudly, then, remembering herself, lowered her voice. 'How does he imagine the queen feels?'

'I do not think it wise to take that tone when discussing the king, my lady,' Thomas said, raising a censorious eyebrow.

Maria bent her head in apology. 'Forgive me my passion, Your Eminence, but it pains me to see the queen so forlorn. The king's presence would soothe her, I am sure.'

'This is out of my hands, my lady.' Thomas edged towards the door.

'But the king always listens to you, Your Eminence,' Maria cried, trotting after him.

It was flattering, this acknowledgement of his influence over the king, but Thomas didn't want to become involved in a reconciliation between the king and his wife. Henry had plenty of friends who could do that for him; indeed, if they couldn't provide the comfort he needed, then they might as well leave the court and do everyone a favour.

Thomas managed to shake off Lady Willoughby and her entreaties to intercede with the king. He left Greenwich Palace, eager to return to York Place.

CHAPTER SIX

A few weeks after the birth of the princess, Thomas had reports from Greenwich that Henry's disappointment in his new daughter, and in Katherine, was lingering. The news concerned him a little, though he had no doubt Henry's mood would eventually lift. He was too good-natured a prince to be perpetually sullen, but Thomas did wonder whether Henry would ever love the queen the way he had when they first married.

And yet, Thomas couldn't help feeling that if Henry did turn away from Katherine, even a little, then it could only be good for him. If Henry stopped listening to Katherine, stopped heeding her advice and listened more to the advice of his ministers, then all to the better. Thomas had good hopes of this. The reports that crossed his desk also told him that the queen's ladies told tales about the court of how Katherine was often in tears, hurt by Henry's indifference and miserable at not being able to give him what he so desperately desired.

But what worried Thomas greatly was hearing that Henry was doing all he could to stanch his sorrow by spending every waking moment hunting, dancing or gambling. This last was becoming a popular pastime at court, with immense sums being won and lost daily. Thomas didn't care what the nobles did with their wealth – they could lose it all, it wouldn't make any difference to him – but he did care about Henry's money. For Henry's money was, in effect, the country's money, and England simply couldn't afford to let it be gambled away.

Thomas asked Tuke for the royal household account ledgers and was greatly perturbed to see that the past few months' gambling losses were three times what they had been the previous year. Henry was losing heavily, and his so-called friends were allowing him to do so.

Thomas decided a visit to consult with the king about this matter was necessary and set off in his barge to Greenwich. When he arrived in the privy apartments, he wasn't surprised to see Henry and his friends at cards. His suspicions confirmed, Thomas asked Henry for a private word. Henry was reluctant, but Thomas was insistent, and his friends were told to leave the room.

Once they were alone, Thomas hesitated. Now the moment had come, Thomas wasn't quite sure how to broach the subject of Henry's excessive gambling.

It was a delicate matter, telling a king he must leave off his spending.

'Well, out with it, Thomas,' Henry said when Thomas remained silent, 'I have a card game to play.'

'It is about these games of cards,' Thomas gestured at the cards on the table, 'that I wish to speak with you, Your Grace.'

Henry laughed. 'You want to play? You need only ask, Thomas. You'll always be welcome.'

'No, Your Grace, thank you, not today. In fact, I'm afraid I must be the voice of censure and ask that you play less often.'

The smile faded from Henry's lips. 'Is it your place to ask me that, Your Eminence?'

His tone was unnerving, the use of his title even more so. Thomas swallowed. 'I speak as your friend, I hope, Your Grace.'

Henry's fierce expression softened. 'I know you are my friend, Thomas. But this,' he gestured at the cards, 'is the only solace I can find at present.'

'I would not wish to add to your troubles, Your Grace,' Thomas continued, emboldened by the return of Henry's use of his Christian name, 'but I would be remiss in my duty were I not to point out how greatly depleted the privy purse has become by dint of this card-playing.'

'My friends will not have me play for cakes.'

'If you will forgive me, your friends should be helping you to find other, less costly diversions. I fear it is for their own pleasure rather than yours that they encourage you in this way.' Thomas saw consideration on Henry's face and decided to press home his advantage. 'I fear they are enjoying seeing how much money they can make from your good nature.'

Henry put his head to one side. 'Do you really think so, Thomas? Is that what they are doing? Taking advantage of me?'

Dear God, was it going to be this easy to break his ties to Bryan, Compton and the others? 'I am sure of it, Your Grace,' Thomas said earnestly.

'They do seem to enjoy it when I lose,' Henry said, nodding.

Thomas kept quiet. He had said enough and didn't want to push his luck.

'I shall think on what you have said, Thomas,' Henry agreed. 'And I thank you for your concern. It gladdens me to know I have such a friend as you.'

'I shall leave you,' Thomas said, feeling a little overcome to hear the king speak so warmly. 'Shall I send your friends back in on my way out?'

'No,' Henry said after a moment's hesitation. 'No, I tire of cards. I think I shall be by myself a little while.'

'Very good, Your Grace.' Thomas bowed and left the room. As he entered the corridor, Bryan, Compton and Coffin made to enter but Thomas held out his hands. 'He doesn't want you. He wants to be alone.'

'What did you say to him?' Bryan demanded angrily.

'Private matters, Sir Francis,' Thomas said, 'none of your concern.'

'You mean to turn him against us,' Compton declared.

'You'll do that without any help from me if you continue to bleed him dry, Master Compton,' Thomas said. 'Treat the king better and you may yet keep his favour.'

'Are we out of favour, then?' Coffin asked, worry evident in his voice.

'All I will say is watch your step, sir,' Thomas said. He looked the others up and down contemptuously. 'Good day to you, gentlemen.'

If they muttered about him as he walked away, he didn't care. Henry had shown the faintest glimmer of uncertainty about his friends, and Thomas knew that, once an idea was in Henry's head, it was difficult to dislodge it. With any luck, these friends of Henry's would be out of favour before the month was out.

~

Despite his warning to Compton, and despite his hopes, Thomas truly had had no idea his words to Henry about his friends would take such deep root in the king's brain. It had been Thomas's intention merely to steer the king away from spending so much money so recklessly, and, if he could, make him less reliant on men who offered so little and took so much. But it seemed Henry had brooded much on Thomas's words and had come to the conclusion that the nobility were taking advantage of his good nature. Richard Pace reported to Thomas that Henry was treating his friends, and some courtiers, with suspicion, so much so that he was worried Henry was not quite right in the head. Thomas wrote back to Pace, telling him he would seek an audience with the king and see for himself.

The king was in the palace gardens, practising his skill with the bow and arrow when Thomas arrived. As Henry raised his bow and arrow and aimed at the target, Thomas felt Pace was right, there was something different about him. The look in his eyes was harder, his brow sterner. Something was definitely plaguing Henry, and Thomas was curious as to what that something was. Surely it was not just his friends' behaviour?

He waited until the attendants had moved away, some to retrieve the arrows the king had shot, some to talk amongst themselves. Henry was examining the callouses on his fingers when Thomas spoke.

'Is there something wrong, Your Grace?' He felt it was the most innocuous opening he could make. Henry could shake his head and declare everything was fine if he wanted, or he could take the opportunity to unburden himself. If he took the former option, Thomas decided he would not pursue the enquiry.

Henry looked off into the distance before answering. 'Do you think some of my nobles are troublesome, Thomas?'

Thomas frowned. What was this now? 'Troublesome in what way?'

'Getting above themselves,' Henry shrugged. 'Taking liberties.'

Thomas felt his heart beat a little faster. He had long believed the nobility were far too powerful and far too ready to abuse their positions to oppress the common man. One of the reasons he had so wanted to become Lord Chancellor was so that he would have the power to redress some of the wrongs the nobility had caused. He hadn't yet found a way of doing this, being so busy on other matters, and Henry's question excited him. Maybe Henry was about to give him the opportunity.

'Well, Your Grace,' he said, stalling a little to collect his thoughts, 'it is quite the coincidence you ask this, and if I may say so, 'tis very astute of you.' A little flattery, he felt, could only help.

'You have thought so, too, then?'

'Indeed. Often in Star Chamber do I hear cases of nobles taking advantage of their power to commit injustices against their tenants and forcing local justices to acquit their servants of crimes that should have been punishable by time spent in the stocks or pillory while innocents are made subject to the full force of the law. This makes your subjects very angry, Your Grace, and I feel your nobles' behaviour reflects badly upon you.'

'How so upon me?' Henry cried indignantly.

'Because they believe you know these injustices are being committed and that you allow them.'

'But I know nothing of them.'

'*I* know that,' Thomas said, putting his hand to his

heart, 'but the people do not. And this is not all. I have had reports that several nobles have been building up their number of retainers despite there being a law against it.'

'Do they mean to threaten me with these retainers?'

'I do not believe so,' Thomas said carefully, not wishing to suggest Henry was in any danger. 'At least, not at present. But, as you know, the law was brought in to prevent any noble possessing a large enough retinue that might threaten a sovereign. That some nobles are building up what actually amounts to private armies is worrying and should be stopped.' He wondered if he had said too much. He studied Henry closely, saw the lines that furrowed his brow, the small mouth tightening.

'This troubles me, Thomas,' Henry said, shaking his head. 'That I should be thought complicit in such abuses pains me to the heart.'

'I agree,' Thomas said heatedly. 'When you are innocent of such wrongs, it is disconcerting to hear of nobles behaving thus.'

'I won't have it, I won't,' Henry said. 'And these are the cases you know about,' he said, jabbing his forefinger at Thomas. 'What about all those that you don't? What about the duke of Buckingham?'

'What about the duke of Buckingham?' Thomas asked, perplexed as to this sudden accusation. Why was Henry worrying about Thomas Stafford? Thomas had informants in every noble household and he hadn't been sent any report about the duke misbehaving.

'You haven't heard anything that suggests he is plotting against me?'

Thomas's stomach lurched. If there was a plot against Henry and he had heard nothing of it, then his informants were failing him miserably. He could not afford to be unaware of plots against the king.

'I have heard of nothing specific,' he said, deciding he better fudge his answer. 'What have you heard, Your Grace?'

Henry snorted impatiently. 'Nothing specific either. I don't get to hear of specifics, Thomas, that is what I have you for.'

Thomas bit the inside of his cheek in his frustration. Henry was right; it was his job to know such things.

'Compton said something the other day about the duke,' Henry continued.

Compton! Now Thomas understood. That blasted Compton had been blabbing and put a ridiculous idea in Henry's head that the duke was plotting against him.

'What did Master Compton say?' he said as equably as he could.

Henry's cheeks coloured and he looked away. 'I once showed favour to the duke's sister. It was some years ago and all perfectly innocent.'

Thomas had heard about the obliging Anne Stafford and knew the king's involvement with her hadn't been innocent at all. Whether the king had only flirted with the lady or had indeed managed to bed her was not known to Thomas, but Henry's intentions had been clear. The king's romantic liaisons, Thomas felt, were not within his purview and so had not concerned himself with the gossip. Now, he could have kicked himself for not having paid more attention.

'Of course, Your Grace,' he said. 'Perfectly innocent, as you say.'

'The duke thought I meant to insult his sister by my showing favour to her, and you know, Thomas, that I would never treat a lady so rudely. But the duke holds a grudge and Compton says he often speaks against me.'

Thomas breathed a sigh of relief. Was this all? 'Speaking against you is not the same as plotting, Your Grace.' He hadn't meant to sound patronising and he hastened to speak before Henry could take any offence. 'But I agree with you. If the duke is saying what he shouldn't, then it displays a significant want of respect.'

'As do these reports of yours that tell you of the nobles' abuses,' Henry said huffily. 'Do all my nobles think they can do what they want?'

Now is the time to move in, Thomas told himself. *Do it, say it.* 'Your nobles have taken advantage of your good nature, Your Grace. It is clear that they do indeed believe they can act as they will without censure and break the law with impunity.'

'They think me weak,' Henry said grimly.

Thomas hesitated. It wouldn't be wise to agree with that remark. 'They think you kind, Your Grace.'

'I am not kind, Thomas,' Henry said, raising his chin a little higher. 'I am the king.'

'Indeed you are, Your Grace.' Thomas cleared his throat. 'If you wish, I will deal with your nobles.'

'How?'

'I shall make an example of some of the more grievous offenders. As Lord Chancellor, I have the authority to prosecute those who have transgressed your law.' He waited, but Henry said nothing. Thomas tried again. 'Your father was right to keep his nobles under control.'

This little nudge worked. Henry nodded. 'Yes, my father was right and you are right, Thomas. Do whatever you think best. But mark me. I especially want you to keep an eye on the duke of Buckingham.'

'I will, Your Grace,' Thomas said, delighted with the way the conversation had gone. He now had the king's authority to act against the men who thought their noble blood gave them the right to abuse the rights of the common man. He bowed to Henry and made to leave when Henry called to him.

'Yes, Your Grace?'

'Keep an eye on the duke of Suffolk as well.'

Thomas wasn't quite sure he had heard Henry right. Had he really just asked him to spy on his best friend? 'The duke of Suffolk, Your Grace?' he asked, just to be sure.

'Yes. Brandon.' Henry shook his head as if he knew he was being silly. 'He's unhappy about the fine

I levied on him for marrying my sister. Says he has no hope of ever paying and that I should remit some of it. I've told him that he will pay me every penny, and he's been surly with me ever since. He may get some silly ideas. Keep an eye on him. Just to be on the safe side, you understand, Thomas.'

'Of course, Your Grace,' Thomas nodded, more than a little taken aback. He could understand Henry being suspicious of the duke of Buckingham – Buckingham had never cared for the Tudors and made no secret of his disdain – but he was being paranoid if he thought Charles Brandon would ever turn against him. Brandon simply didn't have the brains to plot against Henry. He left the king fitting another arrow to his bow and walked away, a little unnerved that Henry could think so ill of those closest to him.

CHAPTER SEVEN

The painted stars on the ceiling twinkled a little in the candlelight.

The Star Chamber was quite a small room in the Palace of Westminster, inappropriately small, Thomas thought, for the matters of great importance that were carried out there. Most days, Thomas dealt with routine lawsuits in Star Chamber – boundary disputes, poaching, property deeds – but today was very different. Today, Thomas was taking an almost unprecedented step against the nobles of England.

Don't lose your nerve, he told himself as the doors were shut on the crowds outside. Thomas nodded to the steward to call the assembly to order. The room fell silent. All eyes were on him, expectant. He cleared his throat.

'It has come to my attention that, for some years now, there has been a lamentable lack of justice delivered in this kingdom. The common man now doubts whether he can ever receive justice when the person against whom he has a grievance has very deep pockets and a great deal of influence. Such a position is not the law of this land. Ever since the time of King Henry the Second, every man in England has known that he has only to seek justice to receive it. But there are those amongst us who are corrupting the law of this land and injuring His Grace, King Henry, by doing so.

'So, I am telling you all now, and a proclamation will be made throughout the kingdom, that those who dispense justice, our country's judges and the landowners, should not consider themselves to be above the law. They are as subject to the law as any other man in this kingdom. The crown is the fount of all justice, and the king would have his subjects know that he will favour no man above another in matters of law. Any person being found to have abused his position as a judge or landowner, aye, even a noble of this land, will have to answer to the king's justice.'

He paused to take a sip of wine to moisten his throat and to give him a moment to try to slow his thumping heart. He took a deep breath.

'To prove to you all that I mean what I say, I order the usher to bring in Henry Percy, earl of Northumberland.'

There was a great muttering amongst the spectators. The door opened and Henry Percy was led to the bar by an armed guard. Percy's expression was furious. He looked about the room, viewing all those gathered with unbridled contempt, but his expression was fiercest when his gaze rested on Thomas.

'Lord Henry Percy,' Thomas began, hoping his voice didn't quiver, 'the Council has discovered you have frequently flouted the king's law and shown contempt for the jurisdiction of law enforcers in and around your lands. There have been several incidences of wrongs done to men who had a right to expect justice from you when your servants, who were to blame, were reprieved under your orders. Such blatant abuses will not be allowed to continue. For your contempt of the king's law, you will be taken to Fleet Prison and incarcerated there until the king and his Council declare you will be set free.'

There was a collective gasp as these words were spoken. Thomas's hands were shaking and he hid them in his lap.

'How dare you!' Percy roared, his hands gripping the bar before him and leaning forward to snarl at Thomas. 'You are a butcher's son, a nothing, a nobody. So what that you wear the robes of the Church. You have no authority to condemn me to prison.'

'I do have the authority,' Thomas said. 'The king, in his great wisdom, has seen fit to bestow upon me, his Lord Chancellor, that authority. Whatever you think of my origins, Lord Percy, you are wrong when you claim I do not have the right to commit you. Guards, take him away and commit him to the care of the warden of the Fleet Prison.'

Percy struggled, but he was no match for the guards who took hold of him and forced him out of the chamber. Thomas reached for his wine cup, almost knocking it over. He clutched it with both hands and brought it to his lips, swallowing all that it held. He set it back down, seeing the steward watching him.

Thomas nodded at him. 'Bring in the first claimant.'

∽

The business of the day was done, and it was time to leave the Star Chamber and return to York Place.

It had been a strange day. Normally, Thomas was able to give all the cases that came before him his full attention, but the Percy case had left him distracted, as though butterflies were fluttering around inside his skull.

He tried to imagine the earl's journey to prison, the people staring from the riverbank, the curses Percy had no doubt spat about Thomas as he was bundled into a boat. It was quite horrible.

As he left the Star Chamber, Thomas saw with dismay that a large group of people had assembled in the hall outside. News had travelled, and travelled fast, about the earl. He scanned the faces. There were nobles amongst them.

He opened his mouth, meaning to call out to his guard to surround him, for he suddenly felt extremely vulnerable. Every noble carried a sword, some a dagger too, and many of them had very short tempers. Thomas knew he was hated, knew too thanks to his informants that many of the nobles had spoken together and fantasised about sticking a knife in the fat cardinal. How easy would they find it to turn those fantasies into reality, feeling sure the king would be on their side?

But Thomas stopped himself from calling his guard. To do so would have been to show he was scared, and he was damned if he was going to do that before all these people. He felt sweat prickle on his top lip and nausea rising up in his throat, but he took one tentative step, then another, and felt the courage to continue.

'You stand there, Wolsey,' a deep, growly voice said.

Thomas halted, his heart beating fast. He recognised the voice. 'My lord Howard,' he said, turning to the speaker. 'You wish to speak with me?'

'I'd rather clean the shit off my shoe than talk with you, Wolsey,' Thomas Howard, duke of Norfolk, sneered, leaning his long, lean face close to Thomas. 'But you've sent Henry Percy to the Fleet. Who do you think you are to do that, eh?'

'I am the Lord Chancellor, Your Grace,' Thomas said as bravely as he could. 'That gives me the right to dispatch whomsoever transgresses the law to prison.'

'What law?' Howard shook his head. 'Laws don't apply to us. You're a butcher's boy. You've no right to act against a noble.'

'The king has given me the right, Your Grace. If you dislike my judgement, then you must take it up with him.'

Howard grabbed Thomas's silken collar. He

thought he heard the silk threads rip and then felt a sharp point at his throat. 'What if I want to take it out of your guts?'

Thomas looked out of the corner of his eyes and saw to his relief that his guards had noticed what was happening and were even now coming to his aid.

'If you do not wish to find yourself in the Tower, Your Grace,' Thomas said, 'you had better remove your dagger from my throat.'

Howard glanced at the guards. 'They won't arrest me.'

'Are you sure of that?'

Howard took another look and noted their very sharp halberds. 'One day,' he promised and sheathed his dagger. He released Thomas and shoved him back, then spat at Thomas's feet, the spittle landing on his red slippers. He walked away, laughing with his cronies.

Thomas could feel he had become as red as his cardinal robes. Oh, the embarrassment, the humiliation of being accosted thus! Even now he could hear the sniggers, the men looking over their shoulders at him and hiding their laughing mouths.

He walked on, holding his head high. He knew what he would do. He would tell the king of this, and then Thomas Howard would be sorry.

~

Thomas didn't return to York Place but went straight to see Henry. He told Henry everything that had happened at the Star Chamber, from Henry Percy's committal to prison to Thomas Howard's attack upon his person.

Henry listened attentively, his chin resting in his hand. When he finished giving his account of the incidents, Thomas leant back in his chair, confident the king would respond with an order for Howard's arrest.

But this response did not come. Instead, Henry drummed his fingers on the table and asked whether Thomas had provoked the duke in any personal manner.

Thomas stared open-mouthed at Henry. 'The duke questioned my authority, Your Grace,' he spluttered.

'It seems to me,' Henry said with a wave of his big hand, 'that tempers were running a little high. That was to be expected, I suppose, after you arrested the earl.'

'Arrested with your permission, Your Grace,' Thomas reminded him.

Henry waved a finger. 'I didn't say you could send him to the Fleet, Thomas.'

What did you think I would do with him? Thomas wondered angrily. *Give him a slap on the wrist and tell him not to be such a naughty boy again?*

'Do you want me to rescind the arrest order?' he asked, his jaw tightening.

Before Henry could answer, the door opened behind Thomas. He turned in his seat to see Pace.

'Forgive me for interrupting, Your Grace,' Pace

said to Henry, 'but several of your nobles are asking for an audience.'

Henry blew out a puff of air, raised his eyebrows at Thomas and went out to meet them.

'Who is out there?' Thomas asked Pace quietly when he had gone .

'Norfolk, Surrey, a few of their friends. They're very angry at you, Your Eminence.'

Howard had obviously rallied his peers to join him in this assault against Thomas. 'You had best join the king in case he wants you,' he said, jerking his head at Pace.

Thomas caught hold of the door as Pace left and let it fall to, leaving it open only an inch. He put his ear to the gap and strained to listen. Unsurprisingly, Norfolk was talking, and loudly, too.

'Your Grace,' Norfolk said, 'the imprisonment of Henry Percy proves what we of your nobility have long suspected. That we are not welcome at your court. And so, I humbly ask your permission to leave.'

The other nobles repeated the request and Thomas held his breath as he waited for Henry to reply. There was a long pause, then Henry spoke.

'You have my leave.'

Thomas gasped. Had the king really given them leave to go? After what he had just said, Thomas had expected Henry to try to soothe his nobles and maybe even appease them by having him arrested. Thomas heard a great shuffling and realised that the nobles were leaving. As he heard footsteps drawing nearer, he hurried back to his seat. As soon as Henry walked through the door, he jumped up again, but said nothing. He needed Henry to speak first, for Thomas hadn't the faintest idea what he was thinking.

'My nobles are leaving court,' Henry said. 'And why are they leaving court?' He jabbed his finger at Thomas. 'Because of you.'

Thomas licked his suddenly dry lips. 'I regret their retreat exceedingly, Your Grace. If I may, why did you allow it?'

Henry banged his fist on the wall, making Thomas jump. 'Why? Because I will not have anyone telling me what I can and cannot do. They leave because they do not like Henry Percy being committed to the Fleet? Well, let them leave. What did Howard think he would achieve? That I would beg him to stay and release Percy?' His fist hit the wall again.

'Kings do not beg,' Thomas said, watching the fist warily.

'No, they don't,' Henry agreed heartily.

'But you could have given me to them,' Thomas said with the smallest of laughs, feeling it dying on his lips as Henry turned to glare at him.

'Don't think I didn't consider it. But I need you more than I need them,' he said, brushing past Thomas and resuming his seat.

Thomas smoothed the silk over his belly and clasped his hands to stop them from shaking. 'They will return, Your Grace, when they have stopped sulking and miss your favour.'

'If I allow them to return,' Henry said petulantly.

He snatched up the book that lay on the table and opened it, sliding out a strip of leather he had been using as a bookmark. 'You can go, Thomas. Just tread a little more carefully in future. You may be cardinal and my Lord Chancellor, but you're still a commoner and nobles do not like to be ordered about by an upstart. You understand?'

'Yes, Your Grace,' he said.

Thomas understood. He didn't like it, but he understood. It was the way of the world. The highest in the land would always stay the highest. No matter how high Thomas climbed, he would never be accepted by the nobility because in their eyes he had common blood.

Thomas bowed and left the room without another word. He realised it was the first time Henry had ever dismissed him.

CHAPTER EIGHT

1517

Please, God, let this year be peaceful.

Thomas muttered 'Amen' and pushed himself up from his *prie dieu*. His prayer was heartfelt. After the year he had had, he felt he deserved a little tranquillity, a year of nothing more than routine paperwork and Church business. Yes, that would be very welcome.

The previous year had not exactly been tumultuous, it was true, but Thomas had found it personally difficult. His actions against the nobility had been unpopular. He was used to unpopularity and could easily have weathered that storm had it not been for Henry's manner towards him after the nobles left court. The way Henry had dismissed him, the lack of support, the lack of warmth, had caused Thomas more than a few sleepless nights.

But Henry's anger had lessened and relations between them had become almost as they had been before when, after a few months, the nobles, one by one, began to return. They came slinking back, and, though they cast sly sideways looks at Thomas, no more threats were made against him. Thomas ordered Percy's release from the Fleet Prison, and he quietly continued hearing cases in the Star Chamber, finding when he could for the common man against the knight or earl, but no more speaking publicly against the nobility. He hoped they had learnt their lesson and would behave. He had no great wish to imprison any more nobles.

Henry also seemed to have got over his disappointment of having a daughter rather than a son. He doted on the little girl, bestowing kisses upon her head, which brought tears of joy to Katherine's eyes. He would still talk wistfully of having a son, though, and Thomas had noticed that he praised the queen less often than he once had, and, on public occasions such as a banquet or a dance, he saw Henry's eyes lingering on the young beauties brought to court by their ambitious parents. The queen noticed it too, but said nothing, at least, not to Thomas, and he suspected not to her husband either.

Then there had been the arrival of Henry's sister, Queen Margaret of Scotland, at his court. The duke of Albany had made good use of the Scottish lords' mistrust of their English queen to force her to flee to England, leaving him to rule Scotland as its regent. Deserted by her unfaithful second husband, Margaret had much to complain of, something she had never ceased to do, in Thomas's opinion, and he had been continually pestered by her for money, clothing and suitable places to live. Though Henry loved his sisters, his love was not so strong that he wished to give Margaret a home for the rest of her life. He wanted her back in Scotland, or, if that was not possible, then available to him as a potential bride for any foreign ruler he wanted to ally with. Thomas had suggested the former was more desirable and had worked hard to broker a treaty with Scotland enabling her to return. With Margaret gone, the burden on the privy purse was greatly lessened and Thomas could once more add up the columns in his household ledger and not baulk or shake his head at the sums spent.

Yes, an uneventful year would be very welcome. He would have time to visit Hampton Court. Thomas was finding with each passing year that he enjoyed London less and less, and he had jumped at the chance to buy the lease on Hampton Court a couple of years previously. He had hopes of making the place his country retreat.

The thought of Hampton Court made Thomas quicken his pace along the corridors of York Place to his office. The architect he had hired to renovate Hampton Court had forwarded his plans a few days earlier, and Thomas had not yet had time to look them over. He decided he would do so now.

Entering his office, he said a brisk 'Good morning' to Tuke and grabbed the leather roll containing the plans from the shelf by the window. He unrolled the pages upon his desk and bent over them, his finger following every line the architect had drawn.

It was immediately clear to Thomas that a great

deal of work needed to be done to Hampton Court, not to make it habitable, for it was already that, but to make it fit for a cardinal. Thomas had been insistent on this. He had plenty of residences dotted around the country. Many houses came with the various Church benefices he held, and this had been the problem. He owned none of them. If he lost the Church title, he lost the building. Not that he had any fear he would lose titles, but it was always possible. He had, on occasion, swapped a benefice when a better one became vacant, and that meant handing the residence over to another priest.

Other residences, such as the first house he could truly call his, La Maison Curiale, had been bestowed upon him by a grateful king. While Thomas had done what he could to make the house his own, he had never felt it belonged to him, coming, as it had, from the estate of an executed man, Sir Richard Empson. Hampton Court would be different. It would represent him through and through.

Joan had tutted when one night he had told her of his plans for Hampton Court.

'You don't need to spend all that money,' she had exclaimed.

Thomas had laughed. 'Joan, when will you understand that I am no pauper? I have money enough to transform Hampton Court and still leave plenty over.'

'But there's no need to spend it at all,' she had insisted. 'There may come a time when you need all the money you can get, and what will you do then?'

Joan's perception of money, the sheer necessity of

it, formed from her earliest years, was difficult to shake. Like Thomas, she came from a class that commonly struggled to make ends meet, not knowing from one day to another whether she would have enough to feed herself and her family. Despite living in high comfort for many years now, Thomas knew she still made economies within his households, scolding the cooks when they bought expensive spices for meals only she and Thomas would eat, using up every scrap of paper so that no white spaces were left, and a dozen other examples of her thrifty house-keeping.

He defended his spending on Hampton Court to Joan. At least he didn't intend to witter his fortune away on pleasure like an idle courtier. No one would find him losing great sums of money on a single card game or taking silly wagers on which archer could hit a target two hundred yards away. No, he would say, squeezing her thigh beneath the bedclothes, his money would be spent on bricks and mortar, something that would provide a fitting legacy for England's only cardinal, and, he secretly hoped, a residence that would make all the nobles who resented his rise green with envy.

Thomas was so absorbed in surveying the plans that Tuke had to poke him in the arm to get his attention.

'Forgive me, Your Eminence, but a letter from the pope has arrived this morning.' He waved a paper beneath Thomas's nose.

Irritated, Thomas straightened, feeling bones

crack in his back. He pressed his fingers to the painful spot and rubbed. 'What does he want?' he asked Tuke, knowing that Pope Leo was always after something whenever he wrote.

'It's the League of Cambrai,' Tuke said, returning to his desk. 'It seems to be playing on his mind a little.'

'It's playing on mine, too,' Thomas muttered.

Following King Francis's victory at Marignano, an alliance had been formed between the three great heads of Europe – Emperor Maximilian, his grandson Charles of Aragon and King Francis – whereby each promised to come to the aid of the other should they suffer attack from an outside foe. Despite the pope's wooing of Francis, and in spite of England's friendly, if not entirely wholehearted overtures, to all three signatories of the League, the alliance had seemed to Thomas a deliberate attempt to exclude not only Pope Leo but Henry, too, and Thomas didn't like that one little bit. Not to be included in the League diminished Henry in the eyes of Europe and in his own eyes, and a humiliated Henry was something Thomas never wanted to have to face. Before Thomas had received news of the League, he had entertained hopes of making England into a power that was, if not exactly equal to either France or Spain, then at least a power neither of those countries could ignore. But this League threatened to return England to the status of an unimportant island once more.

'The pope wants England to join a crusade.'

Thomas heard the amusement in Tuke's voice and he turned to his secretary, who was trying not to smirk. 'A crusade?' Thomas said, incredulous.

Tuke grinned. 'That's what he says. The encroachment of the Turks into the West alarms him, so he wants help in forming an army large enough to check their advance.'

Thomas clicked his fingers for the letter and Tuke handed it over. 'He must be mad,' Thomas muttered as he quickly scanned the text. 'The Turks have enough to deal with. They're not planning to move any further towards Europe.' He tossed the letter aside. 'Come over here, Brian, and have a look at these plans.'

Tuke moved around his desk and joined Thomas at his. He bent over the plans, nodding and making polite noises as Thomas pointed out this feature and that. Thomas knew Tuke had no interest in architecture and that his secretary was merely humouring him, but he wanted someone to admire them. When he sensed Tuke running out of praise, he took the plans and rolled them back up.

'What do you want me to do about the pope's letter?' Tuke asked, moving gratefully back to his desk.

'Oh, I don't know. It's such a lot of nonsense and I don't have an answer for him. I can't tell him what I honestly think, that he's worrying over nothing, but I'm certainly not going to ask the king to go on a crusade to fight the Turk either.'

'The king may like the idea.'

'And that's the last thing I need. No, just put the

pope's letter to the bottom of my unimportant pile. That way, I cannot be accused of ignoring it, just that I haven't got around to answering it yet.'

Tuke nodded and turned to the shelves behind him. In the corner was a large pile of papers, the topmost of these covered with dust, indicative of how little it was attended to. He lifted up the entire pile, let it fall against his chest, and slid the pope's letter to the bottom before returning the pile to the shelf.

~

'Still nothing from England?' Pope Leo asked hopefully, but his secretary shook his head.

It had been months since Leo had written to Wolsey about the Turks. For Wolsey not to have even written a reply confirming receipt of Leo's letter showed a gross lack of respect for the papal office, and for Leo himself. What had happened to common courtesy, or didn't Wolsey believe in such niceties? *Still*, Leo told himself with a shake of his head, I *should expect nothing more from such a man as Thomas Wolsey*, and cursed once more the day he had made the plump, arrogant priest a cardinal. He had known even then that Wolsey would be trouble.

'I am sure word will come from Cardinal Wolsey,' said Lorenzo Campeggio, sitting on the other side of Leo's desk. 'The journey is long, the roads are bad.'

'The roads are not so very bad, old friend,' Leo shook his head. 'No, I know what Wolsey's doing. He's ignoring me.'

'He wouldn't dare,' Campeggio cried, his face aghast at the notion.

'Oh, wouldn't he!' Leo said. He gestured for Campeggio to pass the plate of almond biscuits. 'You know Wolsey better than I. Would you say he is a humble man?'

'No, I would not,' Campeggio admitted, needing no time to consider. 'But I cannot see any advantage to him by ignoring your letter.'

'Aye, there you have it. Advantage. Wolsey only acts when he stands to gain, and he will have nothing personally to gain by joining with me in this action against the Turk.'

'And yet,' Campeggio frowned as he thought, 'his king is young, and young men like to go to war. Will he not be displeasing the king if he fails to respond to your call?'

'Does Henry even know of it?' Leo cried, flinging out his arms. 'Has Wolsey informed him of my entreaty? Every letter that enters England is seen by Wolsey before it gets anywhere near the king, you know that.'

Campeggio shook his head helplessly, knowing it was true. 'Might it not be possible to bypass Wolsey?'

'How?' Leo leaned closer, crumbs hanging from his lips.

'Do not attempt to reach the king at all,' Campeggio shrugged. 'Send your letter to the queen of England instead. Queen Katherine is a devout Catholic, devoted both to you and to the Church. If she knew of your crusade, she would make the king listen and agree, I am sure of it.'

'Yes, you may be right,' Leo nodded. 'But how?'

'Send the letter to her confessor to pass on to the queen.'

The secretary coughed. Both Leo and Campeggio turned in his direction.

'Forgive me, Your Holiness,' the secretary said, 'but, if you remember, we received word that Queen Katherine's confessor had been dismissed from her service.' He paused and looked from Leo to Campeggio. 'By Cardinal Wolsey.'

Leo made a noise of exasperation. 'What am I to do, Lorenzo?' he asked. 'By the Christ, I wish I had never made that man a cardinal.'

'Yes, that decision did surprise me. Why did you?' Campeggio asked.

Leo made a face. 'He had been pestering me for years to make him a cardinal. I promised I never would, Lorenzo, knowing the kind of man he is, but then he got King Henry to do his begging for him. Henry had been loyal to me, and I felt I could not refuse the one thing he asked of me. So, I gave in and made Wolsey a cardinal. And I have regretted it ever since.'

He sighed and pushed himself up from his desk and paced the room. His silk slippers made soft slapping noises on the marble floor. After a few minutes, he came to a stop and pointed a finger at Campeggio.

'I shall send you anyway,' he said decisively.

Campeggio, who had been nibbling a biscuit,

looked up at him in surprise. 'Send me?' he said uncertainly. 'Send me where?'

'To England,' Leo said, resuming his seat. 'Wolsey won't dare refuse to see you once he knows I have sent a papal legate to see the king. He couldn't turn you away. That would be a huge insult to me.'

'Are you sure Wolsey won't turn me away?' Campeggio asked, a lump rising in his throat. 'I am not.'

'He would not dare,' Leo said again. 'It shall be well, you shall see.'

Campeggio reached towards his left foot. 'My gout is quite painful, Your Holiness—'

Leo waved that away. 'It can't be helped, Lorenzo. I trust you to deal with Wolsey, there is none better. Yes, you will go.' He clicked his fingers at the secretary, who knowing what was coming, hurried to his desk and snatched up his quill. 'Make arrangements for Cardinal Campeggio to travel to England. Ensure he will have accommodation wherever he needs to stop. And send word to Cardinal Wolsey,' he almost spat the name, 'that he is coming.'

If Leo noticed the dejection upon Campeggio's face, he made no comment. Cardinal Campeggio was going to England, whether he liked it or not.

CHAPTER NINE

Richard Williamson peered through the tiny wooden bars at the two birds fluttering inside the cage and smiled. Nice plump birds, they were. They'd make a lovely supper for the wife's birthday. Margery deserved something better than the usual pottage for her special day after all she'd had to bear of late, her sister and father dying of the fever and their son having trouble keeping up at school. Yes, Margery would like the doves, boiled and served in a juniper sauce. Richard asked the stall-holder how much he wanted for the birds.

The man named his price, and, in no mood to haggle, Richard handed over the requisite coins and put his finger through the ring at the top of the bird-cage. He was about to lift it from the bench when someone at his side drawled, 'What is this?'

Richard turned. The accent had been strange, unfamiliar. As he looked the speaker up and down, taking in the brightly coloured doublet and hose and the tall, curling white and black feather in his bonnet, he realised he was French.

The Frenchman spoke again. 'Tell me, what is a peasant like you doing buying such fine birds?'

Richard's mouth opened in outrage, at the same time realising the Frenchman was not alone but had several of his countrymen huddled behind him, all laughing and pointing at him. 'What business is it of yours? I can buy what I like,' he said, summoning up his courage. 'And who are you to call me a peasant?'

'I am calling you a peasant. All English are peasants,' the Frenchman said with a sly twist of his lips. 'And these birds,' he put his finger in the ring, wrenching it from Richard's finger, 'are fit only for a Frenchman. They are so fine, in fact, I think I shall have them for my master's table.'

'Give them back.' Richard made a grab for the cage.

But the Frenchman held the cage aloft and with the other hand drew a dagger from his belt and held it to Richard's throat. The point cut into the skin, drawing blood. 'I think not, peasant. They are mine now.'

The Frenchman pushed Richard away, and he fell backwards over the bench. Signalling to his countrymen to follow, the Frenchman walked away from the stall, laughing at his victim.

Richard straightened, jerking his arms away from the stall-holder, who was trying to help. 'French whoreson,' he yelled after his attacker.

The Frenchman heard him and turned. He

shouted something in French, which Richard didn't understand, but which he could tell from the tone wasn't polite.

A crowd had gathered around him. Richard felt his face growing red with shame. He should have stood up for himself, knocked the blade away and kneed the Frenchman in the groin. Instead, he had quivered like a maid and let him walk away with the birds, the birds he had paid good money for. For a moment, he considered asking the stall-holder to return his coins, but as the words of sympathy and outrage swelled around him, from people who could have helped him had they had the courage they were swearing they possessed, he knew he had to get away.

Richard pushed his way out of the marketplace, furious impotent tears misting his vision. *We are all afraid of these foreigners*, he thought as he walked, he knew not where. Not one of his fellow Englishmen had come to his aid, and yet there had been more English than French. Together, they would have got the better of the blasted foreigners easily.

But they had all cowered and dared not speak, dared not act. 'What cowards we English are,' he said to the air. He looked up and saw he was outside a tavern. He needed a drink; a jug of beer would set him up. How could he go home to his wife and tell her what had happened without her being ashamed of him? And she would be right to be ashamed, he told himself as he stepped inside the tavern.

It was night when Richard emerged. The moon was out and casting her silvery light to guide him home. He reached his front door and, after taking a deep breath, lifted the latch and stepped over the threshold. His wife was standing in the hallway, a handkerchief to his eyes.

'My dear, what's wrong?' Richard asked.

Before she could answer, two constables stepped into the hallway from the parlour. The elder of the two asked, 'Richard Williamson?'

Richard's throat had gone dry. 'Ye... yes.'

'You are to come with us. You're under arrest for insulting a member of the French ambassador's establishment.'

'Me! Insult them!' he cried, hardly able to believe what he was hearing.

'Oh, Richard,' his wife sobbed as the constable took hold of Richard's arms and set shackles around his wrists. 'What have you done?'

～

Dr Beale, Canon of St Mary's, had had enough. What was happening to London? Everywhere he turned he heard foreign tongues spoken, foreign, probably heathen, religions being practised and the formation of small foreign communities behind walls that permitted no English person to see in or enter. It was wrong, all wrong. Whose bloody country was this? Dr Beale was sure that any visitor to London would wonder what country he had set foot in because it certainly wasn't England.

He knew he wasn't alone in thinking this. He had

friends and acquaintances, and they all said the same, that they all felt like strangers in their own land. And it wasn't just the imposition of foreigners that was the problem. If it was, perhaps he could, as a Christian, have borne that. No, it was that the foreigners weren't at all grateful for the home they had been given in England. They acted as if it were their right to live here. And that didn't include those who came over from the Continent to visit. They were even worse. Why, there was that poor man his friend John Lincoln had spoken of, that Richard Williamson, who had been wrongfully imprisoned on the say-so of a Frenchman!

Dr Beale didn't mind admitting he was becoming frightened. He didn't feel safe walking through the streets of London anymore. Something had to be done. But no one seemed to be brave enough to do anything. He had looked about him, to the aldermen of his parish, to his merchant parishioners, men who had voices in the local community and were not afraid to use them to slander one another or to demand their legal rights. But not one had offered to speak against the foreigners. And so it was left to him to speak on behalf of all Englishmen.

He didn't want to have to be the voice of reason, but he felt he had no choice. He wasn't sleeping properly because of the injustices he kept hearing about, and his conscience would not let him have peace until he spoke out.

Beale felt the sweat on his neck and beneath his arms as he climbed the pulpit in St Paul's. When he made his speech, he knew he would be speaking against the king's wishes. The king wanted foreigners in his country. It was good for business, it was claimed. Why, only the previous year, King Henry had ordered an enquiry to be made into the person or people responsible for putting up bills all over the city that claimed the king had lent money to Florentine merchants only to have those same merchants use the loan to beat their English counterparts down on price. Was it true? Beale didn't know, but he wouldn't be at all surprised if it were so. That was just the kind of sneaky, underhand, thoroughly un-English thing those Florentines would do.

He put his hands on the stone, feeling the cold seep into his skin, and looked down on the crowd beneath. The church was always busy, but it wasn't always that people stopped their business to listen to whoever climbed the pulpit to preach. Perhaps no one would pay him any attention. He didn't mind that. He would have said his piece; maybe then he would be able to sleep of a night. But say it he must. Beale closed his eyes and murmured, 'God, give me the courage to stand before these people and tell them the truth, even though it be against my king.'

Opening his eyes, he took a deep breath. 'Good people,' he cried loudly, testing his voice. It sounded firm, commanding. A few of the passers-by halted and looked up at him. Their interested faces gave him courage. 'I have something to say to you if you will hear me. I have long been troubled by what I see around me, and that is the decline of this, our great country, being brought low by the actions of strangers in our midst. God gave England to Englishmen, but now we English are being made poorer and poorer by the immigrants that have come to this country, set up homes in the city, and then taken all the work away from honest Englishmen.'

There were nods and a few encouraging grunts. They spurred him on.

'And not only do they take our ancient crafts and corrupt them with their foreign ways, but they endanger our very lives by closing their doors against us, allowing no Englishman to know what goes on behind them. Do you know what happens in their closed communities?'

A few angry shouts of, 'No!'

'No, nor do I. For all we know, they could be plotting crimes against us, against our king. My fellow Englishmen, we must act against these invaders. Have compassion for the poor people, your neighbours, and also for the great hurts, losses and hindrances and the extreme poverty of all the king's subjects that inhabit this city. These aliens and strangers take the bread from our poor fatherless children and the livings and business from all English merchants, thereby increasing our poverty, and causing every man to bewail the misery of another, for craftsmen are brought to beggary and merchants to need. This land was given by God to Englishmen. As birds would defend their nests, so ought Englishmen to cherish and defend themselves and to hunt and grieve these aliens for the common weal.'

The crowd were with him. He had raised his arm in the air with his final words, buoyed up by the faces beneath that seemed to hang on his every word, and he held it there now, as if it were a standard waved on a battlefield.

There were cheers and shouts and applause. Beale looked down on the men and women he had inspired and basked in their appreciation. He had not had such a reception before and he enjoyed it. He had been right to speak out, he thought joyfully. He had not been alone in his outrage; the people of London had just needed a voice to speak up for them. His had been that voice.

He brought his arm back down to his side and looked over the crowd. Yes, they were all with him, all of them smiling up at him, all – no, not all. There was that man leaning against the wall, arms folded, cap pulled low. He wasn't cheering or applauding. He didn't even seem to be smiling. A twinge of unease gripped Beale's stomach. Perhaps he was a foreigner and thinking of how he could do him harm.

Beale quickly descended the pulpit steps, his joy of only a few moments before rapidly receding. He had said what he had wanted to say, got the crowd on his side. It was enough. His courage only went so far. Now all he wanted to do was reach the safety of his home before word of what he had preached got around and foreigners in their hundreds sought him out to stick a dagger in him.

~

They were lined up in front of him, like schoolboys summoned to the headmaster's study to be whipped: Lord Mayor John Rest and the aldermen of the capital. It would have been amusing, Thomas thought, if the matter were not so serious.

Thomas held up the bill poster one of his servants had delivered to him that morning. It had been pasted onto a church door and discovered by a church warden jangling his keys to open up. It was a poorly printed publication. Some of the letters were the wrong way round and there were large ink blots covering a few of the words, but the majority of the text was perfectly readable by those who had the education to read it. It was a call to arms. The English were being roused to attack the foreigners in their midst. 'How many of these have been posted?' he asked.

'We've taken down forty-three so far,' John Rest replied. 'I have men out searching for others.'

'These bills were put up during the night. So we have no way of knowing how many have been seen and read.'

'That is correct, Your Eminence.'

'Then we must act on the assumption that they have been widely read and spoken of to others.'

'I'm sure it's just the apprentices up to their usual mischief,' Rest said, waving his hand dismissively at the bill Thomas held.

'Are you?' Thomas looked up at him, making the old man quail. 'I don't think we can afford to take that chance.'

Rest clamped his hands together and ducked his head, not willing to say another word that would earn the scorn of the cardinal.

'This is not the only incident of this kind,' Thomas continued. 'This has not been bruited abroad, so I don't expect you to know, but several men of the highest degree have been threatened because of the discontent surrounding foreign communities in London. I myself have received threats. Which is why we must treat this,' he set the bill down on his desk, 'with all seriousness.'

'You have a suggestion, Your Eminence?' one of the aldermen asked.

'I have instructions,' Thomas replied curtly. He held out a sheet of paper to Rest, who took and read it, his lips mouthing the words he read there. 'I am imposing a curfew on the capital. From nine o'clock to seven in the morning on May Day Eve, all citizens are to remain indoors. If anyone is discovered abroad during these hours, the watch is to place them under arrest. Meanwhile, Master Rest, you are to arrest this Dr Beale.'

Rest lowered the paper. 'On whose authority, Your Eminence?'

'On mine,' Thomas snapped. 'What other authority do I need? Good God, Rest, *you* had the authority to arrest him. You should not have allowed Beale to speak at all, let alone finish his sermon. Let us hope, gentlemen, this will all come to nothing.'

John Rest and the aldermen all nodded their

hearty agreement and shuffled out gladly when Thomas dismissed them.

'Fools,' Tuke said as he closed the door upon them. 'Of course that man Beale should have been arrested. I know that and I'm only a secretary. Why are men like that given high office if they can't do the bloody job?'

Thomas's lips twitched at Tuke's derision. He felt the same. If only all men were as assiduous as he at their work. Joan often asked why Thomas didn't delegate more. In John Rest and those aldermen, she had her answer. No one else would do the work as well as he.

'Let us hope this Dr Beale was just getting a grievance off his chest and we'll hear nothing more of him or his cause.'

'Not if the apprentices have anything to do with it,' Tuke said. 'They'll use any excuse to start a fight.'

'Yes,' Thomas said grimly, 'in that I fear you are right.'

Tuke took up a letter from his desk, the death threat Thomas had spoken of. 'Do you really think you are in danger, Your Eminence?' he asked, gesturing with the letter.

Thomas gave it the merest of glances before carrying on with his work. 'I think it would be sensible to take the threat seriously, Brian. I've ordered the men to arm themselves. If anyone does think to make good on that threat, then I will be ready for them.'

~

Alderman Munday left his office in a very bad mood. It had been humiliating to stand before the cardinal and be told off for not taking such-and-such action when it wasn't his job to do so. The Lord Mayor gave the orders for keeping the city safe and quiet; Munday and his colleagues merely had to follow them. *But try telling that to His Eminence and see how far you get,* Munday thought bitterly. *It's all very well for him, sitting in his office in his scarlet finery, dozens of secretaries to carry out his every command, guards on the gates at York Place. Let him come down to Bucklersbury or Eastcheap and see how easy it is to maintain order.*

In some respects, he sympathised with Dr Beale. There were too many foreigners in London. Oh, he knew they weren't all bad, but it was true that they kept themselves to themselves. Why weren't decent Englishmen allowed to go into their communities and see for themselves what went on? What did these foreigners have to hide?

Of course, Munday would never advocate civil disobedience. If he believed in one thing, he believed in law and order. He agreed with the imposition of a curfew if it would stop trouble from starting, but he wasn't sure how easy it would be to enforce it. The Lord Mayor had few men at his command. There was the watch, of course, but many of those men were elderly and took the job expecting to have nothing more to do than patrol the empty streets and keep an eye out for fire. They certainly wouldn't be able to fight a mob.

Munday turned a corner and stopped dead.

Ahead of him, near the end of the street, was a group of young men. Even in ordinary times, Munday would have preferred to avoid such a crowd. He wished vehemently that he had paid attention to the noise they were making a street or so back. He would have taken a different route home.

But it was too late now. They had spotted him. And besides, the curfew was approaching. Cardinal Wolsey had made it very clear that it was his job to enforce the curfew. If he failed at this, he would feel the full force of the cardinal's displeasure, he felt sure. One humiliation was enough for him. He would not endure another in the same day.

'You there,' he called to the two young men nearest to him, who were playing with wooden swords, 'don't you know there's a curfew? The hour is almost nine. You must get home at once or risk arrest by the constable.'

One of the men thumped his companion on the shoulder and jerked his head at Munday. 'Who's this now, telling us what to do?' he said with an ugly grin.

'I am Alderman Munday,' Munday said with as much dignity as he could muster. 'It is my duty to remind you of the curfew.'

'Your duty, eh?' the youth jeered. 'And is it your duty to walk us home too?'

His friends laughed loudly.

Munday felt his stomach turn over. 'No,' he said, forcing a smile onto his face, 'but it is my duty to fetch the constable if you do not go home, young man. And you don't want me to do that, do you?'

The young man's face turned serious, and he stepped up to Munday. 'You got no right to talk to me like that, alderman.'

Over his shoulder, Munday saw the rest of the youths come towards him. His legs were turning to jelly, and he truly felt that he would have collapsed had not the youth grabbed his cloak and held him up by it.

'You will unhand me, young man,' he said, and he knew his voice came out tremulous. 'The cardinal has ordered—'

'The old fat man has ordered what?' the youth yelled in Munday's face.

Munday was appalled at hearing the cardinal spoken of so. He rebuked the youth severely and tried to pull his cloak out of the young man's grip. But he was held tight and could do nothing but hang there.

'Let's send the cardinal a message,' one of the group said to the others and picked up a stick from behind a barrel that stood against a wall. It was a very heavy stick and Munday had visions of it coming down and crashing his skull in.

'No, please,' he whimpered, unable to take his eyes off the stick. 'I am an alderman.' It was his only defence.

'This one's nothing,' the youth said sneeringly. 'What say you, lads? Let us go have some fun with some foreigners, eh?'

His words were greeted by a hearty cheer, and Munday found himself thrown into the gutter. He landed with a splash and tasted the filth of the street as it entered his mouth. He lay there for a long moment, eyes closed, praying the youths were leaving him alone.

They did leave him alone. He heard their shouts and laughter grow fainter as they moved away and he opened his eyes.

He was on his own. He felt his stomach lurch and, a moment later, spewed its contents over the ground. He knew he had come close to death this night, and was thankful, though God forgive him, that his attackers had not thought him worth the effort and instead had gone off to hurt the very people he had been ordered to protect.

The cardinal would never forgive him.

~

Joan came rushing into his office. 'There's armed men at the gates, Tom. And the cooks in the kitchen are saying we're going to be attacked.'

Thomas went to her, arms outstretched to take her into an embrace. 'Joan, Joan, there's nothing to worry about. The house is secure, and no one is going to get in.'

'You mean it's true?' she cried, her eyes growing wide in fear. 'We *are* going to be attacked?'

'There is some trouble in the city,' Thomas nodded, moving her to his chair and pushing her into it. 'But it will be under control very soon.'

'Someone told me you had been threatened.'

He would have preferred that that little piece of

information had been kept from Joan. She did worry so about him. 'Nonsense,' he lied. 'That's just kitchen gossip. I've told you before not to listen to what the cooks say. Now, I want you to go back to our rooms and stay there.'

Joan clutched at his hands. 'Come with me.'

He shook his head. 'I can't. I have to stay here.' Thomas glanced over to Tuke and gestured towards Joan. Tuke nodded and came around the desk. He put his hand beneath Joan's armpit, encouraging her to rise.

'Come with me, Mistress Larke,' he said. 'I'll see you to your rooms.'

Joan allowed herself to be propelled towards the door, looking back over her shoulder at Thomas with fear in her eyes.

'Get someone to sit with her,' Thomas called to Tuke, 'then come straight back here. I will need you.'

Tuke nodded and closed the door behind himself and Joan.

Thomas moved to the window and stared first down the river, then across to its other side. That side seemed quiet, but he knew that wasn't where the trouble was. The trouble was to the east, near Eastcheap, and he had no doubt that if he had the power, he would be able to hear screams and shouts, the crackle of fires, all the noises of a mob on the rampage. *So much for my curfew*, he thought. *Too little, too late.* Tuke had been right about the apprentices. The report Alderman Munday had sent confirmed that the apprentices had begun all this trouble.

But they weren't the only ones causing trouble. The reports he had received told Thomas that the apprentices' mob had swelled considerably. There had been several ugly incidents, none so ugly as the attack on Flemish merchants that had resulted in their bruised and battered bodies being thrown in a ditch and left for dead. The perpetrators of that particular incident had been arrested and incarcerated, but that was a small consolation. In fact, the only thing Thomas was thankful for was that neither the king nor the queen were in London but had moved to Richmond the previous week because of the rumours the dreaded sweat had returned.

He heard the door open and close and turned away from the window to see Tuke returning.

'Is she well?' Thomas asked.

Tuke nodded. 'She'll calm down, I'm sure. I sent Martha to sit with her.'

Martha was an elderly woman in charge of the laundry, and Thomas knew she and Joan were friends. Martha would calm her, he knew, and was glad. He moved back to his desk.

'I need you to write to the duke of Norfolk and the earl of Surrey,' Thomas said. 'They are both in London and they have large retinues.'

'To see off the rioters? Will they come?'

Thomas knew Tuke was thinking of both nobles' affirmed hatred for him and whether they would obey a summons from the cardinal to gather armed men. 'They had better,' he growled, 'or I shall tell the king how they failed him.'

There was a knock on the door and it opened immediately. One of the clerks from the outer office poked his head around the door and handed Tuke a paper before disappearing again.

'What news?' Thomas asked.

Tuke read quickly. 'The rioters have broken into the prisons. All the prisoners have been freed. The gaolers couldn't do anything to stop them.'

'What do you mean, they couldn't?' Thomas cried. 'They're armed, aren't they? Are not the prison walls and gates secure?'

'The rioters outnumbered the gaolers, Your Eminence.'

Thomas shook his head. 'And what of the gaolers now? I suppose next it shall be that they've joined the rioters.'

'It doesn't say here,' Tuke said.

Another knock at the door. Another clerk poking his head round and delivering reports.

'This one says the rioters have left Cheapside and are making their way to St Martin le Grand.'

'To where most of London's foreign communities reside,' Thomas said through gritted teeth. 'God help those poor people if the rioters are not stopped.'

'And this…' Tuke held up another paper.

'What is it?'

'It's from the Lord Mayor. He dispatched Sir Thomas More as under-sheriff to apprehend the rioters as per your orders, but Sir Thomas refused to take armed men with him.'

'He refused? How dare he do so?'

'Apparently, Sir Thomas told the Lord Mayor that he would use reason to make them desist.'

Thomas stared in utter incomprehension at Tuke. 'The man's a bloody fool. How can one reason with a mob?'

'Sir Thomas More can be very persuasive, I understand.'

'Not that bloody persuasive,' Thomas said, moving back to the window. He pressed his forehead against the glass, enjoying the chill creeping into his skin. 'Oh, let him try what he can. It's his life he's playing with. Send those letters to Norfolk and Surrey at once. It sounds like Under-Sheriff More is going to need all the help he can get.'

∼

The night wore on and the riot worsened. News came in that More had failed to persuade the rioters to lay down their weapons and go home and that they had, in fact, increased in number and ferocity.

Thomas had Tuke write out an order to the Lieutenant of the Tower to fire the cannons into the streets surrounding the grim fortress, certain that cannon fire would scatter the mob and have them scurrying in all directions. Once broken up, the rioters would be easier to deal with. Thomas knew that lives would be lost, English lives, but the rioters had forsaken any kind of consideration when they had begun their attack. He didn't like the idea of ordering the killing of Englishmen, but it couldn't be helped.

He breathed easier when Tuke reported that Norfolk and Surrey had taken their retinues to the street, along with the earl of Shrewsbury. Thomas hoped that seeing so many men in livery would make the rioters quail and realise the nobles were not with them, they were with the king. Even if the rioters were not dispirited by such opposition, they would find themselves hopelessly outnumbered.

By three in the morning, it was all over. Thomas ordered the night watch to arrest as many of the rioters as could be found, and he received word that more than three hundred had been sent to the prisons that were once more under the gaolers' control. Thomas was astonished at the number. So many arrested. How many more had escaped back to their homes?

He had Tuke enquire as to how much damage to buildings and other property had been caused. There had been considerable breakages of windows and doors, mostly in the foreign quarters where the rioters had forced entry, and some small fires that had been swiftly put out, to Thomas's great relief, for he well knew how dangerous fire could be to the city. On the whole, though, it seemed that they had got off quite lightly. There was nothing damaged that could not be put right, and only a few lives had been lost.

Thomas had not left the office since the trouble began, neither had he eaten or drunk a thing. When Joan put her head around the door a little after five, when the grey of the dawn was bleeding through the windows, Thomas realised just how tired he was. He was pleased that she had gone to bed, for she was still dressed in her nightgown and cap, but her eyes looked tired.

'I've been waiting up there for hours,' she whispered, glancing anxiously at Tuke, who had fallen asleep at his desk, his head on his folded arms. 'What's happening?'

Thomas waved her in, putting his finger to his lips to tread quietly. 'It's over,' he said as she sat on a stool by his desk.

'Oh, Tom,' she sighed. 'Thank God.'

'I will,' he assured her. 'As soon as I can.'

'You must get some sleep first,' she said, putting her finger to his chin and tilting his head to the light. 'You look exhausted.'

'Just a few more letters to write and then I shall come to bed.'

'Promise me it will be just a few letters, Tom.'

He kissed her. 'I promise. Now, go before anyone sees you.'

Thomas watched her leave his office, closing the door as quietly as she had opened it. He had meant what he said to her. He had just a few more letters to write – letters of congratulation to Norfolk, Surrey and Shrewsbury, and to the king to assure him that the mob had been defeated – and then he would go to bed very willingly.

It had been a very long and very unpleasant night.

CHAPTER TEN

Thomas had been summoned to Richmond.

Joan protested. 'But you're exhausted, Tom. You've sent reports to the king, I know you have. Are they not enough that he must drag you up the river to ask you what he already knows?'

Thomas shook his head and told her he could not ignore a summons from the king, however pointless it might seem. She had continued protesting even as he climbed down into his barge, and he wished she would stop.

Joan meant well, but she knew he must go; this nagging only delayed and aggravated him. He swayed a little as he bent to enter the canopied rear of the barge and almost fell onto the cushioned seat. A wave of nausea came over him and he held himself still as he thought he might vomit. The feeling passed, but the incident proved Joan right. He really did need to rest if merely moving made him dizzy. Maybe, after all this was over, they would go to the country for a few weeks.

Tuke clambered onto the barge after him. 'Do you want the curtains closed, Your Eminence?'

Thomas nodded. If he was feeling dizzy and nauseous, it would be better not to watch the river go past.

Tuke took hold of the curtains. 'Why don't you get some sleep? I'll wake you when we near Richmond.'

'Thank you, Brian. I think I will.' And Thomas twisted his body round so he could lean against the seat. He stuffed a small cushion between the back of the seat and his cheek and closed his eyes.

The next thing he knew was Tuke shaking him awake. 'We're here, Your Eminence.'

Thomas blinked, wincing as the sunlight coming through the gap in the curtains hurt his eyes. He held out his hand to be helped up and he heard Tuke groan as he pulled. Maybe he should do something about his weight as well, Thomas mused, as he lifted his robes away from his damp legs, shaking them to make them drape properly.

'Good day, Your Eminence,' someone called as he moved along the centre of the barge to climb out onto the river steps.

'Richard,' Thomas cried with genuine pleasure, for he liked the king's secretary a great deal. 'Have you been sent to greet me?'

'I insisted,' Richard said. 'The king would like to

see you as soon as you are able. Would you like to rest, to eat—'

'That would be very welcome,' Tuke began.

'No,' Thomas said, putting a silencing hand on his arm, knowing Joan would have told him to keep an eye on his master, 'we must not keep the king waiting.'

Tuke opened his mouth as if to argue but shut it again at Thomas's stern expression.

'It's been a tiring few days, I imagine,' Richard said as he led them towards the rear of the palace.

'Very,' Thomas agreed, 'but we got through it without too much harm done. Tell me, is there a reason why the king wanted to see me? I sent him detailed reports of all that happened.'

'And he read them all,' Pace said. 'He seemed satisfied with all you wrote. To tell the truth, Your Eminence, I think it was the queen who insisted you come here, not the king.'

Ah, yes, Katherine had made Henry send for him, that made sense. She was ever likely to doubt him. Another wave of nausea hit him, stronger this time, and Thomas came to an abrupt halt, his hand pressing against his stomach. A cold sweat broke out over him.

'Your Eminence, are you ill?' Tuke asked, taking hold of his elbow.

Thomas couldn't answer at once; he was trying to keep the vomit or bile, or whatever was threatening to rise up his throat, down. 'The river journey has upset me, I think,' he said when he felt a little better. 'Perhaps, Richard, a sit down and something for my stomach would be advisable.' He had no desire to vomit in front of the king and queen.

'Of course, Your Eminence. Follow me.'

Pace led them to the kitchens. A cardinal in their midst flummoxed the kitchen staff a little, and Thomas was aware of the quiet that descended over what was normally a hive of activity and continual noise. He sat down on a bench at the kitchen table and closed his eyes. The dizziness passed, but his stomach was still lurching. A few minutes went by and then a cup was set before him, steam rising from the contents. He picked it up and sniffed. Ginger in the liquid. That was good, that would settle his stomach. He sipped at the hot drink, then tested the volatility of his stomach with a few deep breaths. Nothing happened, and he relaxed.

'Better?' Tuke said in his ear.

Thomas nodded and took a few more sips until the cup was half empty. The kitchen staff were still quiet, going about their work with shifty glances at one another. Thomas knew his presence unnerved them, and he thought it only fair to leave them alone. He rose and Pace pointed to the kitchen's exit into a dark corridor.

'Say nothing of this to the king or queen,' Thomas said to Pace as they walked.

''Tis nothing to be ashamed of, Your Eminence,' Pace protested.

'I know, but I do not want the king to think I

cannot conduct his business. He doesn't need to know, Richard.'

Thankfully, Pace understood. He nodded and said nothing more. A few moments later, they were standing outside the double doors of the king's privy apartments and he nodded at the guards to open up. Thomas entered, leaving Tuke and Pace to wait in the corridor.

'He's here at last,' Katherine muttered to Henry as the doors closed behind him. She was sitting at a small table, an embroidery upon her lap. Henry stood beside her.

'Forgive me if I am late, Your Grace,' Thomas said to Henry. 'I set out as soon as I received your summons.'

'Then why did it take you so long?' Katherine asked.

'I could not say, madam. Perhaps the river was against us?' Thomas suggested, annoyed that she was making such a fuss.

'It matters not, he's here now, Kate,' Henry said, putting his massive hand on Katherine's shoulder. She looked up at him, took an indignant breath at his censorious expression, and returned her gaze to her embroidery. Henry looked back to Thomas. 'A troubling business, all this, Thomas.'

'Indeed, Your Grace, though it is all under control now.'

'A pity matters had to be got under control,' Katherine said pointedly. 'Could this whole affair not have been avoided?'

'We tried to avoid it, madam. I instigated a curfew as soon as I learnt of the rioters' intentions. Admittedly, the preachers should have been arrested earlier. I have reprimanded the Lord Mayor and the aldermen for their slowness in responding to the threat. The preachers are now under arrest.'

'A case of too little, too late.' Katherine stabbed her embroidery with her needle, and Thomas wondered if she was imagining it was his eye.

Thomas drew in a breath. 'If I may, my lady, it is very easy with hindsight to say what should have been done and when it should have been done. It is not so clear when one is in the midst of such an event.'

Katherine's eyebrow rose, but she said nothing.

'How many arrests have been made?' Henry asked.

'More than three hundred malefactors, including women, have been arrested, Your Grace,' Thomas said, relieved to be spared talking further to Katherine. 'The majority of these were taken by Norfolk, Surrey and Shrewsbury.'

'It seems to me that we have our nobles to thank for our deliverance rather than yourself, Cardinal Wolsey,' Katherine said. 'And yet these are the men you are so eager to persecute in your Star Chamber.'

Thomas's jaw tightened. 'I agree that much thanks should be given to those gentlemen, my lady, and I have done so. Though I do not think I am wrong in saying they were only able to make arrests because of my coordination and instructions.'

'Oh, of course,' she nodded, her eyes narrowing. 'You are to be praised, none other.'

'Kate,' Henry growled.

At least Henry is on my side, Thomas thought, sliding his gaze from Katherine to her husband. 'The question is, of course, what happens next.'

'Indeed,' Henry agreed. He chewed his bottom lip for a moment. 'Executions?'

He says the word so easily, Thomas thought. *Can he really countenance the execution of three hundred souls without any qualms?* 'I agree that the ringleaders, the ones who urged this action on, should be executed, Your Grace. But I wonder if there is not more to be gained by showing mercy to the others?'

'What?' Katherine cried.

'Mercy?' Henry burst out.

Thomas held up his hands. 'If you will bear with me, Your Grace. This event will be reported throughout Europe. It will be known that a few unruly subjects challenged your authority and were swiftly put down by true and loyal servants.'

He glanced up at Henry, seeing if he understood that this would not remain a purely English affair. Others would judge Henry's standing as king, and, if he was not careful, he might come out wanting.

'It is expected for traitors to be executed,' he continued. 'In France and in Spain, I do not doubt, the traitors would be executed in the most horrible way possible, without trial, merely on the king's command. But you are not a French or Spanish king,

Your Grace. You are an English king, and English kings are not such tyrants.'

'Certainly not,' Henry agreed vigorously.

'When a king has an opportunity to show mercy, he should show mercy,' Thomas went on, taking pleasure in the furious expression on Katherine's face. She hadn't liked him suggesting the Spanish were cruel. 'Imagine what your counterparts on the Continent would say if you were to pardon those who rioted?'

'They would say my husband is weak,' Katherine said.

'No, my lady,' Thomas wagged a finger at her, 'they would say King Henry has no fear of his subjects.'

'Would they really, Thomas?' Henry asked.

'You are a Christian king, Your Grace. The Bible instructs us to show mercy. You would be following the law of God and ensuring that those whom you had every right to punish with death are grateful to you for their lives. They will never act counter to your rule again, I assure you.'

Please, believe me on this, he silently urged. He didn't want to have to order the death of three hundred people, no matter how much trouble they had caused.

Katherine looked up at her husband. He looked down at her. Thomas waited.

'You are right, Thomas,' Henry said at last. 'No, my dear,' he shook his head at Katherine, who had opened her mouth to protest, 'I have decided.'

'My father would never have pardoned traitors,' she said.

'I am not your father,' Henry said, and Thomas was surprised by the malice in his words. 'How do we go about it, Thomas?'

Thomas breathed a sigh of relief. 'Well, the malefactors must be held to account. Their offences must not go unrecorded. I have been thinking that, with Your Grace's agreement, we have them all brought to Westminster Hall. We do not tell them they are to be pardoned. We let them think they are to be sentenced to death. Both of you,' he nodded from Henry to Katherine, 'are present to show your unhappiness at their treason. They must be made to feel how greatly they have transgressed the natural order.

'We must also, while we are about it, do what we can to protect the foreigners they took against so. Your Grace and I both know how vital such people are to our economy and England's wellbeing abroad. We don't want them leaving. We must let the foreigners within our country know they are safe. I suggest you make a speech explaining how greatly you pity the foreigners and how you will not tolerate any further animosity towards them. You are so angry, you order the malefactors' executions at once.'

'And when they are about to be hanged, I rescind the order?'

'No, Your Grace. The cost of making a scaffold large enough to hang so many at one time would be wasted. And besides, I think it necessary to show that you are persuadable, unlike your brother kings. I suggest, therefore, that I, and if my lady agrees, the queen, beg you to show mercy to the malefactors.'

'I will not plead for traitors,' Katherine declared.

'Kate,' Henry said sharply, 'you will do as I ask you.'

'You mean to go along with this... this charade?'

'I believe this is an excellent plan, Thomas,' Henry said, ignoring her.

'Well, I do not,' Katherine said, crossing her arms across her chest.

'But, my lady,' Thomas said, 'think what we will have achieved by doing this. I, who represent the Church, plead for the prisoners. Womanhood, represented by yourself, pleads for the prisoners. And the king, persuaded by the gentle words of his queen, a foreigner by birth, a woman who has every right and reason to hate the malefactors, who, had she been of lower birth, would have had no mercy shown to her by the prisoners, agrees to show mercy to them.'

Katherine could not argue, he saw, as her mouth opened to retort. There was no argument she could make. He had laid it out so very neatly; all three of them, he, Henry, Katherine, would emerge from Westminster Hall with reputations even greater than before. He knew Henry would not be able to resist that.

'Very good, Thomas,' Henry said, his face breaking into a smile. 'Return to London and make the arrangements. Send for us when all is ready.'

'I will, Your Grace, thank you.'

Thomas bowed and exited.

'Well?' Pace asked as he emerged into the corridor.

138

'The prisoners are to be pardoned.'

Pace's mouth fell open. 'You are joking, surely, Your Eminence? The king was all but foaming at the mouth when he heard about the riots.'

'He must have calmed down,' Thomas said modestly.

Pace laughed and shook his head. 'I don't know how you do it, Your Eminence.'

'By virtue of a lifetime of working with men greater than I,' Thomas said. 'I will send instructions in a day or two, Richard. I know I can trust you to keep the king informed.'

'You can. Come, let me take you back down to your barge. I know you are keen to return to York Place.'

Keen to return, yes, Thomas thought as he and Tuke followed Pace out of the palace. And keen to rest. When all this is over, he promised himself.

~

Henry and Katherine were sitting beneath their canopies of estate, both suitably grim-faced as befitted the occasion. Thomas had briefed them thoroughly the night before at Baynard's Castle, telling them what was going to happen at Westminster Hall and what they were to do. He had even written Katherine's speech for her. She had accepted the paper with bad grace, but Thomas hadn't cared. Just as long as she played her part, she could loathe him all she liked.

It had been a busy couple of days – weren't all of

his days busy? – since returning from Richmond. As soon as he was back behind his desk at York Place, he had begun dictating letters. The first two were to the Lord Mayor and Lieutenant of the Tower. He informed them of his plan to bring all those arrested for rioting to Westminster Hall and charge them with treason and gave them instructions on how to make the prisoners ready. The next three letters were to Norfolk, Surrey and Shrewsbury, advising them to be ready to give evidence before the king and queen and to thank them once again for their help in subduing the mob. It never hurt to butter up the nobility, especially when thanks were due.

Thomas took his seat to the right of Henry and Katherine, his chair set lower than theirs but raised above the floor of Westminster Hall where the prisoners would stand. He signalled to the Lord Mayor to begin the proceedings.

The prisoners were led into the hall, all three hundred and forty-one. Thomas saw with satisfaction that they were dressed according to his instructions. They had all been stripped down to their shirts or shifts, and every one of them had a horse's halter around their neck to show that they were prisoners and had been subdued by the authorities. Thomas recalled the Lord Mayor's worried reply to his letter that to find so many halters at such short notice would be a problem. Thomas had told him to apply to one of the nobles to supply the deficiency, shaking his head that he had to think of such minor details as those. In addition to the halters, the prisoners' hands were tied behind their backs. Every one of them, without exception, Thomas judged from the pitiful expressions on their faces, expected the worst.

The Lord Mayor called for quiet. The charade, as Katherine had called it, was about to begin.

Thomas rose and read out the indictment, calling all the prisoners traitors and stating the nature of the punishment for those who committed treason against their king. Many of the women, and some of the men, began to weep.

First, the Lord Mayor and aldermen were called upon to give their accounts of what had happened on what was becoming known as Evil May Day. Then Norfolk, Surrey and Shrewsbury made their statements of how they had acted upon the cardinal's instructions to gather all their retinues and march them onto the streets of London to quell the mob. The evidence was damning. No one spoke in defence of the rioters.

Then Thomas rose and moved to stand before Henry. Bending his body, he lay flat on the ground, feeling the cold of the flagstones penetrate his silk robes, the large gold cross pressing uncomfortably into his stomach. When he spoke, he felt his words bounce back against his face.

'Most gracious sovereign, I appeal to you now to spare these men and women. Though they are guilty of acting against the laws of your kingdom and of showing you the greatest disrespect, I beg you to show mercy and let them go free.'

He heard gasps from the spectators and the

breaking off of sobs as the prisoners realised what he was asking. He waited for Henry's response, the one he had respectfully asked him to make, hoping Henry didn't have any ideas of his own to make this more difficult.

'My lord cardinal,' Henry said, 'rise.' He waited for Thomas to clamber to his feet, an awkward twenty seconds or so. 'You have pleaded most eloquently for these prisoners, but they have offended me greatly with their treason and the enmity they expressed against the foreign communities to whom we, as fair and generous Englishmen, give shelter. Is it not my duty to punish those who transgress the law?'

'Indeed it is,' Thomas said with relief. Henry had stuck to the speech.

'Then I am not minded to pardon the prisoners.'

It was Katherine's cue to speak. She rose from her chair, sedate, regal, not liking what she had to do now one little bit.

'My lord,' she began, Thomas knowing she had moved as near to him as she could bear and no nearer, 'I too beg your kindness for these prisoners. Their minds and their hearts were roused by the misguided sermons of men who should defend the foreigners who have sought sanctuary in your king- dom. Let those men alone be punished and show the great depth of your love for your people by pardoning them, entrusting them never to act against your authority again.'

She is magnificent, Thomas thought as Katherine finished. She had delivered her speech perfectly with grace and poise. If he didn't know better, he would have believed she meant every word she said.

Henry took a few moments to consider his wife's plea. He drummed his fingers on the pommel of his chair, thrust out his bottom lip and narrowed his eyes.

'Very well,' he said, and Thomas felt the prisoners' relief flood the hall. 'My wife the queen and my lord cardinal have moved me with their words. The prisoners are pardoned and shall be set free.'

Almost as one, the prisoners began calling out 'God save the king'. Through their tears, women cried out their thanks and fell to their knees. They thanked Henry, they thanked Katherine, and they thanked Thomas. It was all very gratifying and rather moving.

Thomas turned to the prisoners and raised his hand for silence. 'The king in his great mercy has pardoned you. You are free to return to your homes but be warned. Such treason may not be forgiven twice. You must obey the law in the future and treat all foreigners with the same respect and brotherly love you would show your English neighbours. Mark what I have said.'

He gestured for the guards to untie the prisoners' hands. This took quite a while, for the prisoners greatly outnumbered the guards, but when it was done, some of the prisoners took off their halters and threw them in the air with a cheer. Most, however, were eager to leave before the king changed his mind, and there was a great scurrying towards the hall's doors.

Thomas watched them go with immense satisfaction. His mind travelled back to the ceremony when he had been made cardinal and John Colet had told him his duties. He had saved three hundred and forty-one lives this day with no measurable gain to himself. How was that for bestowing Christian love?

Joan was waiting for him in his office. 'How did it go?' she asked when he was barely through the door.

'Very well,' he said.

Joan sighed extravagantly. 'Is that all you can say? What about the king and queen? The prisoners? What did you say? What did they say?'

Thomas slid the skullcap from his head, noticing that the red silk was damp between his fingers. He snatched up a cloth from his desk used to clean his pens and rubbed it over his head. It too came away damp. He stared at it stupidly.

'Tom!'

'I don't have the time to tell you all about it now, Joan, please,' he snapped.

'You never have time for me. You're always too busy.'

'Joan!'

'Don't "Joan" me,' she carried on remorselessly.

Thomas saw Tuke move to his desk, trying to pretend he wasn't there. Years before, Tuke might have made an excuse to leave, but Thomas knew he had grown used to Joan's outbursts and these days paid them little heed. Moving to the window, Thomas poured himself a cup of wine. Joan was still talking at him but he was no longer listening. He took a mouthful of the wine. It didn't seem to ease the soreness of his throat. He supposed he had talked too much at Westminster Hall, and he touched his fingertips to his neck gingerly, experimentally. He winced at the pain the pressure caused. He tried again, changing the angle to use the pads of his fingers. There were lumps there, either side of his Adam's apple. They were rather large. They hadn't been there earlier.

Oh God, I'm ill. It all made sense now. The sweating, the nausea, the dizziness, now the throat. No doubt, if he undressed, he would find lumps beneath his armpits too. *Not now, not me. I can't have this.*

Fear ran through him like a trickle of water. He knew the sweating sickness was back. There had been several cases of it in London in the previous month, and its presence was partly why the royal court had decamped to Richmond. But Thomas had thought he was safe, he so rarely caught anything.

Joan's voice was washing in and out of his ears like the going out and coming in of the tides. He closed his eyes and swayed where he stood.

Then Joan's voice stabbed into his brain, sharp, urgent. 'Tom! Tom! What is it, what's wrong? Oh, my God. Brian, help him.'

Her panicked words were the last thing Thomas heard as he fell to the floor.

This is home, Thomas realised as he looked around the room. There above his head were the green and white striped wall hangings, to his side the sloping wall of the attic room, opposite the bed the banisters going downstairs. But this wasn't his home, not anymore, not that it had ever really been his home. But it was his family's home. *And this is my parents' bedchamber. What am I doing here?* He lifted his head, expecting pain. His head felt light, no weight at all.

'Father?'

Robert Wolsey was sitting in a chair by the bed, staring at him. He looked bony and coarse, the grey stubble of his beard giving him a dirty look, and his nightshirt was grey and stained.

'But you're dead,' Thomas protested, not liking this vision at all, 'you can't be here.'

'I'm not here, you idiot,' Robert said with the vigour of a man very much alive. 'I'm where you left me, in Purgatory, while you lust after that Finch wench.'

'No, no, you're not in Purgatory, Father. I paid a priest to say masses for your soul and you're in heaven. And Alice is gone, long ago. She was never mine. But… but I never told you about Alice Finch, so how do you know of her?'

'How? I know everything here,' his father said scornfully. 'I know that you're not working as hard as you could be.'

'But I am, I am.'

146

'I won't have him at court,' a woman's voice said, and he snapped his head to the other side of his bed. There was Lady Margaret Beaufort, sitting prim, as if she had a poker inserted into her bodice, her thin face pinched as though she had an unpleasant smell in her nose.

But she was dead too.

'He's an ugly, fat fellow,' she said. 'Not fit to advise my son, the king.'

There came heavy footsteps on the stairs, and suddenly his mother was flying at Lady Margaret and whacking her about the head. Lady Margaret tumbled onto his bed, knocking against his legs.

'How dare you say that about my son?' his mother screeched, and the women struggled with one another until a figure emerged from the shadows. It was tall and white, and Thomas had to stare to try to make out the face. But the figure didn't have a face, just darkness where the face should be, but he recognised the clothes the figure wore. It was the pope, and he was sprinkling holy water over him and the bed.

Thomas felt the water droplets hit his face and they hurt a little. He put up his hands to shield himself, and he cried, 'Stop it, don't, please, stop it.'

And then they were all gone. The room was gone, and he was alone in the darkness.

~

Thomas opened his eyes, with difficulty and pain for the lids were stuck together and needed to be pulled apart. He felt hard crust sticking to his lashes. The light, sunlight, he thought, not a candle, for it was warm and everywhere at once, hurt his eyes and he closed them again until the pain receded.

He tried them again, and it hurt a little less this time. He kept them open, it taking a moment for him to be able to name what he was looking at. A tester. *So, I'm in bed*, he realised, and had a moment of fear that he was back in Ipswich and his father would be there, and his mother fighting with Lady Margaret and, and… *But no, it's my bed. Those are my favourite colours, blue and yellow, and the silk. That's the silk I ordered last year, the one Joan told me off about because she said it was too expensive.*

And now he could hear voices, soft, murmuring. Whose voices were they? He listened harder, feeling unable to turn or lift his head. A woman's voice. Joan's voice, yes, that was Joan, but who was she talking to? Brian Tuke? It sounded like Brian, but it was hard to tell.

Thomas closed his eyes, for they felt tired already. He tested moving his legs, managing only the smallest of movement. Then he tried to lift his right arm, but he couldn't even get his elbow off the mattress.

'Joan,' he croaked. The padding of feet, a shadow falling across him.

'Tom?' Joan's hot hand lifted his fingers and gripped them. 'I'm here.'

'Thirsty.'

Joan looked up and said, 'Brian, help me,' and Thomas felt himself pushed up and a pillow stuffed behind his back. He groaned as his muscles protested and sighed as he sank into the soft feather pillow.

'Here.' Joan put a cup to his lips, and he drank. He couldn't tell what it was, water, beer, wine. It tasted of nothing.

'Am I dying?' he asked.

'No,' Joan said, hitching herself up on the bed and blocking out much of the sunlight. 'But you gave me such a fright, Tom. You've been very ill.'

'Was it the sweat?'

'Yes. You had a fever. You were raving. I didn't understand half of what you were saying. You talked about your father and mother, the pope and—'

'I saw my father. He told me he was in Purgatory.'

'You quite frightened me, I can tell you.'

'I'm sorry. Was I the only one to become ill?'

Joan shook her head, her chin wobbling. 'No, six of the household staff had it too. They died.'

I didn't know them, he thought, *otherwise she would tell me their names.* 'I am sorry for that. That I should be saved and they should die. That's not fair.'

'There isn't any fairness in this world, Tom. There's just God's will. He has work for you here.'

Work!

Thomas tried to sit up. 'I must get back to work.'

Joan held him down. 'All is well, Tom. Brian and the other secretaries have managed everything. Everyone who needed to know was told you were ill.'

'The king—'

Tuke stepped up to the bedside. 'The king and queen are at Windsor. They went there as soon as it

149

was known the sweat was back. They are safe and well.'

'So, you needn't worry yourself about them,' Joan told him sternly. 'And the king has written.' She held up a letter and showed him the king's seal. It was broken.

'I opened it, Your Eminence,' Tuke said apologetically.

Thomas waggled his fingers for the letter.

'No,' Joan shook her head, 'I'll read it to you. "My beloved Wolsey, I have been informed you are ill with the sweat. I cannot say how worried this news made me, but the latest reports" – that's Brian's doing. See, I told you he was taking care of things – "I've had say that you are through the worst and will recover. I prayed every day that you would live and God heard my prayer. The queen sends her best wishes, and I look forward to our next meeting when the danger is completely passed. Your friend, Henry Rex." There, what do you think of that? Such a lovely letter. The king values you highly, does he not?'

'He is a most gracious sovereign to have been so concerned for me,' Thomas agreed.

'And your sister wrote too. I wrote to tell her you were ill and she wrote back. I did think she would come and visit you, but apparently not.'

'She was right not to come, Joan. She would only have put herself in danger and there was nothing she could have done for me.'

'I would have come to see my brother if he had been as ill as you were.'

There was no point trying to explain his relationship with Elizabeth. Joan was a good-hearted creature who had nothing but fondness for her family. Thomas and Elizabeth were bound by blood only; they felt a duty to one another. If there had been love once, absence had diminished it.

'Are you hungry, Tom?'

'No. I'm tired.'

'Then go back to sleep. When you're stronger, I should like to go to the shrine at Walsingham. We must give thanks to the Virgin Mary for your deliverance. Please don't say you will be too busy to go.'

'We should give thanks,' Thomas agreed. 'And it will be good to get out of London, even for a little while.'

'Yes, it would. But look, you can't keep your eyes open. Go to sleep now, Tom.'

He didn't need any persuading.

~

The journey to Walsingham had been a torment to Thomas. Foregoing his usual lavish procession, he and Joan had left London in a coach, damask curtains drawn against nosy passers-by, and only two dozen attendants with a handful of chests. Once out of London, the journey had become very hard. The further they went, the worse the roads became. With every fall into a pothole or swerve of the horses to avoid an oncoming vehicle, Thomas burrowed deeper into his woollen cloak and took a swig of the simple

Joan had made up to soothe him. The simple hadn't helped a great deal. His body ached terribly, and he was still so very tired, but his discomfort in the coach seemed to prevent him getting any rest at all. It was with the greatest relief that Thomas staggered down from the coach when they arrived at Walsingham.

He and Joan spent a week at the shrine, Joan officially present as his nurse, and no questions about her were asked. Thomas gave fervent thanks to the Virgin Mary for his life being spared when so many had not.

Thomas had left Tuke in charge back at York Place, and Tuke dutifully sent on any papers that needed Thomas's attention. On the day before he and Joan were due to leave Walsingham, Thomas received a letter forwarded by Tuke from Master Stubbs, the man he had hired to oversee the building works at Hampton Court.

'Do you know, Joan,' Thomas said, tapping the letter against his chin thoughtfully, 'Tuke is managing everything so well in London, I think we can indulge ourselves and pay a visit to Hampton Court before returning to London.'

Joan agreed readily to his suggestion. She was of the firm belief that Thomas needed all the time he could get to recover from the sweat.

They prepared well for the long journey, one of the secretaries ensuring sufficient stops at roadside taverns along the way for he and Joan to rest. It was over a week after they had left Walsingham that they arrived in Richmond and turned into the long drive that led to the house.

'Tom,' Joan cried as she stuck her head out of the coach window, 'how big is this place going to be?'

Thomas chuckled. If Joan was impressed now, when only the first stage of his improvement plan had been executed, how much more so would she and others be when Hampton Court was complete?

The coach came to a halt, its wheels scrunching over the damp stone and sand of the drive that was constantly being churned over by the passage of workmen and carts laden with building materials. Joan opened the door before the driver could jump down from his seat and hurried around to the other side to help Thomas out. As they started to walk towards the house, she slid her arm around Thomas.

'Not here,' he hissed, and Joan withdrew, taking a step away from him to create a distance of at least a yard. It was more than was necessary, but Joan was making a point. He knew he had hurt her with his rebuke, but such familiarity between them would be seen and commented upon. He couldn't afford gossip. He began talking about the building works to cover up the incident, and soon Joan mellowed enough to move a little closer.

'What do you think?' he asked, as they both stood before the gatehouse that loomed five storeys high above them.

'It's magnificent, Tom,' Joan replied, craning her neck to see to the very top.

It was magnificent, he thought, as his critical eye studied the deep red bricks interspersed at one course with black diaper work, the feature he had insisted upon to show his membership of the Catholic Church. It had taken such a lot of research to decide on the design for Hampton Court. The idea for its appearance had come from a visit he paid to Layer Marney in Colchester, where Lord Marney had employed Italian sculptors to create terracotta decorative friezes in the latest fashion. 'Say what you like about Italians,' Thomas had said, 'but they certainly know how to build,' and he had instructed Master Stubbs to hire a team of Italian workmen to help build a house that would rival any cardinal's palatial residence found in Florence or Rome.

'Are we going to live here?' Joan asked as they moved slowly through the gatehouse, emerging into a large courtyard with arcades in the Italian fashion.

'Eventually,' he said, nodding at the workmen who stopped their work to bow to him. 'You can see that there's a lot more to be done before it can become truly habitable. This court here will be for guests.' He counted on his fingers, testing his memory. 'There are more than twenty bedchambers in this court alone. Not all of them are ready, but there are enough for us and the servants.'

'That's good. I was wondering where we were going to sleep tonight. I thought we would have to go on to the More or ask the king at Richmond Palace if we could have a bed.' She gave a little laugh.

Thomas shot her a disapproving look. 'I'm more than able to provide a roof over your head, Joan.'

'I'm teasing, Tom,' she said with a sigh. 'Can't you tell?'

Thomas didn't answer. He knew he was being irritable with her and she didn't deserve it.

'How much is all this costing?' she asked.

'A great deal, but it will be worth every penny. There won't be another place like it in England.'

'What will happen to York Place? Will you sell it?'

'No, I will always need a London residence. And besides, it's not mine to sell. It goes with the archbishopric. But this will be all mine.' He said this with a great deal of satisfaction.

'Will the king and queen stay here?'

'I will have apartments suitable for them,' he nodded, 'but this isn't meant to be a house for entertaining guests.'

'What is it for, then?'

'For me. For us,' he corrected. 'I intend this to be a retreat, Joan, somewhere I can come to get away from everyone.'

'You, get away?' Joan laughed. 'That'll be the day.'

'I thought you would like the idea.'

'I do. I'm always saying you work too hard, but the truth is, Tom, you enjoy it.'

'I don't like being pestered all the time,' he said. 'I get so much more done when I'm left alone.'

'And you can't do that at York Place?'

'Hardly. At York Place, we don't have any privacy. Even our bedchamber can be accessed by anyone who wanders past. And there are always people waiting to be seen, hanging about in the corridors, in the courtyards, in the garden. I want somewhere private, where there are whole rooms and corridors between me and the people who want to see me.'

'I think it's a lovely idea, Tom. I just doubt it will happen.'

I'll make it happen, he promised himself as they explored further.

CHAPTER ELEVEN

1518

He was still feeling a little weak and, seeing this, Joan had ordered him to take it slowly. But Thomas had no idea what 'taking it slowly' truly meant. Work was work. It had to be done and done as quickly as possible because it never stopped, it just kept on coming.

When he had walked into his office at York Place that morning, the sight that had captured Thomas's attention was his desk, piled high with papers. He had looked around and seen the room was nothing but piles of paper: on the windowsills, on the secretaries' desks, on the shelves, even on the floor.

'Take it slowly,' he muttered as he edged around the paper obstacles to sit down. 'Chance would be a fine thing.'

'I've tried to keep only the most urgent matters for you to deal with,' Tuke said, trying pointlessly to tidy Thomas's desk. 'All the other routine matters I have dealt with. I hope that is acceptable, Your Eminence?'

'Perfectly,' Thomas nodded, reaching for the pile before him. This pile seemed to be letters and dispatches from England's ambassadors. Routine, yes, but still important papers, he realised, that had been neglected during his illness. He sighed. He would not get to his bed before the morning, despite Joan's concerns for his health.

'Before you begin, Your Eminence,' Tuke said, seeing Thomas take the first letter, 'could I ask what you want to do about Cardinal Campeggio?'

Thomas looked up at Tuke. 'Campeggio?'

'Yes,' Tuke said, 'if you remember, before you became ill, the cardinal had reached Calais on the pope's embassage. You refused him a passport to enter England, Your Eminence, after consultation with the king. It was during the rioting,' he added carefully. 'It would be only natural if you didn't recall—'

'Not at all,' Thomas cut him off. The fog was clearing, the memories coming back. 'I do remember, Brian. He is still there in Calais, is he? I had thought he might go home back to Rome.'

'No, he is still there, Your Eminence,' Tuke said with a smile, 'and growing ever more impatient to leave. He writes at least three times a week.'

Thomas didn't doubt Campeggio found Calais uncomfortable – the cardinal was like him, fond of comfort, and Calais was decidedly not comfortable – and he could almost sympathise with his plight. In truth, Thomas was extraordinarily grateful to Leo for sending Campeggio when he knew he wouldn't be guaranteed a passport to England. Sending Campeggio had provided Thomas with an opportunity he might otherwise not have had, that of pressuring the pope to give him something he wanted in return for admitting Campeggio to England. Thomas wanted to be a papal legate and, before he fell ill, had sought an audience with Henry to convince him he needed to ask the pope to make Thomas one before he would agree to meet with Campeggio. Only when Henry had his own papal legate would he agree to meet with the pope's.

'The pope has not written regarding making me a papal legate?'

Tuke shook his head. 'Not yet, Your Eminence.'

'Then, regrettably, Cardinal Campeggio must stay where he is, Brian.'

'Yes, Your Eminence,' Tuke said, returning to his desk, 'I will write and tell him so. How shall I phrase the letter, Your Eminence?'

'Any way you please, Brian,' Thomas said, bending his gaze to the letter he held from the Spanish ambassador. 'So long as you use unambiguous language and make it clear that I will not budge on this matter.' He met Tuke's eye. 'I will be a papal legate, Brian, or the pope can forget his bloody crusade for good and all.'

~

'Who does he think he is?' Pope Leo cried, banging his hands down on his desk in his exasperation. He

159

looked up at the secretary as if he were to blame. 'The impertinence of the man.'

The secretary, shrinking beneath Leo's furious glare, shrugged his thin shoulders helplessly. 'Cardinal Wolsey's letters are always impertinent.'

'But this!' Leo flapped the letter beneath the secretary's nose. 'This is… is…' He simply didn't have the words to describe how Thomas's letter made him feel. Oh, if Wolsey was standing before him now, he would put his hands round that thick neck and squeeze.

'King Henry does have the right to refuse entry to a foreign papal legate, Your Holiness. There are precedents for refusal in our archives.'

'I don't care if there are,' Leo snapped, wondering whose side his secretary was on. 'Neither the French nor the Spanish rulers would refuse me so. What makes England so proud, eh? I'll tell you. Cardinal Thomas Wolsey, that's what.'

He felt the blood pounding in his ears and willed himself to calm down. He wouldn't allow Wolsey to upset him like this; he wouldn't give him the satisfaction. But the unpleasant truth was that Wolsey had him right where he wanted him. To get permission for Campeggio to cross to England, he must make Wolsey a papal legate, however much the very idea vexed him. Leo picked up the letter and read it again. He hadn't noticed before that there was a postscript written in a different hand to that of the rest of the letter. Was it Wolsey's own writing? Had he actually taken the time to scribble a few words to his Holy

Father? He read the postscript, thinking it would be some sort of apology, but it was not.

'He wants the bishopric of Bath and Wells too,' he cried and screwed up the letter and threw it against the wall.

The secretary cleared his throat, and Leo snarled, 'What?'

'Would it not be good for you if you were to bestow the bishopric upon Cardinal Wolsey, Your Holiness? Considering your feelings about the present incumbent of Bath and Wells?'

Leo glared at his secretary. The skinny little thing was right, of course. Leo hated the current bishop of Bath and Wells, Cardinal Castelessi, who had recently conspired to assassinate him. It would serve the vile wretch right to have his bishopric taken away from him. But to give it to Wolsey! It would be playing right into his hands. Could he bear to do that? *But can I bear not to have my crusade?* he asked himself.

'Oh, let Wolsey have his legateship and his bishopric,' he said, throwing his hands up in a gesture of resignation. 'Campeggio must be allowed to speak to the king and get his support. I must have the backing of all the European heads, else I cannot act against the Turk.' He gave a hollow laugh. 'So, Wolsey becomes bishop of Bath and Wells and a papal legate in one blow.' He looked up at his secretary standing mournfully by the desk. 'I expect Wolsey will want to be pope next, eh?'

It was rather disconcerting to see the secretary nod in agreement.

Thomas had allowed himself one blessed hour of rest. It was a lovely day, and Joan had tempted him to join her in York Place's kitchen garden. The garden had become her particular joy. She would lose herself for hours there, tending the herbs and vegetables that would make their way onto Thomas's table and into the simples she made.

The scents of lavender, rosemary and other herbs filled Thomas's nostrils as he closed his eyes and let the sun warm his face. He told himself that when Hampton Court was finished he would do this sort of thing, take an hour or two for himself, more often.

He heard footsteps crunching along the gravel path and knew his time in the garden was probably coming to a premature end. A shadow fell across him.

'What is it, Brian?' he asked, not opening his eyes but recognising the tread of his secretary.

'A letter from Rome, Your Eminence,' Tuke said. 'I thought you would want it.'

At the mention of Rome, Thomas had opened his eyes. He now held out his hand, and Tuke put the pope's letter between his fingers. The seal of two crossed keys was broken and Thomas unfolded the thick paper. He scanned the lines, past the greetings and the enumeration of the pope's various trials, to reach the paragraph confirming Thomas's new appointments.

'Very satisfactory,' Thomas said, handing the letter back to Tuke.

'Shall I write to Cardinal Campeggio, Your Eminence?' Tuke asked. 'Give him your leave to come to England?'

'Yes,' Thomas said, deciding he could allow himself another half hour in the garden. He put his head back to rest against the brick wall and closed his eyes once more. 'And send to Master Pace at Greenwich to tell him to prepare the king for Campeggio's visit. He'll know what he needs to do.'

He heard Tuke's footsteps on the gravel again, moving away.

'What was all that, then?' Joan asked from the other side of the path.

Thomas opened one eye and lifted his head. 'We'll celebrate tonight, my dear. I'll have the best of my wines brought up from the cellar, you know, the one you like.'

'The one that makes my nose go red,' she said. 'What will we be celebrating, Tom?'

'The pope has made me a papal legate, Joan. And bishop of Bath and Wells.'

'Oh yes?' she sounded distinctly unimpressed. 'And what does that mean?'

'The bishopric is quite profitable, I've been after it for some time. But it was the legateship that I really wanted. What it means, Joan, is that I can act on my own authority in regard to Church matters without having to refer them first to Rome. It's a very important title for me.'

'Oh, well then, I'm glad for you, my dear,' Joan

said, bending to trim the lavender. 'But I thought you did that, anyway.'

'Not quite,' he said, smiling a little, 'but I'm glad you're glad, my sweet. And the king will be glad too.'

'Why will the king be glad?'

'Because he now has his own papal legate, just like the other kings of Europe.'

'Oh, I see,' Joan nodded, her eyebrows rising. 'So, you wanted to be a papal legate to please the king, is that it? Not for yourself at all?'

'That's right,' he said, 'mock me if you want. I can take it.'

Joan gave her girlish laugh and Thomas smiled to himself. So what if he had wanted the legateship for himself? It wasn't hurting anyone to have it, and, by having it, he had done his king some good in the process. He supposed others would think as Joan did, that he had insisted on the titles for his own benefit and his own benefit only, but what went on in other people's minds about him was no concern of his. He had achieved a great deal for himself and Henry with very little effort. He called that a good day's work.

CHAPTER TWELVE

Thomas had arranged for Campeggio to stay at Bath Place while in London, and he had travelled the short distance from York Place to greet him when he arrived. Posting a boy at the river steps, Thomas retreated to a small private room to wait and consider what he would say to his fellow cardinal and legate.

Settling into a chair by the fireplace, he tried to anticipate what Campeggio would say to him. Undoubtedly, he would begin with complaints. To be fair, Campeggio had plenty to complain about. Thomas knew he had been a little unkind to keep him waiting in Calais, but it had been necessary to gain the titles he sought. It wasn't personal. He made no apologies for Calais.

But what he couldn't excuse was the debacle of Campeggio's journey to London. It was important that, as legate, Campeggio's journey to London be stately and dignified. To be any less would be to impugn the office of the papal legate, and, having become one himself, Thomas was keen to avoid making the office appear insignificant. So, he had ordered that seven mules, the animal always used by cardinals to demonstrate their humility, were waiting at the dockside for Campeggio, each carrying empty boxes to take all the gifts the people would imagine the pope had sent to King Henry. As far as Thomas knew, Pope Leo had sent nothing other than Campeggio, but the legate couldn't appear to arrive in England empty-handed. People would talk and they would criticise, saying the pope didn't consider Henry worth any gifts. Thomas wasn't having that. With nothing to put in the empty boxes, Thomas had ordered his secretary to have them discreetly filled with anything to hand, it didn't matter what, as long as the contents made the boxes heavy, and no one would be any the wiser.

But there had been an accident at Cheapside. Some of the mules had stumbled on the uneven streets, and the boxes they were carrying had fallen to the ground and broke. Their contents spilled over the road for all to see.

And what the spectators saw were not silks or goblets of gold but old raggedy clothing and shabby leather shoes, rancid meat and foul-smelling eggs. The onlookers had held their noses and laughed. Thomas's secretary had reported that Campeggio had done his best to pretend he had not minded the incident but that in private he had complained bitterly, convinced it had been intentional, that Thomas had always meant to dishonour him in this way.

It wasn't true, and Thomas knew he would have to be almost grovelling in his apology to convince Campeggio of it. He didn't mind; perhaps a little grovelling would appease Campeggio and stop him asking to see Henry at every opportunity as his secretary reported the legate had been doing. Thomas was keen to avoid giving Campeggio any private audience with the king. The last thing he wanted was the legate persuading Henry of the rightness of the pope's cause and the king agreeing to join the crusade without consulting him first.

There was a knock on the door and it opened to reveal the steward of Bath Place and, behind him, a very tired and aged Campeggio.

Thomas got to his feet and held out both his arms. 'Lorenzo, my dear fellow, how good it is to see you.'

Campeggio did not return the greeting. He merely nodded and headed for the chair opposite the one Thomas had been sitting in. Thomas told the steward he could go and resumed his seat.

'How are you?' he asked, pouring a cup of wine for Campeggio and handing it to him.

'Not well,' Campeggio said, taking the cup and downing most of it in one gulp. 'You kept me waiting in Calais for weeks.'

'Yes, I know.' Thomas made what he hoped was a suitably sorrowful face. 'I'm afraid it could not be helped. Certain matters had to be settled before you could come over.'

'So I heard.' Campeggio glared at him over the

rim of his cup. 'I should congratulate you. Papal legate and bishop of Bath and Wells.'

Thomas bowed his head in acceptance. 'I am sorry about what happened on your journey here.'

Campeggio waved his hand to silence him. 'It is done, over. I do not wish to be reminded of that… that farce.'

That was good enough for Thomas. He would say no more of it. He sipped his wine.

'When am I to see the king?' Campeggio asked.

'The day after tomorrow. I've allowed a day for you to rest, I thought you would appreciate that.'

'It is to be a private audience, I trust? Just myself and the king?'

Thomas shook his head. 'The king would prefer it if I were present, and indeed, as legate, it is right I should be with you.'

'I see.' Campeggio made a noise of displeasure. 'Can you at least give me an indication of what the king's response will be? Is he favourable towards the pope's proposal?'

Thomas smiled and shook his head. 'Let us not talk of it for the moment, Lorenzo. I can see you are weary, and no doubt hungry. There will be time enough tomorrow, or the day after, to talk about this matter.'

Thomas was grateful Campeggio didn't argue. *He really must be tired*, he thought. *Either that or he already believes this mission to be a lost cause.* He was rather pleased at the notion. It should make it easier to say no.

Thomas rose early the next morning and took his barge to Greenwich to see the king.

He found Henry in the gardens, the friends Thomas so loathed gathered around him, laughing and jesting while musicians played. Despite the participants, it was a pleasant scene and Thomas found himself wishing he had the leisure to enjoy it. Oh, what it was to be a king or an idle courtier.

He sent one of the attendants over to Henry to tell the king he wanted to see him. Henry glanced in Thomas's direction and Thomas did not miss the slight annoyance that crossed his face. He hoped that was because he was disturbing him and not because he was out of favour. Thomas never knew what those damned friends of Henry's said about him when they were alone but he had no doubt none of it was good. Henry strode across the lawn to Thomas.

'Yes, Thomas?' he said, his hands going to his hips in a stance that was becoming very familiar. 'What brings you to Greenwich?'

Henry was so large, he blocked out the sun, throwing Thomas into shadow. 'Forgive me for disturbing you, Your Grace, but I wanted to inform you that Cardinal Campeggio has arrived in London.'

'He's here at last, is he?' Henry nodded. 'Made him comfortable, have you?'

'He's at Bath Place.'

'Good, good. What now, then?'

'He has already asked when he will be meeting

with you and I have told him not before tomorrow, if that is convenient.'

'I suppose so.' Henry turned back to his friends at the sound of female laughter.

Thomas peered around him and saw that a group of women had arrived and were being invited to sit by the men. The women were young, pretty and elegant, dressed in the latest fashions, not the type of clothes worn by the queen's ladies, who dressed very sombrely. Thomas coughed to regain Henry's attention. 'We should discuss our response to the pope's request.'

'Oh, must we do that now?' Henry made a face. 'See,' he gestured towards his friends, 'I am being called for. Just tell me what you want me to say to him, Thomas. You say it's not a good idea, this crusade of the pope's, and I agree. I trust you to do what's best.' He hurried back to the merry group.

Which one of those pretty young things has taken your fancy? Thomas wondered, running his eyes over each girl as she bobbed a curtsey. Henry had always been very discreet in his affairs, taking care that not only the queen never knew of them, but that most of the court was unaware he strayed. Thomas doubted Katherine was as ignorant of his amours as Henry believed, but guessed that she made a decision not to know of them. But Henry had been growing less considerate of her feelings of late, and perhaps he was even now wondering how best to woo the lady of his choice with his friends looking on.

Thomas was happy to let Henry focus on flirtation, as it left the running of the country in his more than capable hands.

~

'How was the king, Your Eminence?' Tuke asked as Thomas entered the office.

'Distracted,' Thomas said.

'But what did he say about Cardinal Campeggio?'

'That I need only tell him what to say and he will say it.' Thomas flopped down into his chair and grinned. 'Which works out rather well, I should say.'

'Indeed,' Tuke agreed.

The silence Tuke fell into was unnatural and Thomas looked up from his desk, frowning. 'What is it that troubles you, Brian?'

'Oh.' Tuke looked embarrassed. 'I'm not troubled, Your Eminence, just a little confused. Is not this proposal of the pope's actually a good idea?'

Thomas threw down his quill and leant back in his chair. 'What makes you ask that?'

Tuke rose from his desk and came nearer. 'It seems to me the Turk should be stopped if he's threatening Christendom. Spain and France have agreed to join the pope's crusade. If it's good enough for them, why is it not good enough for us?'

Thomas pointed Tuke to the chair by the desk and Tuke sat expectantly, waiting for Thomas's explanation. 'Spain will always agree with the pope, Brian, that is a given, but, possessing a great empire, Spain has the wherewithal to finance such an expedition. As

Holy Roman Emperor, Maximilian will feel it is his duty to agree, but he, as we know to our cost, will promise much and do nothing. King Francis has indeed agreed to join the pope but only when he has a son and heir to follow him should he be killed whilst on crusade. That happy event is yet to happen, so King Francis will be going nowhere. Only England will feel duty bound to honour her promise, and only England cannot truly afford to take part at present.'

'I understand all that,' Tuke nodded, 'but if you'll forgive me, lack of funds has never stopped us before.'

Thomas smiled. It was true, of course, and Tuke was right to point that out. 'The pope's proposal is not without merit,' he admitted, 'and indeed, I do not dismiss it lightly. I have thought about it a great deal. This is simply not the right time. But tell me, Brian, do you not think the proposal is a little unambitious?'

'I don't see that. The pope proposes that peace is made between the powers of Europe and unites them against the infidel. That seems not at all unambitious to me.'

'You're right, of course, and the alliance is not what I think unambitious. It is the timescale, I mean. The pope wants peace for five years.'

'Yes?' Tuke pressed, frowning.

'Five years!' Thomas cried. 'What's five years? It's nothing. And it is self-defeating. Just think, Brian. If we and the other nations were to embark on this crusade this very day, all the kings and emperors would be thinking that in four and a half years it will all be business as usual. They'll be planning to invade the others' countries, hamper trade routes and seek dynastic alliances that will improve their own positions. In five years and one day, I promise you, all the good work of the previous five years will be undone.'

'I see,' Tuke said, rubbing his chin. 'But what else could the pope do to prevent that?'

'Why not seek a much longer peace?' Thomas offered with a smile. 'A peace that could last the rest of our lifetimes. Think what we could do then, the progress that could be made if we didn't have to worry about which country was going to declare war on us every time spring came round again.'

Tuke looked doubtful. 'Could such a peace ever be engineered, Your Eminence?'

Thomas chewed his bottom lip for a moment. 'Perhaps, Brian. Perhaps.'

∼

The first thing Thomas did upon entering the Great Hall of Greenwich Palace was check that his dais with his chair was at least six inches higher than that given to Campeggio. He wasn't about to get out a rule and measure the height, that would make him look ridiculous, but he could tell by eye it was. Good, his orders had been followed. It might be a petty gesture, and he had seen that his carpenters had thought so when he gave the order, but he knew that even a little thing like who sat the highest could give him a profound psychological advantage over his fellow legate. The king, of course, would be seated higher than both he and

Campeggio, as was fitting, but it should be clear to all the spectators that though he and Campeggio were equal in the eyes of the pope, he, Thomas, had precedence in England.

Campeggio shuffled into the hall, his left foot swaddled, his right encased in a large red slipper. Thomas went to greet him.

'I hope my barge was comfortable enough for you, Lorenzo.'

'It was,' Campeggio nodded, 'but my foot pains me greatly.' He pointed at it. 'This weather of yours makes it worse.'

Am I supposed to apologise for the rain, now? Thomas despaired as he gestured Campeggio towards his chair on the dais. He saw Campeggio study the dais, look at Thomas's set a few feet away, then back at his own. So, he had noticed the difference. Quite remarkable that he should, and Thomas made a mental note to not ever take Campeggio for a fool or a dim-witted old man. Thomas waited for a remark, but Campeggio only looked at him, raised a grey eyebrow and stepped up gingerly onto the dais. Thomas saw him seated comfortably, then walked away to greet the king, who had just entered.

'I received your notes,' the king said, referring to the papers Thomas and Tuke had put together to apprise Henry of what Campeggio would likely say and what Henry should say in response. 'I cannot say I think we are treating the pope very well, Thomas, but I will go along with you, all the same.'

'The pope will get over it,' Thomas murmured, so

174

low he wasn't sure if Henry had heard him. 'Was everything clear to you, Your Grace? Do you need me to explain any item?'

'I'm not an idiot, Thomas, I understood every word. Let's get on with this, shall we?'

Thomas quickly introduced Campeggio to Henry, who had hobbled over as quickly as he could to the king, perhaps hoping for a private word, but Thomas took his elbow and steered him back to his seat.

It had been agreed that Campeggio would speak first and put the pope's proposal to the king. He rose from his chair and Thomas saw him look around as no one in the room got to their feet. That was Thomas's doing too. He had given instructions that no one was to rise when Campeggio got up to speak. Thomas half-expected Campeggio to protest, but no, he merely joined his hands and turned to Henry.

'Great lords, I am come to England on behalf of His Holiness, Pope Leo, to request that the king of England lend his support to his decision to stand fast against the infidel. His Holiness asks that England shows her duty to the Holy See and to God and agrees to join the other European sovereigns in a pact of mutual amity and toleration of each other and fight the Turk to entirely subdue them and so free Christian Europe from their pernicious influence and territorial ambition.'

He bowed his head and returned to his chair. Thomas was surprised that Campeggio had said so little. He had expected the legate to speak for much longer, expounding on the loyalty all Christian kings owed to the pope, the need for offensive action against the Turk, the rightness of the pope's cause. What would Leo say if he knew how little Campeggio had tried to persuade Henry? he wondered.

It was Thomas's turn to speak. He rose from his chair and there was a great shuffling as everyone in the room, even Henry, got to their feet. Thomas saw Campeggio out of the corner of his eye look around the room in open astonishment, and only belatedly, when he saw that the king had risen, did the legate rise too. Thomas had to suppress the smile he felt threatening to burst out upon his face.

Thomas bowed to Henry, folded his fat hands over his stomach and began. 'We all give welcome to the papal envoy, Cardinal Campeggio, and applaud His Holiness's desire to stop the ravages of the Turk. However, Constantinople is very far from England, and we wonder how greatly the Turk threatens us on this island. The king, in his great wisdom, has deemed this a remote possibility, and as for a pact of peace with our European neighbours...' he paused and looked around the room, resting lastly on Campeggio. 'Well, England and her king are all for amity, but we cannot speak for our neighbours.'

'Aye, the pope should keep a close eye on King Francis,' Henry declared, nodding at Campeggio.

'And so,' Thomas continued, 'England is not ready to join a papal alliance at this time. We will, of course, have the care of the papal see at the forefront of our considerations, should the need arise in the near future.'

Thomas nodded to Henry, and he turned back towards his seat. Henry sat down and everyone else in the room did the same with another great shuffling. Campeggio sat down with a grunt and scowled at the floor.

It was Henry's turn to address the hall, echoing Thomas's words and assuring Campeggio of his great admiration for the pope's desire to rid Christendom of the Turk while expressing his regret that it was simply not possible for England to become involved. Everything, in fact, that Thomas had suggested he say, and he was glad Henry had followed his advice to the letter. Henry didn't linger long after his speech and, once he had left, the hall swiftly emptied.

'You never intended to agree to the pope's call for an alliance against the Turk, did you?' Campeggio said as Thomas rose and stepped down from his platform.

'It is a pointless endeavour, Lorenzo.'

'Pointless? To fight the infidel?'

'Sultan Suleiman has territory enough. I do not honestly believe he has his sights set on conquering Europe as well.'

'Then why did you not write to the pope and tell him so from the first?' Campeggio said crossly. 'You could have saved me an uncomfortable and unnecessary journey.'

'You know that wouldn't have served my purpose, Lorenzo.'

'No, you negotiated very well for those new titles

of yours,' Campeggio said without admiration. 'Tell me, how many titles do you now hold?'

Thomas shrugged. 'A fair few.'

'More than a few, Thomas. But you should be careful. You're getting a reputation.'

'For what?'

'For rapacity. You should be careful not to over-reach yourself.'

'I am in no danger of that, Lorenzo,' Thomas assured him, 'but I thank you for your concern. Come back with me to York Place and we shall dine together.'

'Why not?' Campeggio agreed. 'You always have the best wine. And maybe you will tell me what you are really planning. I know you have something you're keeping to yourself and I mean to know it.'

Thomas clapped him on the back and they began to walk. 'All in good time, Lorenzo.'

CHAPTER THIRTEEN

The pope's crusade may well have been quashed, but Thomas couldn't get the idea of an alliance out of his mind. It was a good idea, he kept telling himself. Its only problem, as he had said to Tuke, was that it didn't go far enough. Thomas didn't want just five years of peace; he wanted twenty-five years if he could. But was peace for so long even possible? Could he really expect all the rulers of Europe to persevere with peace and not declare war on each other for so many years? It was highly unlikely, he had to admit, but what if...?

It was no good. The idea wouldn't go away. He had to work it out, get it down on paper and see if it was as absurd as he feared.

Pulling a clean sheet of paper before him, Thomas dipped his quill in the ink, hesitated for a moment to collect his thoughts, then put the nib to the page. Firstly, he made a list of all the crowned heads of Europe whom he would want to join the alliance: France, Spain, the Netherlands, Belgium, Portugal, Denmark… It proved to be quite a list, quite daunting, in fact. He moved on to making a mark against those who would join such an alliance readily, leaving unmarked those who would need more than a little persuading and noted down what inducements he could offer to make them join. Lastly, he drew a line down the centre of the page to create two columns, heading the first column 'Advantages' and the second 'Disadvantages'.

When he was done, Thomas set down his pen and lifted the page up to his face. The Advantages column was only a few lines longer than the Disadvantages column, but it *was* longer and that was good enough. He wanted Europe to have such an alliance, and he was sure he could make it work. And if he did – no, when he did – all of Europe would revere him. He would be talked about as the greatest statesman of the age.

All he had to do now was convince Henry. In his youth, when he had first become king, Henry had been keen to demonstrate his prowess on the battle-field and he had done that to, some might say, less than glorious effect, in France. But a few years had passed and Henry, although still martial in spirit, spoke of war less and less. To Thomas's way of think-ing, Henry was more interested in the pleasures to be found at home in England than the discomfort of campaigns in foreign fields. No, Thomas didn't think he would have any trouble in persuading Henry to

180

become the symbol and head of his new idea of a universal peace.

~

'But I thought we believed the idea of a European alliance was unworkable,' Henry said, frowning.

There was a hint of irritation in his voice and Thomas gave him a tight smile. 'You are quite right, the pope's plan was indeed unworkable. The plan I have devised for Your Grace to consider is better.'

'How is it better?'

'Because it will last longer.'

Henry sighed and shook his head. 'You had better explain it to me, Thomas. Your words have me all in a whirl.'

Thomas doubted he was the true cause of Henry's confusion. If Henry was in a whirl, then it was because of his new mistress, Lady Elizabeth Blount. Bessie, as she was known, was very young, no more than sixteen or seventeen, beautiful, intelligent, highly accomplished at music. Thomas could almost believe God had created her solely to attract the king, she was so perfect a match for him.

Thomas had been glad when he had learnt of Bessie and her relationship with the king. He had been growing quite concerned at the reports Pace sent him. Henry had become moody and irritable, snapping at Pace and his other servants for little reason, and even finding fault with his closest friends. Thomas thought the most likely cause of this irritability was his lack of a son, as Pace reported the king had begun speaking of the queen in less than complimentary terms regarding her childbearing abilities. But Bessie seemed to have changed him, cheered him up. No doubt feeling guilty at betraying his wife, Henry had become solicitous of Katherine once more, and was rediscovering his old enjoyment in music, dancing and general merrymaking. Thomas had no doubt Katherine knew of this latest affair but averted her eyes and pretended not to know.

Henry settled back in his chair, and Thomas smoothed his robes over his lap before beginning. He explained his plan in as much detail as he thought Henry could bear, of how he would bring Europe together in a peace treaty that would have no end date, in which all the signatories would swear to come to the aid of the others should they ever be threatened by enemies. In this way, he told Henry with a smile, no king would declare war on another because he would realise that he would have many opponents, not only one. No king would dare enter into a war he had no chance of winning. He went on to explain how such a peace treaty would benefit all the signatories. Money would not need to be spent on defences. Instead, it could be spent on trade and commerce, and privy purses would grow fat rather than lean.

And finally, Thomas gave Henry what he hoped would be the most important aspect. While he, Thomas, was the peace treaty's architect, Henry would be its figurehead, and he would be revered by his fellow rulers as the greatest of men.

Henry's eyes glistened. 'Will they all agree, Thomas?' he asked eagerly, and Thomas thought he read insecurity in the young king's eyes.

'I believe King Francis will be more than ready to accept the hand of friendship from you, Your Grace,' Thomas assured him. 'The others will follow suit.'

'A universal peace treaty with me as its head,' Henry mused dreamily. 'I must confess, Thomas, that would make me very proud. Is that not sinful?'

Thomas shook his head. 'No, Your Grace. I do not consider pride a very great sin. In fact,' he smiled broadly, 'I don't consider it a sin at all.'

~

King Francis watched his mother as she read the letter that had arrived from England that morning. He had sent for her as soon as his chief minister had read aloud the approach made by Cardinal Wolsey, deciding they needed her wise counsel.

'Well?' he asked as she put the letter down. 'What do you make of it?'

Louise de Savoie steepled her fingers beneath her chin and looked at her son as she considered. 'An intriguing proposal. Audacious, even.'

'It cannot be possible, can it?' Francis said. 'How can all of Europe agree to be at peace?'

'His Holiness thought it possible when he put forward such an idea, an idea which, I remind you, you agreed to upon the birth of a son. You now have your son, and yet you are reluctant to keep your end of the bargain.'

Francis waved that remark away. 'But it is Wolsey who has told the pope England will not join him in his action against the Turk. Why did he do so if he means to propose a treaty that is, in essence, the same as the pope's?'

'It is similar,' Louise mused, running her forefinger along the lines of text, 'but not quite the same. Wolsey makes no mention of the Turk.'

'Yet I sense some trick in this, Mother,' Francis said, looking around the table at his ministers, some of whom nodded in agreement. 'Wolsey is up to something.'

Louise gave a little laugh. 'Oh, my dear, I don't doubt His Eminence is always up to something. He is that kind of man. But no, I do not think this to be a trick.'

'What, then?'

'Why, my dear, I think it perfectly clear. He wishes to draw you away from Spain and the Netherlands. Wolsey will not have liked his king being left out of our treaty with Maximilian and Charles. I do not doubt he seeks to make King Henry master of this new proposal to bolster his poor reputation. We cannot blame him for that. If only your own ministers were as mindful of your reputation as Wolsey is of his king's.'

There was a clearing of throats around the table as Louise's words touched a few nerves.

'You're sure?' Francis asked.

'As sure as I can be. As sure as years of rule can make me,' she added pointedly, reminding Francis of her years as regent while he was in his minority.

'Then I trust in your advice, Mother. If you say this is no trick, I will consider Cardinal Wolsey's proposal.'

'You would be wise to.' Louise sighed. 'I know men like war but, as a wife, and especially a mother,' she touched Francis's hand and smiled fondly, 'I would thank any man who wants to bring peace to our lives.'

'The cardinal wants my son to be betrothed to the Princess Mary.'

'As to that,' Louise said, 'we will wait and see. What interests me most is this.' She drew Francis's attention to a single word in the letter.

'Tournai,' Francis nodded. 'Yes, I want the town back, Mother. To think that there is land in my kingdom that belongs to the English pains me terribly.'

'I know it does. And Wolsey is offering to give Tournai back to us, though the price he asks is high.'

'You think it too much?'

'I think we should negotiate a lower sum, certainly.'

'So, we should agree to hear this proposal for the sake of Tournai?'

'Not just Tournai. The title of emperor is also at stake. A new emperor will be elected when Maximilian is dead.'

A cough came from one of the ministers.

185

'Madame, it is almost certain that Charles of Spain will succeed Maximilian.'

'Almost certain,' Louise agreed. 'But there is always hope the Electors will show some courage and originality and vote for a man who actually deserves the title.'

The ministers tittered obsequiously.

'It would be helpful to have King Henry's support when the time comes,' she continued. 'Write to England, my boy. Let them know you are interested in this alliance and would like to discuss it further.'

Francis clicked his fingers at the Council's clerk, an instruction to start scribbling.

'To whom am I writing?' the clerk asked. 'King Henry or Cardinal Wolsey?'

'Young man,' Louise said, 'they are one and the same thing.'

~

It had been an anxious three weeks for Thomas while he waited for the French response to his proposal. His letter to King Francis had taken an age to phrase, had gone through several drafts, and only when no fault could be found had he dispatched it.

It had been perfect, he told himself as he watched the knight and horse charge down the list, his mind only half registering the cheers that accompanied the charge. He brought up an image in his mind: Francis being shown the letter by his Council, probably distracting him from a bevy of women, for Thomas knew the French king's reputation for womanising. Would Francis have ceased his dalliances long enough to pay attention to Thomas's letter? Or would he wave his Council away, telling them not to bother him with trivialities?

But Francis would read his letter eventually and then what? He couldn't dismiss it, Thomas knew that. Simply including congratulations on the dauphin's birth had ensured Francis would have to answer the letter personally. Would Francis be intrigued by the offer of the return of Tournai? Surely he would be? The English ambassador had often reported to Thomas how Francis fumed over the loss of Tournai. He desperately wanted it back. For his part, Thomas desperately wanted to be rid of it. The town had no strategic value nor produced anything of worth, and yet it cost the Exchequer a small fortune to maintain. England would be well rid of it. He thought offering it to Francis therefore a masterstroke. Admittedly, Thomas would miss the income he received as Tournai's bishop, but he felt sure Francis would compensate him very well for the loss.

Thomas reassured himself with the knowledge that even if Francis wasn't ready or willing to ally with England, his mother would see the benefits. Louise de Savoie was too intelligent a woman not to even consider Thomas's proposal. Even if it all came to nothing in the end, Thomas was sure some good, preferably for both himself and Henry, would materialise between France and England.

The crowd was clapping, and the noise shook

Thomas out of his thoughts. One of the riders had been unseated. He peered over the wooden balustrade and squinted at the shield lying fallen on the sand. Thomas recognised Compton's device and felt immeasurably cheered by the sight. He clapped heartily, smiling down at Compton as he picked himself up and lifted his visor to show Thomas his scowling, blood-streaked face.

'Never mind, Compton,' Henry, sitting alongside Thomas, called to his friend with a grin. 'You'll get your own back next time.'

Compton didn't reply, stomping off to the combatants' tent instead, no doubt to be tended by a sympathetic girl who thought him handsome and charming, and whom Compton would have on her back before the day was out. The poor girl. Henry really should choose his friends with greater care. The girl would become pregnant, the outraged parents would appeal to Henry, and Henry would tell Thomas to deal with it. Which he would, of course, finding a suitable husband for the girl, throwing the father some land to keep him quiet and gifting the mother some silks for a new dress.

A movement behind drew his attention from the sulky Compton. Thomas turned to see Tuke peering around the green and white canvas that enclosed the pavilion. Thomas's heart beat faster. Before leaving for Greenwich, he had told Tuke to let him know at once if news came from France. Thomas gestured him over and Tuke self-consciously stepped inside and edged around the benches until he stood behind his chair.

'Is it news from France?' Thomas asked eagerly.

Tuke nodded and handed Thomas a letter. Thomas, feeling the king's eyes upon him, unfolded the letter as calmly as he could and read. He had to stop himself from crying out in triumph. King Francis was interested in Thomas's alliance and looked forward to hearing further details. To that end, King Francis was dispatching High Admiral Bonnivet to England to meet with the king's Council.

'Good news, Thomas?' Henry asked.

Thomas refolded the letter and smiled. 'Very good, Your Grace. That matter regarding Europe we spoke of? King Francis is interested and is sending an envoy to learn more.'

Not even the new riders entering the lists could draw Henry's attention from Thomas at hearing this news. 'Is he, by God? Well, you said he would be interested, Thomas, and you were right again. When will this envoy arrive? We shall have to put on a good show, shan't we?'

'Indeed, we must,' Thomas agreed. 'Next week for the envoy's arrival if the Narrow Sea allows. I shall make the arrangements to receive him.'

'Good, I know can leave that all to you,' Henry said and began clapping as Bryan entered the lists.

~

The French envoys had arrived and Thomas had been the perfect host, providing rooms for them at York Place, introducing them to the king and queen, and on their last night in London holding a sumptuous feast for the entire delegation.

Thomas had reason to treat the Frenchmen well. It had become clear very quickly to him that King Francis wanted to be allied with England and that he needed no further information as his letter had claimed. All Thomas had to do was set out the terms of the alliance and wait for Francis's proxy, High Admiral Bonnivet, to agree to them. The return of Tournai – agreed. The betrothal of Princess Mary to the dauphin – agreed. The new alliance to be set down on parchment and signed by both England and France – agreed. *Can it really be this easy?* Thomas wondered, as Bonnivet nodded to all his conditions.

But on the last day of the French visit, as they walked to the river steps to say goodbye, Bonnivet said something which took Thomas a little by surprise.

'Our two kings must meet.'

'Must?' Thomas said, alarmed by the idea. He had not considered Henry and Francis meeting at all, there was simply no need.

'But of course. My king is very keen to meet with King Henry. He has heard so much about him, he feels he already knows him well.'

'King Francis's feelings are entirely reciprocated by King Henry,' Thomas said hurriedly, not even stopping to consider the lie in his words.

As he watched Bonnivet climbed into the barge,

he tried to work out whether there was any advantage to the two kings meeting. His instinct told him it was a bad idea – the two had long considered each other rivals in chivalry and kingship, and both were young and liable to speak or act before considering consequences – but Bonnivet had made the statement in a tone that seemed to brook no refusal. He made a decision. 'I'm sure something can be arranged.'

He bid Bonnivet farewell and watched as the French envoy and his party were rowed away. When he deemed he was out of their sight and need wave no longer, Thomas returned to his office. He ordered Tuke to take down a letter, and began dictating his words to the king, informing him that the French had now left. Thomas decided he wouldn't mention the suggestion of a meeting with King Francis just yet. Henry would only badger Thomas with questions, and Thomas could do without those. No, he would hold the meeting idea back for the time being until he had thought about it some more.

CHAPTER FOURTEEN

It was October, and England was once again playing host to the French. Thomas was busier than ever. He knew that the French had intended to bring many more representatives than before when Bonnivet and his few associates had visited, but even he was surprised at the size of the French entourage when it arrived in London. It turned out that King Francis had decided to send many of his close personal friends to meet with Henry, not just the ambassadors, secretaries and clerks Thomas had been expecting, and they all needed to be found beds.

Thomas lodged the ambassadors in the Merchant Taylors' Hall, saw they were comfortable, then ordered his men to commandeer rooms in the homes of the merchants who lived nearby. This caused a mild uproar. The merchants did not appreciate being told they had to give space in their homes to the king's guests, and those guests Frenchmen to boot, but Thomas promised them they would receive compensation for the inconvenience and, satisfied, their complaints ceased.

After that, Thomas barely had time to breathe. Every day brought a new event to be managed, whether that was a feast, an entertainment, or the main reason for the French visit: the treaty.

And yet, despite all the extra work, despite all the worry, despite everything that could go wrong, it all went smoothly. A week after their arrival in London, the French and English swore their allegiance to Thomas's treaty, and a few days after that the Princess Mary was officially betrothed to the dauphin. To celebrate the betrothal, a tournament and banquet, hosted by Henry and Katherine, was held at Greenwich a few days later. As he watched Henry and Katherine dance with their French guests, Thomas allowed himself to finally relax and had his wine cup filled to the brim.

Thomas could not help but be proud of his king. Henry had been the perfect host; there had not been a word he should not have spoken nor a gesture he should not have made. When the French ambassadors wrote their reports to their king, Thomas knew they would write of Henry's friendliness and generosity, of the love he engendered in his courtiers and, most importantly, his professed commitment to keeping friends with France. Henry had done everything Thomas had asked of him and done it well. He had been an exemplary king. It didn't even bother Thomas that Henry was now leading Katherine back to her seat so he could dance the next dance with Bessie. Henry had earned a dance with a pretty girl.

Thomas felt someone drop down into the empty chair beside him and turned. 'Bishop Fox, good evening.'

Fox nodded a greeting. 'You were looking very pleased with yourself just now, Thomas. Not that you don't have good reason. This is a very great thing you and the king have accomplished.'

'Thank you,' Thomas said, turning his gaze back to the king, who had in truth done very little to bring the treaty about. Thomas would have liked it if he could be credited with the whole enterprise, but he knew that was asking for too much. 'I think it is the most important treaty ever to be devised.' He saw Fox's raised eyebrows out of the corner of his eye and bristled. 'You think I sin in taking pride in this treaty. But this treaty will prevent men being killed on battle-fields, improve trade, and make our king respected by all the heads of Europe. I think I should be allowed a little pride.'

'There's no need to be so defensive, Thomas,' Fox said, patting Thomas's arm. 'I don't think you sinful. I agree with you entirely. I truly believe it is the best deed ever done for England. I realise the king must take the glory for it, but I know who is the real architect of this peace.' He rubbed his eyes and gave a quiet groan.

'Your eyes are no better?' Thomas asked kindly, mollified by his old friend's assurance. He studied the milky film that had been encroaching across the bishop's irises for some time now.

Fox sighed. 'They will never be better. I know this to be true, for my father suffered with this malady. In a little time, I shall be quite blind. If I haven't died first, that is.'

'I am sorry for it.'

'It is God's will, and I must bear it. Thomas,' Fox leant forward to speak low, 'I want you to know, I'm thinking of retiring.'

Thomas did not pretend surprise. 'I think you are wise to do so, bishop.'

'What?' Fox laughed, pretending hurt. 'No words to compel me to stay? No assurance that I am irreplaceable?'

'I would not have you work until you drop dead,' Thomas said quietly. 'You have earned some peace.'

'And I know you do not need me.'

'You will not be so very far away,' Thomas said. 'And you will always answer my letters?'

'Of course,' Fox nodded, adding, 'should you send me any.'

'I'm sure I shall have cause to send you many.'

Fox gave a little laugh. 'You flatter me, Thomas, I know it, and thank you for it. But we both know you have no need of me or any of the Council.'

There came laughter from the room and both men turned to watch Henry and his friends bantering with Francis's friends as they danced. They all seemed to be getting along very well.

'Do you think I could slip away without anyone

noticing, Thomas?' Fox asked, stifling a yawn. 'I confess a yearning for my bed.'

'Go, bishop,' Thomas said. 'The king is very well attended and will not notice your absence.'

'Thank you, Thomas.' Fox rose. 'I shall bid you good night. Congratulations once more, old friend. I only hope both the kings prove worthy of your ambitions.'

Thomas watched him leave the chamber and wondered what on earth the old man had meant by that last remark.

~

The French embassage had left only the day before and Thomas had gone to his desk that morning even earlier than usual, hoping to make a dent in the work that had gone unattended during their visit. He had hoped to enjoy several hours of uninterrupted labour, many of them answering the letters from foreign ambassadors asking for their countries to join the Treaty of London, the name given to his new Anglo-French alliance, and had been annoyed when, after only an hour or two, Tuke showed Richard Pace into the office.

'Richard, what's wrong?' he asked as soon as Pace stepped inside his office. Pace had a worried look upon his face and Thomas immediately feared something was wrong with the treaty.

Pace held up his hands. 'It's not my fault, I assure

you, Your Eminence. The king had me draw up the commissions. I could not disobey him.'

'What commissions? What are you talking about?'

Pace took a deep breath. 'King Henry has appointed his friends to new positions. He's calling them his Gentlemen of the Privy Chamber and they are to serve him. He got the idea from the French.'

Of course he did, Thomas nearly snarled. He should have seen it coming, should have known that Henry would have noticed the French king's friends and their appointment to become *gentilshommes de la chambre*. Not wanting to be outdone by Francis, Henry would want his own set of *mignons*, as the men were known. Thomas had already had a note from Henry that he wished to be addressed as 'Your Majesty' from now on, rather than the centuries-old 'Your Grace', having heard that Francis was addressed so.

Pace delved into his leather satchel and pulled out several pieces of parchment. He passed them to Thomas. 'These are the commissions.'

Thomas unfurled them and scanned the text quickly. He found the names of Compton, Bryan, Wyatt, Coffin and a few more of Henry's friends there, naming them all as his new Gentlemen of the King's Bedchamber. Was anything more absurd than these rogues, these layabouts, being given salaried positions at court? And not just any positions, but positions that guaranteed them unrivalled access to the king at any time of day and night?

'I cannot but wonder why the king made these

appointments without discussing the matter with me first,' Thomas said.

'I suppose the king did not think consultation was necessary,' Pace said.

Thomas glared at him. 'And you did not think it was necessary to give me fair warning that the king was doing this?'

'I am obliged to do my duty by the king, Your Eminence,' Pace said defiantly. 'I knew you wouldn't like it and that is why I am come to you now, to tell you. I do not think the salaries to be too great,' he added as a solace.

'It's not the expense that concerns me,' Thomas said, scribbling his name on the papers to confirm the appointments, and throwing them back at Pace. Thomas knew he shouldn't take his anger out on Pace but the secretary had the misfortune to be standing before him and he needed someone to shout at. 'Although I have taken great pains to reduce the expenses on the privy purse.'

'I am aware of your efforts, Your Eminence.'

'Are you? Do you know how much the king was spending when I became Lord Chancellor, Richard? I must admit, when I first saw the ledgers, I was appalled. Seventy-four thousand pounds, that's how much was being spent, in one year alone! Do you know what the privy purse expenses are now? Fifty thousand pounds. And that only by dint of my most careful scrutiny and control. If the king has his way, he would be spending double that.'

'He *is* the king, Your Eminence.'

'And that gives him licence to do as he pleases, does it?' Thomas snapped.

'It does give him the right to make appointments,' Pace replied bravely.

Thomas grunted and nodded. 'Yes, you are right, Richard, though I do not like this. I do not like this at all.'

'Because of the expense?'

'Because of the influence they will have upon the king. God knows what they'll be telling him to do.'

'But they are already an influence upon him,' Pace said, frowning.

'Aye, and before this, will have spent only a few hours a day with him. If they are to be his constant attendants, with him from the moment he rises to the hour he retires, just think of all the opportunities they will have to persuade him to do this and that. Just think what damage they could do.'

'Perhaps you could persuade the king to change his mind?' Pace said, his tone hopeful, but Thomas heard the doubt behind the words. They both knew there was little chance of that.

'No, the king can have his minions, if that's what he wants,' Thomas said, waving Pace towards the door.

'Thank you, Your Eminence.' Pace paused at the door and looked back at Thomas. 'And it's *mignons*, like the French.'

Thomas looked back at him with a sly smile. 'Oh, I think "minions" is more apt, don't you?'

CHAPTER FIFTEEN

For late October, the day was unusually warm, and the sun shone brightly, bleaching a little the sand of the tilt-yard and making the pennants and brightly painted woodwork arrest the eye. Thomas knew he too would catch the eye, dressed as he was in his customary scarlet robes and the large gold cross around his neck that glinted with every subtle movement. That was good, he wanted to be noticed.

Henry, it seemed, had not had enough of festivities while the French were in London and had ordered a tilt at Greenwich. Perhaps he was keen to make the most of the autumn while it lasted; there would be little outdoor entertainment once the cold set in. Thomas was glad of the opportunity for a few hours away from his office. He could do with the break from work and an afternoon watching the tilt was a not unpleasant way to pass the time.

Charles Brandon, still at court, opened the tilt. Thomas knew Brandon was out of practice, living as he did mostly in the country, and yet he had done well, displaying the skill that had once made him a fearsome opponent to Henry. He was followed by Compton and Bryan, both of whom were always willing to show off their prowess. There were a few other young men who also tilted, new to court and eager to prove themselves, and the shadows lengthened as the horses charged up and down the lists. It was all most enjoyable.

Thomas frowned as there was a muttering to his left. He had been so interested in the last charge that he had not been paying any attention to Henry and Katherine sitting a little way to his left, and turned his head now to see Henry rising. There was a great scuffle as everyone else in the pavilion got hastily to their feet, Thomas included, and he watched as Henry held out both his hands to Katherine and pulled her to her feet, not all that gently. Thomas was surprised at Henry's roughness. It was most unlike him to be so rough with a lady, especially when that lady was so big with child.

The elder and most faithful of Katherine's ladies proceeded to fuss around her, while the younger ones all held back with forlorn expressions. They knew that for them the entertainment was over. If Katherine was leaving, they would have to leave too.

As Henry released Katherine, Thomas heard him say that she must summon the doctor to attend her, but Katherine flapped her hands at him in what seemed to be annoyance. It was a rare sight. In Thomas's experience, Katherine rarely found fault with Henry and never in public, but he supposed this latest pregnancy was taking its toll on her temper.

With Katherine and her ladies gone, the pavilion was half empty. Henry waved for those waiting to tilt to continue, then resumed his seat. Thomas kept one eye on the tilt-yard and one eye on Henry. The king's mood seemed to have altered with Katherine's departure. He wasn't missing her, Thomas could tell that. No, it was as if he was irked by her. Thomas knew it annoyed Henry that Katherine didn't enjoy the same things as he, for she had never been interested in hunting or archery, or even tilts for that matter. That had been a bone of contention between them ever since their marriage, but in the early days Henry had been prepared to overlook his wife's disinterest. Now, it seemed to Thomas, the differences in their persons and in their tastes were becoming more marked and harder to ignore.

After a few minutes, Henry turned his head slightly towards Thomas, and Thomas gave the king an enquiring smile. Henry considered a moment, then gave the slightest jerk of his head, an instruction for Thomas to draw near. Thomas gestured at Katherine's vacated chair and Henry nodded for him to take it. It was still warm.

'The queen was feeling tired,' Henry said.

Why are you bothering to make an excuse? Thomas wondered. 'That is to be expected, Your Majesty.'

Henry grunted. 'I need you to do something for me, Thomas. I'm asking you because I need you to be discreet and I know you will be so. You see, a young lady of my acquaintance is with child.' Henry paused to rub his chin. 'It is my child she carries.'

Ah, so that was it. Katherine had no doubt noticed Bessie's swelling stomach and realised her husband had put a child in her lady's womb, hence her unusual display of anger at Henry. 'Mistress Blount, I presume?'

Henry nodded. 'I would have preferred to keep this from the queen, but she has discovered the lady's unfortunate condition and is a little upset. I cannot have the queen upset at such a time as this. The smallest anxiety could harm the child she carries.'

'I understand you wish Mistress Blount to be removed from court?' *Out of sight, where the queen need not see her*, Thomas thought, *and where you need not be bothered by either lady.*

'I do,' Henry nodded, and leant a little closer, 'but Mistress Blount must also be cared for. For the sake of the child, you understand.'

'I know of a suitable place for the lady to be confined,' Thomas said. 'There is a friary near Barking that is very comfortable and the friars very discreet.'

Henry nodded. 'See it done tomorrow, will you? I would have Mistress Blount gone as soon as possible.'

The matter settled, Henry's attention returned to the tilt. He cheered and clapped loudly as the rider nearest the pavilion was unseated. A cloud of sand rose and seemed to hover in the air. Henry got to his feet as the rider was helped up by servants wearing green and white tabards and limped away.

'I shall tilt,' he said to Thomas, there being no Katherine present to plead with him against taking such a risk, and made his way down the wooden steps to the cheers of the crowd, who had realised what he was about.

Thomas returned to his seat, feeling a little sorry for the women Henry had made the bearers of his children, and not a little sorry for himself. He was not looking forward to telling Bessie she had to leave court.

~

Thomas plumped up the cushion and replaced it in the bowl of the chair. Ladies liked cushions, he knew, and he wanted Bessie to be comfortable in body for he knew she would not be comfortable, once he had spoken with her, in mind.

He wondered if she would cry as he resumed his seat, hearing footsteps in the chamber beyond. He really hoped she would not, for he wouldn't know how to deal with her. Thomas wasn't used to women in tears. His sister Elizabeth had hardly ever exhibited any emotion but resentment, and the only time Joan had ever cried was when she had been parted from their children. He supposed it would depend on what Henry had told Bessie in their intimate moments. If she was a sensible young girl, then she would under-stand that she had been nothing more than a pleasant diversion for Henry and would retire from the scene with good grace. But if Henry had sworn love and devotion, as Thomas supposed he had, then it was likely Bessie would be upset by being sent from court and he was in for a very unpleasant interview indeed.

He prepared himself as the door opened and Tuke entered. 'Sir John Blount to see you, Your Eminence.'

Thomas tried to hide his dismay as Sir John strode in. He hadn't been expecting the father. Bessie followed in his wake, head down, the dutiful little daughter. To Thomas's eyes, Sir John looked ready for a fight; no doubt he knew what was coming. Thomas offered him a chair and for a moment Sir John looked as if was going to refuse it. *What does he think he can do?* Thomas wondered, as he turned and smiled at Bessie.

She tried to smile back, but there was fear in her expression. *She is still a girl*, Thomas thought, looking at her pensive face, *behaving as if she has been summoned by her parents to be chastised.*

'It is good of you to spare the time to accompany your daughter, Sir John,' Thomas said, nodding to Tuke that he could leave.

'I thought it best,' Sir John said stiffly. Bessie was taking too long to sit and he patted the seat of the chair next to him impatiently. She hurried into it.

'I'll get straight to the point,' Thomas said. 'The king has told me of your daughter's condition and he wishes to ensure Lady Elizabeth's comfort by having her leave court.'

Bessie gasped and turned to her father open-mouthed. Sir John refused to look at her, keeping his eyes firmly on Thomas, but he placed his hand on her knee, not a gesture of tenderness, Thomas thought, but one of control. Sir John wanted his daughter to be quiet.

'For how long will she be from court?' he asked.

'That is not yet known,' Thomas said carefully. Did the man not understand that it would be for good, unless the queen failed to provide an heir and Henry needed the son he hoped Bessie would bear? Then Bessie would be welcomed back as the mother of a future king.

'Is the king displeased with me?' Bessie burst out.

Her father shushed her angrily. 'Your Eminence, my daughter has been discreet in her relationship with the king. It is not possible he could find fault with her.'

'I assure you, the king has no complaint to make about your daughter, far from it,' Thomas said, holding up his hands pacifically. 'But you must understand, the queen is near her time and nothing must be allowed to upset her and so endanger her child. Your daughter's condition must not become common knowledge.'

Sir John drew himself up. 'What you actually mean is that my daughter must be got out of the way. I expect Katherine has complained about her.'

'The queen has always been very kind to me, Father,' Bessie said.

'Be quiet, girl,' Sir John said, frowning at Thomas. 'What if I refuse to take her away from court?'

Oh, you foolish old man, must you dig your heels in over this? Thomas leant back in his chair and folded his hands over his stomach. 'Let me be clear, Sir John.

This is not a request. The king orders your daughter's removal.'

Sir John jumped up from his seat. 'What you mean is that the king has had his fun with my daughter and now he's done with her. Well, let me tell you, Your Eminence, I will not let the king discard my daughter as if she were nothing. He took her maidenhead.'

Thomas saw Bessie blush and hide her head. He wasn't having this. He took a deep breath and fixed her father with a hard stare. 'If the loss of her reputation was so important to you, Sir John, perhaps you should have instructed your daughter to refuse the king. She was very young when she went to the king's bed, and I have no doubt that she did so with your agreement, perhaps even at your instigation. Do you think that a proper thing for a father to have done?'

Sir John fell back into his chair. 'Well... I... that is...'

'I think you've said enough, Sir John,' Thomas said, beginning to sort through his papers to imply he had more important things to attend to. 'I appreciate that your daughter could be considered tainted by her affair with the king in terms of a future marriage. Let me allay your fears in that regard. Your daughter will have the king's child and, after a suitable period has elapsed, I will find a husband for her. Mistress Blount will also be cared for financially. I trust this is acceptable.'

'Quite acceptable,' Sir John said, entirely subdued now.

'Good,' Thomas said, smiling and turning to Bessie. 'My lady, I have made arrangements for you to go to St Laurence's Priory. It is a very pleasant place and you will be taken very good care of.'

'But I don't want to go there,' Bessie said, sniffing. 'Why can't I go home to have my baby?'

'If the child is a girl,' Thomas continued adroitly, ignoring her question, 'you will be permitted to retire to your family home with her. It is possible that if the child is a boy, the king will formally acknowledge him and give him his own household.'

'Acknowledge him as his heir?' Sir John asked with renewed interest.

'I do not speak of that,' Thomas said sharply. 'The child will be a bastard. I speak of a possibility only. The king has not said anything on this subject.' *And I shouldn't have said anything about Henry acknowledging a boy*, he chided himself, but he knew why he had done it. He had wanted to give Bessie something for all he was taking away.

'But he doesn't have an heir,' Sir John said. 'If the queen miscarries or has another girl—'

Thomas held up a hand to cut him off. 'Sir John, I think you cannot be in your right mind to speak so.'

Sir John looked aghast. 'I didn't mean to sug... Forgive me for my rash words.'

'They will be so forgotten so long as you make no further objections to these arrangements. If you persist, however—'

'No, no,' Sir John shook his head. 'Bessie will leave the court. Everything will be as you say.'

'As the king says,' Thomas corrected. 'Well then, if we are agreed…' He rose, and his visitors did the same. Thomas came around his desk and took Bessie's hand. 'My very best wishes to you, my lady.'

He could tell Bessie couldn't wait to be gone. She did not look up at him, and Thomas saw wet streaks running down her pale cheeks. Bessie dipped a curtsey, slipped her hand from his, and headed for the door, casting a quick look behind to ensure her father was following.

'Thank you, Your Eminence,' Sir John said, looking determinedly at the cross that bobbed on Thomas's stomach rather than at his face. 'I know my daughter will miss being at court, but I understand the necessity for her leaving. I trust the king will appreciate her sacrifice.'

Thomas wanted to tell him the truth, that he doubted whether Henry had given his bonny Bessie another thought since asking Thomas to deal with her, but he wouldn't say so to her father. 'I will be sure to inform him of it,' he said instead, and showed Sir John out.

CHAPTER SIXTEEN

Katherine's child had been born dead. Yet again, the queen had failed to provide her husband with an heir.

Katherine had suffered greatly. The labour had been long and tortuous. The baby had died within her womb, and the doctor had had to wrench its corpse from Katherine's writhing body. There had been so much blood, there had been concern that Katherine would die.

Perhaps, Thomas had thought, *it would have been better if she had died*. That would leave Henry free to take a new wife, a younger woman, or a widow who had already borne children and so proved fertile. It was a cruel thought, and Thomas berated himself for it. It was God's will that Katherine lose the child, they all had to remember that. But God's will or not, it did not alter the fact that Henry still had no male heir. All that he had to hope for was a bastard son from young Bessie, but maybe that would have to do.

Thomas put the lack of an heir to the back of his

mind for the moment. He was very busy answering the enquiries of the rulers of Portugal, Denmark, the Netherlands and others who all wanted to join with England and France in their new treaty. It was very gratifying. He doubted whether the pope had been so petitioned when he had wanted all of Europe to rise against the Turk.

But there were also reports coming from court that perturbed Thomas not a little. The king's unhappiness was evident to all. Thomas did not blame him for being unhappy, nor for showing it, but it was how it was manifesting itself that worried him. Henry was finding consolation, or at least temporary freedom from thinking about his lack of a son, in the company of his newly appointed Gentlemen of the Privy Chamber, none of whom Thomas had any affection for. Bryan, Compton, Sir Nicholas Carew, Sir Thomas Wyatt, Henry Norris – these were some of the men Henry had chosen to surround himself with, and every one a rascal to some degree or other. That Henry needed companions was undeniable, but that he needed these kinds of companions was debatable. They encouraged all that was weak in Henry. They nurtured his love of gambling, knowing that Henry was no clever card player and expecting him to lose heavily. He did lose consistently, and Henry's privy purse grew leaner while his friends' purses grew fatter. He was also drinking much more, and Thomas heard of late-night revels with much vomiting and raucousness. Such behaviour did not make for an attractive king.

The matter was discussed in Council. Concerns were raised, questions asked. Should the king be allowed to continue in this manner? Should someone, and by someone the counsellors all meant Thomas, not speak to him about regulating his behaviour and that of his friends?

But Thomas neither had the time nor the inclination to talk to the king. Henry was grieving, he said to the Council, and must be allowed to spend his grief how he felt fit. If his behaviour continued to be detrimental to his honour, then and only then, would Thomas act. The Council agreed on this course of action, and Henry's behaviour and that of his friends were no longer a matter of great moment.

But Thomas had no doubt they would become so, sooner or later. For the moment, however, Thomas had other things on his mind. Word had come from Bishop Gurk. The Emperor Maximilian was ill.

$\sim$

'So, he's dead at last,' Thomas said when Gurk wrote a second letter to deliver the latest news of his master. 'It's strange. He's been around for so long, I just assumed Maximilian would recover when we heard he was ill.'

'I know what you mean,' Tuke said, rereading the bishop's letter. 'I wonder what this will all mean.'

'For whom?'

'Why, for Europe, Your Eminence.'

'That's obvious, Brian,' Thomas said. 'Charles of Spain will become Holy Roman Emperor.'

'How can you be so sure? The emperor has to be elected, doesn't he?'

'A mere formality. The German Electors will go through the motions, but I guarantee they will elect Charles. He is Maximilian's grandson and they will always opt for continuity. And I expect Bishop Gurk will pay them a great deal to elect Charles.'

Tuke looked shocked. 'He would bribe them?'

Thomas chuckled. 'Of course he will. That's how it's done.'

'I see.' Tuke stared at his desk and frowned. 'But will the Electors ignore King Francis? I mean, he is as powerful as Charles, is he not? Even the pope courts him.'

'I suppose Francis may try to be elected Holy Roman Emperor. Yes, you might have something there, Brian.' Thomas made a noise of annoyance. 'Why did Maximilian have to die now? The timing couldn't possibly be worse. This will divide Europe again, after all I've done to bring her together.'

'You mean your peace treaty will suffer?'

Thomas nodded. 'It will be every king for himself again. I will tell the king that he mustn't announce his support for any candidate, so in essence England will be neutral, but it's still going to make a mess of every-thing, you wait and see.'

'You have to look on the bright side, Your Eminence,' Tuke said cheerily. 'If the election is a foregone conclusion, there won't be any need for rivalry between King Henry and King Francis.'

'You're very optimistic, Brian. I envy that.'

Tuke smiled. 'I suppose no one else will be in the running. Just Charles of Spain and King Francis?'

'Who else are you thinking of?' Thomas murmured, running his finger down a column of figures.

'Oh, just of the king.'

'Which king?'

'Ours, of course. King Henry.'

Thomas looked up, his eyes widening in surprise. 'As Holy Roman Emperor?'

'Why not? Wouldn't you like King Henry to be the emperor?'

'No, I would not,' Thomas declared emphatically. 'It's an empty title, Brian. Lots of ceremonies to hold and attend, many obligations and no real power. It's really not worth the having, I promise you.'

'Sounds good, though, doesn't it?' Tuke persisted. 'Henry, King of England, Ireland and Wales, and Holy Roman Emperor!'

'It will never happen,' Thomas assured him and told him to get back to his work.

CHAPTER SEVENTEEN

'A letter's come from that popinjay Boleyn,' Tuke said as Thomas returned to his desk after a morning spent drowning in Star Chamber legal cases.

Thomas allowed himself to smile at Tuke's description of their new ambassador in France – it was very apt. Boleyn *was* a popinjay. He always walked with his nose in the air as though there was a bad smell emanating from his fellow courtiers, and yet he had no right to act so high and mighty. Boleyn was only a little grander in blood than Thomas. Boleyn's not-so-distant ancestors had been in trade, not the bloody trade of butchery and farming as Thomas's had, to be sure, but trade was trade when all was said and done.

Thomas did allow that Boleyn was rather more intelligent than most of the other courtiers. He was well read and fluent in French, and that latter talent set him apart. It always surprised Thomas to discover how ignorant many courtiers were. They revelled in their ignorance, and that was something Thomas simply couldn't abide. How could a person not want to learn and increase their knowledge? It was incomprehensible to him. Boleyn was different, perhaps because he was so newly ennobled, and it had been his fluency in the French tongue that had led to him being chosen to be the new ambassador. That and the fact Thomas thought he would fit in well at the French court with all its affected airs and graces.

Thomas pressed his fingers into his eyes, weary from staring at papers all morning. He had been feeling the strain lately. He could still work all day and most of the night, but he was getting lots of headaches behind his eyes these days.

'Read it to me,' he told Tuke.

Tuke cleared his throat. 'I shall spare you all the opening words, they are just the usual courtier's patter, all wind and piss. Ah, here we are. "King Francis greeted me with great warmth and sincere good wishes. He wished me to pass on his thanks for the great friendship and hospitality extended to his friends in October of last year when the treaty was signed and offered his congratulations to Cardinal Wolsey for the management of the whole affair."' Tuke snorted. 'I wager he hated having to write that.'

'Just his words without the commentary will do, Brian.'

Tuke smiled and continued. '"The handover of Tournai is progressing well. The first instalment of twenty-six thousand livres has been received without any attempt to lessen the sum, which I understand the Council feared. I would like to allay their fears. The French cannot have been more welcome or honest in their dealings with me."'

'France agrees with Sir Thomas very well, it seems.'

'We knew it would. Ah, now he's writing about the meeting between Henry and Francis. "King Francis is anxious for the meeting with his brother king to go ahead and has mentioned that he would prefer it to be an intimate affair, with as few attendants as possible, as he believes this will allow he and King Henry to know one another better."' Tuke looked up from beneath lowered lids at Thomas.

Thomas was pouting. An intimate affair was not what he wanted for the meeting of Henry and Francis. Having at first doubted the wisdom of allowing the two young men to meet, he had decided it would be a very good thing indeed, a chance for England and, yes, he, to show what they could do, an opportunity to show their importance. This alliance and the meeting that would celebrate it was going to be perhaps the most important summit of the century, and he wanted everyone to know about it. Oh, no, it was not going to be an intimate affair.

'Take a letter, Brian,' Thomas said and waited impatiently for Tuke to find his pen and ink beneath the papers on his desk. 'To Sir Thomas Boleyn. Under no circumstances will King Henry countenance an informal meeting with King Francis. Such a meeting deserves much ceremony, and His Eminence will not allow either King Henry or King Francis to be demeaned by their sovereignty not being celebrated. His Eminence appreciates that this will mean a great deal of money must needs be spent, but he feels that not to make this meeting magnificent will defeat its ultimate purpose. You must explain to King Francis that a subtle affair will not do.'

Tuke finished scribbling a minute later. He looked up. 'Do you want me to read out the rest of Boleyn's letter before ending yours? In case you want to say something else?'

Thomas had forgotten the remainder of the ambassador's letter in his indignation. He nodded. 'Yes, carry on.'

Tuke found Boleyn's letter again, found the place he had read up to, and scanning the next few lines, realised Thomas was unlikely to care for the remainder any more than he had liked what he had already read out. He cleared his throat and began to read. '"King Francis has made it clear to me that he would welcome the support of King Henry in his candidacy to become Holy Roman Emperor and reminds us of the great amity between our two countries so recently professed."'

'You don't have to continue, Brian, I understand both Sir Thomas Boleyn's and King Francis's meaning. The treaty will be upheld so long as we help King Francis become emperor.'

'That makes things rather difficult, doesn't it?' Tuke asked. 'You wanted us to remain neutral.'

'It seems I am not to have the luxury of not getting involved. If we must take sides, then I am all for King Francis as emperor, as is the pope, but I cannot see it coming to pass. Maximilian paved the way too well for Charles of Spain, although admittedly the Electors are taking time to make up their minds to elect him. Still, I suppose we can lend our support to King Francis as he asks. It will not hurt us to do so. Add that to my letter. What?' he asked as he saw Tuke hesitate, pen hovering over the page.

'I was wondering about the queen,' Tuke said. 'Will she not object to our support for France? Charles of Spain is her nephew, after all.'

Thomas fixed him with a steely stare. 'But the queen does not rule England, Brian, and has no right to object to our support for France. Unless you are suggesting she rules the king?'

'Certainly not, Your Eminence,' Tuke said sheepishly.

'I'm very glad to hear it,' Thomas said, and meant it. With Henry paying Katherine less and less mind, Thomas could almost believe he had the king all to himself.

Sir William Tyrwhit was crushing his cap in his hands as he stood before the Council table and told the assembled counsellors his complaint. Thomas knew Tyrwhit had hoped to see him alone, for the matter was personal, but he had picked his moment poorly, and now there was no option but for all the Council to hear.

Tyrwhit had lost the widow he had been hoping to marry. Thomas already knew of his suit to the lady, as Tyrwhit had asked him to put in a good word for him, which Thomas had been happy to do. Sir William Tyrwhit was a good servant to him and deserved to be wed to a woman with a decent fortune. So, he had written to Mistress Vernon and told her what a fine man Sir William Tyrwhit was and how pleased he, Thomas, would be if she accepted his proposal of marriage. The letter written, Thomas had not given the matter another thought, believing that with his backing Tyrwhit would be married to the widow within the month. But no. Tyrwhit was standing before the Council telling him he had lost out to one of the king's Gentlemen of the Bedchamber, one William Coffin.

Thomas could hardly believe it. That Mistress Vernon would have ignored his good advice and chosen a man like Coffin was absurd. Coffin was like all the king's friends: arrogant, raucous, a gambler, a drinker, a womaniser. That she should prefer such a man to a decent, upright fellow as was Sir William Tyrwhit! What was the world coming to?

'The lady must be quite mad,' Thomas said when Tyrwhit had finished.

'I don't know about that,' Tyrwhit said sadly. 'I think it was the king's letter that made her agree to Master Coffin.'

Thomas looked up at Tyrwhit, frowning. 'What letter?'

Tyrwhit shifted uneasily. 'Coffin got the king to write to Mistress Vernon to press his suit, Your Eminence.'

All heads at the table turned to Thomas.

'Before or after I wrote to Mistress Vernon?' Thomas asked.

'After,' Tyrwhit said.

Thomas felt his neck growing red. That the king should have interfered in this way and undone all his work was hugely embarrassing. What could he say before all these men? That the king had no right to write to the widow? He couldn't do that, but really, what had the king been thinking? Thomas grunted as he realised what had happened. That rogue Coffin had got to him, whispered in his ear that he should have the widow, no doubt not mentioning Thomas or Tyrwhit at all. And the king, in his good nature, agreed to help the widow make up her mind.

'I daresay Master Coffin did not acquaint the king with all the facts in this case,' Thomas said carefully. 'Had the king known of my letter to Mistress Vernon, he would not have agreed to write on Master Coffin's behalf.'

'You sound very sure of that, Your Eminence,' Sir Thomas Lovell said.

'I am sure of it, Sir Thomas,' Thomas snapped. 'The king and I think as one in all things.'

'Providing the king is aware of your thoughts.'

Lovell nodded, sharing a smile with the counsellor sitting opposite.

'I shall speak to the king about this matter, Sir William,' Thomas promised Tyrwhit, 'but I fear that the widow may have made a promise to Coffin she is now duty bound to keep.'

'I have lost her, then?' Tyrwhit asked pitifully.

'Don't worry, Sir William,' Lovell said jovially, 'His Eminence will find an even richer widow for you to marry, you see if he doesn't.'

Everyone around the table laughed, even Tyrwhit, who seemed to believe Lovell spoke the truth.

I will find him a very rich widow, Thomas thought savagely as Tyrwhit was shooed out of the door by a clerk. *That'll teach you all to laugh.*

'For all the humour in Tyrwhit's situation,' Bishop Fox began when the door had closed, 'it is an example of the problem we have already spoken about. That of the king's Gentlemen. I don't believe we can ignore this problem any longer.' He looked meaningfully at Thomas.

Thomas gestured for him to continue.

'Some of the king's Gentlemen have been gaining notoriety,' Fox said, 'not just here at court and in London, but abroad too. We have had reports from our ambassador in Paris.' He clicked his fingers and the clerk hastily found a sheet of paper and handed it to him. 'You remember how the king sent some of his friends to escort the French back to Paris last month. Here, he writes of what they got up to once there.' He cleared his throat and began reading from the paper. "'Sir Francis Bryan and Sir Nicholas Carew donned disguises and proceeded to rampage through the streets of Paris. Without thought or care for the king's reputation, they pelted the people with eggs and stones, and whatever else they could find to throw. I have received numerous complaints that several people were injured during this childish behaviour and I beseech the Council to do something about it. These gentlemen must be made to understand that, when abroad, they represent the king, and any bad behaviour on their part reflects poorly on our king." There, we cannot have it put more plainly than that.'

'Why was I not told of this?' Thomas demanded, snatching the paper from Fox's hand.

'You had said that you didn't think the Gentlemen's behaviour was anything to be concerned about,' Fox reminded him. 'And at the time it seemed a rather minor matter, one we told the ambassador to patch over with the French. But this today with Tyrwhit, and several other incidents that have reached our ears this week, well, we think it is time something is done about these men.'

'When you say something must be done about these men,' Thomas said, 'what exactly do you mean?'

'I mean he must be made to give them up. They are ruining him, Thomas.'

'Bishop Fox,' Lovell said, his brow creasing in worry, 'we cannot make the king do anything.'

Fox smiled back at Lovell. 'Sir Thomas, His

Eminence can make the king do anything.' He turned, grinning, to Thomas. 'Isn't that right?'

Thomas glowered at him.

~

Thomas sought an audience with the king as soon as the Council meeting was over. When he entered the privy chamber, he found the very men Fox had mentioned, Carew and Bryan, lounging around, cups of wine in one hand, cards in the other.

Henry came out of the inner room a moment later. 'Good morning, Thomas. What do you do here?'

'Good morning, Your Majesty. I would like a word in private, if I may.'

'Of course. Come into the other room. I know how you loathe these two lazy dogs.' He grinned at Carew and Bryan as Thomas followed his gesture and went into the inner chamber. 'Well, what is it?'

Thomas took the chair Henry offered. 'I'm afraid I must speak with you about Carew and Bryan, Your Majesty, and your other Gentlemen.'

A frown appeared on Henry's face. 'What about them?'

'Your Majesty should be made aware of an unfortunate incident that occurred in Paris last month.'

'You don't mean that scrape those two out there got into, do you?' Henry said, his face breaking into a grin.

'It was rather more than a scrape,' Thomas said,

determined not to be put off by the king's playing down of the incident. 'And it was by no means an isolated incident.'

'But they told me all about it,' Henry said, waving his hand at Thomas. 'A bit of fun, that was all.'

'I fear the French did not consider it in that light. They made a complaint to our ambassador, and bearing in mind our alliance with them, it is not something we can ignore. Not when your reputation is at stake.'

The smile dropped from Henry's face. 'My reputation?'

Thomas held out his hands, palms up. 'What are the French to think if it is known that friends of yours are allowed to abuse them without reproach, possibly even with your agreement?'

'But I didn't know anything about it until they got back to London,' Henry protested.

'That is not an acceptable excuse as far as the French are concerned.' He watched Henry and waited to see how he would take this comment. When Henry seemed to be considering it, Thomas felt emboldened to continue. 'And as I said, there have been other incidents that reflect badly on you. This matter with Master Coffin and Mistress Vernon, for example.'

Henry looked up. 'Coffin wanted to marry the widow. What could possibly be wrong with that?'

'Your Majesty would not have been aware, at least, I am assuming Coffin did not inform you, that I had petitioned the widow Vernon to become the wife of one of my servants, a Sir William Tyrwhit. It was my understanding that she was very warm towards the idea of becoming Lady Tyrwhit but that a letter from yourself persuaded her to agree to marry Master Coffin instead.'

The frown returned. 'I didn't know about Tyrwhit. Coffin never told me. He just said there was a lady with a fortune he wanted to marry and would I put in a good word for him. I didn't see any harm in it, Thomas.'

'Indeed, why should you? You believed your friend had told you all. You could not know that he had misrepresented the matter.'

'You mean he deliberately misled me?'

Thomas gave the slightest of shrugs in answer.

'Well, what if he did? He wanted the lady. Am I to consult you on every little personal matter?' Henry laughed, almost as if he was daring Thomas to contradict him.

'You need not consult me if you do not wish, Your Majesty,' Thomas said, hoping it was clear to Henry how put out he was. 'I would hope, however, that you would welcome my opinion on such matters and not put yourself in a position where you could be easily manipulated by a man who has only his own interest at heart.'

That hit home, Thomas could tell. Henry's small mouth pursed. 'Coffin has been false to me, you say?'

'I would not go so far,' Thomas said, not wishing to appear too eager to criticise Henry's friend, 'but he

226

has been guilty of taking advantage of your good nature.'

'I should remind him who is king here,' Henry said heatedly.

This was good. This was Henry as Thomas would have him be: outraged, indignant that he had been used. Thomas folded his hands on the table before him. 'And yet, the damage has been done. I would not want you to be made to look foolish in the eyes of Mistress Vernon. I fear Sir William Tyrwhit must concede defeat with good grace in this matter. But it has highlighted a concern to me. Whilst I understand Your Majesty's desire to have your friends about you – and far be it from me to deprive you entirely of their company – I fear they do occupy a position of great influence that may not always be to your good. This matter of a marriage may seem trivial, but it represents a greater danger. At least, that is how it seems to me, who does have your best interests at heart, Your Majesty, I assure you.' *Unlike your friends*, he added mentally, trusting Henry to think the same. Thomas made to rise as though he had said his piece and would say no more, but Henry waved him back into the chair.

'I know you are always thinking of me, Thomas. I know how much I owe you. But what do you suggest?'

'That you dismiss your friends as Privy Gentlemen of the Bedchamber.'

'And leave me without servants?' Henry cried.

'You would not be without servants,' Thomas said smoothly. 'Merely that if you were to allow me to choose your Gentlemen for you, you would have servants that would serve you rather than themselves.'

Henry sighed despondently, and for a moment Thomas saw in the dejected expression the miserable little boy he had comforted in a window embrasure after the death of his mother.

'If I may say so, Your Majesty,' Thomas continued, sensing an opportunity to speak of something that had been on his mind for a while, 'there is a great need for reform in England. Allow me to explain. The court here is barely any different from that your father presided over, hardly different, in fact, from any that every previous king of England presided over. I believe we should look on your kingship as an opportunity to improve things here in England.'

'Of what do you speak, Thomas?' Henry asked, curiosity roused.

'Of many things. The law courts, for example, greatly favour the wealthy and influential. The poor man or woman has little chance of justice if they are pitted against those who have both. I sought to redress that in the Star Chamber a few years ago when you gave me leave to act against those nobles who practised abuses. But your nobles are sliding back into their old ways, and I would have them know who is king here in England. I would provide justice for everyone, regardless of station, and I would want it known that I do so at your behest. Just think, Your Majesty. Every man and woman in England would know that they could receive justice because the king of England insisted on it being so. No more would nobles escape punishment or retribution simply because of their blood.'

Thomas watched Henry carefully, saw the young man's face almost glow with the idea, and felt encouraged.

'Then there are the monasteries,' he continued before Henry could speak. 'It pains me greatly to talk of the great corruption inherent in such places. Places that should be beacons and examples of Christian benevolence are instead examples of greed and dissipation.'

'We would have a new England,' Henry breathed.

'Your England,' Thomas said emphatically. 'And such reforms must begin with your own self. Make an example to all your nobles. Show them you will not tolerate corruption and self-serving by cleansing your privy chamber.'

He had said enough. If he said more, he would be in danger of pushing his luck too far. Thomas waited for Henry to speak.

'You are right, Thomas,' Henry said. 'But I will not be without my friends, I tell you. Those that have offended will be dismissed, but those that have not will stay.'

It was enough. The main troublemakers, Bryan, Carew, Coffin, Compton, would be sent packing. 'Your Majesty is most wise,' Thomas said.

The Gentlemen stood before the Council table, all dressed alike in their black damask doublets and gowns. Coffin, Norris and Compton had serious faces. Bryan and Carew seemed to think their being summoned before the Council highly amusing. Thomas doubted if they would still be smiling by the end of this meeting.

Thomas nodded to Fox to begin. Fox stood, cleared his throat portentously and said, 'Gentlemen, you are hereby charged with being over-familiar with His Majesty the King, for having played such light touches upon him that you have quite forgot your true station and presumed upon the generous nature of the king. You have played upon his good nature, inducing him to gamble and divest him of his treasure of gold.'

'This is ridiculous,' Bryan scoffed laughingly. 'Henry knows what he is doing.'

'The king, Sir Francis,' Fox reminded him. 'You will refer to him as such.'

'He might be the king to you, old man,' Bryan said, 'but to me he is Henry.'

'Sir Francis,' Thomas said, spurred to speak by Bryan's insolence, 'you would do well to hold your tongue.'

'Would I, Your Eminence?' Bryan challenged.

'You would.' Thomas smiled sweetly. 'Who do you think ordered us to hold this meeting?'

Oh, the joy of seeing the smile drop off Bryan's face. Bryan fell silent as the others looked at him in wonder at seeing their brave speaker silenced.

'You see, gentlemen,' Thomas continued, as Fox, realising he was no longer needed to speak, sat down, 'the king is a man of such gentleness and liberality that he has not had the heart to rebuke or reprove your behaviour. But be assured, he has felt your misdemeanours keenly. He has given us, his Council, the authority to do what is necessary for the maintenance and defence of his honour.'

'We meant no dishonour to His Majesty,' Norris burst out.

'Nevertheless, you have been the cause of it,' Thomas said. 'But no longer. You are dismissed from your posts as Gentlemen of the Privy Chamber with immediate effect.'

'You cannot do that,' Carew declared.

'I can and I do,' Thomas said calmly. 'And what is more, the king orders you to leave court. You have until the end of the day. If you are still here at nightfall, you will be forcibly removed.' He flicked his fingers at them. 'You are dismissed.'

He had half-expected some argument from the young men, but they filed out of the Council room as meekly as women.

'Congratulations, Thomas,' Fox said as the door closed upon the last of them. 'I knew I said you could persuade the king to do anything but I must confess, I had not thought you would have bent the king to your will as quickly as this.'

Fox's language troubled Thomas a little. 'I did not bend him to my will, bishop,' he said a little testily. 'I merely pointed out to the king how his friends were damaging his reputation. His sense of honour did the rest.'

'Yes, of course,' Fox said, appeasingly. 'So, is the king to be unattended from now on?'

'Certainly not,' Thomas answered promptly. 'I think it was a very good idea of his to have personal attendants. He just chose the wrong men to serve him.'

'Who shall choose the right men?' Fox asked.

Thomas suspected the bishop already knew the answer, but it pleased him to be able to voice it. 'I will, of course.'

~

Tuke coughed to draw Thomas's attention. When Thomas looked up from his desk, he wondered at the smirk on his secretary's face.

'What has amused you, Brian?'

'Do you remember when we talked about the election of the Holy Roman Emperor?' he said. 'Well, Pace is outside and asks if he can have a word.'

'Bring him in,' Thomas said, intrigued as to what Pace wanted to see him about. 'Good morning, Richard,' he said as Pace and Tuke entered the room. 'Brian seems to think you have news regarding the election. Something amusing.'

Pace shot a look at Tuke. 'I don't find it funny.'

Tuke was still smirking and Thomas was growing annoyed. 'Brian, stop grinning like a loon and get on with your work. Take a seat, Richard. Is it the king?'

'Yes,' Pace said, then sighed. 'No… well… sort of.' He took a deep breath. 'You see, the thing is, the king is sending me to Germany.'

Tuke's amusement suddenly made sense. 'He wants to be considered as emperor, doesn't he?' Thomas said, understanding.

Pace nodded. 'It's that letter from the pope that started it. The one where he wrote that he would like there to be a third candidate in the running besides Charles of Spain and King Francis. King Henry thinks the pope meant he wanted him to stand.'

'The pope didn't mean him at all,' Thomas cried. 'He meant one of the German princes. Leo is worried that if either Charles or Francis becomes emperor, he won't be able to control them.'

'I know that, Your Eminence, but the king doesn't,' Pace said. 'Could you not persuade him of there being no hope? I haven't been well, as you know, and I don't really feel up to a long journey to Germany, especially on a wasted enterprise.'

Thomas shook his head. 'I sympathise, Richard, I really do, but if the king has ordered you, there's nothing I can do.'

That wasn't strictly true. He could have spoken with Henry, explained that there really was no hope of his becoming emperor. Henry might listen, but he might not. Either way, he would know that Thomas felt he was no match for Charles or Francis, and Thomas felt that that would do him no good at all. No, best to let Pace go and not have any success. That way it would be Pace's failure, not Thomas's.

Pace bit his bottom lip and nodded sadly. 'No, I suppose not. I thought I'd ask, but…' He smacked his hands on his thighs and rose with a sigh. 'I shall not detain you any longer, Your Eminence.'

'Have a safe journey,' Thomas called as the door closed upon Pace. He met Tuke's eye. 'Aren't you glad you work for me and not the king, Brian?'

Tuke raised both eyebrows. 'I thank the Lord for it every day, Your Eminence.'

Thomas smiled as he bent his head to his work once more. 'Carry on behaving foolishly and I might send you to him.'

CHAPTER EIGHTEEN

1519

There had been no procession this time, no train of three hundred servants, no splendidly bedecked mule for him to ride out on. Such a procession would attract attention, and attention was what Thomas wanted to avoid. After all, he didn't want the whole world to know he was on his way to visit the king's mistress in her hour of labour.

With the stillbirth of the queen's last baby, the child growing in Bessie's belly had become rather more important to the king. Thomas received intelligence from his agents at court that Henry had taken to speaking wistfully of Bessie and the child she carried. Katherine, it seemed, featured hardly at all in Henry's mind these days.

There would be more mistresses in the future, Thomas reasoned. Henry had been more than uxorious to the queen since their marriage, and his mistresses had hitherto been few, but as Katherine grew older and less physically appealing, Thomas knew Henry's eye would begin to wander. Soon, he would begin to emulate King Francis and take many more young women to his bed. *This visiting of young women in childbirth might become a regular excursion for me,* he reflected ruefully.

Thomas found himself enjoying the trip from London. He realised he was liking the capital less and less these days. He found it noisy and crowded now, whereas before he had revelled in its bustle, even its squalor. But more to the point, he was never allowed to be unavailable in London. If the king sent for him, he had to go and go at once. Petitioners and claimants haunted his corridor day and night. In London, he knew he had to be seen if he was to stay in control. But in the country…

His thoughts turned fondly to Hampton Court, and he swore to himself that he would make an effort to spend more time there. At Hampton, he fancied he could almost be a private gentleman. It was a state he was finding increasingly appealing.

After an hour or so in his carriage, he arrived at his destination, the priory where Bessie had been lodged for the last six months. A friar was waiting for him at the gates. The friar was all obsequiousness, clearly excited to be greeting one so exalted as Thomas. Thomas immediately asked after Bessie. The friar told him Bessie was still in labour and asked if His Eminence would care for some refreshment while he waited?

Thomas hoped he hadn't been summoned too early. He had heard of some women being in labour for days. He accepted the offer of food and wine, and the friar led the way to the abbot.

As Thomas took a seat, he could not help but note the bounty of the table. The friars of this priory were supposed to be mendicants, holy men who had to beg for their sustenance, but there seemed little evidence of beggary. He did not bother to chide himself for hypocrisy. He had recently audited his account books and realised that his personal fortune amounted to more than thirty thousand pounds. Only the king came close to possessing such a sum. But as Thomas saw it, he was a cardinal, the king's most trusted minister. If he were to go about as a pauper, it would diminish the king's magnificence. He had to put on a good show to enhance and maintain the king's image at home and abroad. But the friars of this priory had no such need. They should not dine so well.

The repast had come to an end when an elderly friar shuffled into the room and whispered in the abbot's ear. The abbot's face broke into a smile.

'Excellent news, Your Eminence. The lady has been delivered of a healthy child.'

'Boy or girl?' Thomas asked at once.

'A boy.'

Thomas's breath caught in his throat. Henry had a son, a healthy son. He got to his feet. 'I must see the lady.'

The abbot rose hurriedly, not expecting this haste, and led Thomas to the rooms Bessie occupied. The abbot, in his eagerness to please his most important visitor, forgot to knock on the bedchamber door, and

Thomas saw the startled and weary face of Bessie appear in the doorway as she struggled to sit up in the bed.

Thomas entered. Lady Blount stood by the bed, and he was glad Bessie had had her mother's company for the birth. Lady Blount dipped a curtsy but said nothing to him. On the other side of the bed was an ornate cradle and Thomas headed for it. He peered inside. A red-faced, wrinkled creature lay in the cradle, a small thing, ugly. Thomas searched for any resemblance to the king. Save for the florid complexion which Henry acquired after only a little exertion, Thomas could discern no similarity between father and son. For the briefest of moments, he wondered if this was Henry's son, but a glance at Bessie convinced him that, though she had been happy to go to the king's bed, she was chaste enough to have denied others.

'The child is well, I am told,' he said to her.

'I thank the Lord he is,' Bessie said, her voice a little cracked.

'And you, my lady? You are well too?'

'I am, thank you.'

'You are tired, of course,' Thomas nodded understandingly, 'but I wanted to acquaint myself with the king's son. I shall let you rest.' He started for the door.

'Will the—' Bessie called after him.

He turned. 'Yes, my lady?'

She blinked rapidly and he hoped she wasn't about to cry. 'Will the king be pleased, Your Eminence?'

'The king will be exceedingly pleased.'

'And I will be able to return to court?'

Thomas glanced at Lady Blount, who, by her downcast expression, understood the true state of affairs.

'I fear that will not be possible, my lady,' Thomas said as sympathetically as he could. 'But as your child is a boy, the king will establish him in his own household and you will live with him. You will wish to be with your son, I am sure.'

'But the king will visit me?'

'Bessie!' Lady Blount said sharply.

'What, Mother?' Bessie turned wide, uncomprehending eyes on her.

Lady Blount looked to Thomas for help.

It was time to be blunt. 'My lady,' Thomas began, 'you must realise that you will meet with the king no more. Your liaisons will not resume. You will, however, be treated with all the respect due to the mother of the king's son, bastard though he be.'

Inevitably, he supposed, tears started to fall from Bessie's beautiful eyes. Thomas sought for some kind of solace.

'In due course, I will arrange a marriage to someone suitable for you. You have done good service to the king and you will not go unrewarded. Now, if you will forgive me, I must return to London and inform the king of the child.'

As he closed the door of the bedchamber, Thomas heard the bed creak and the rustle of silk as

Lady Blount climbed onto the bed and tried to console her distraught daughter.

~

Henry was playing bowls when Thomas arrived at the palace. Katherine and five of her ladies were seated nearby, applauding dutifully. Thomas waited until there was a break in the play, then stepped forward and coughed politely.

Henry strode over to meet him. 'What news?'

Thomas glanced over at the queen. Katherine was watching them both with intense curiosity. He kept his voice low. 'Mistress Blount has been delivered of a son, Your Majesty.'

'Thank the Lord. A son, you say.' He clapped his hands over his mouth and took a deep breath. 'Healthy?'

'Very robust.'

'I knew it wasn't my fault,' Henry said heatedly. 'All those doubters, Thomas. All those who said I couldn't father a boy—'

'I am sure no one has said that,' Thomas lied smoothly. He too had heard the gossip.

'I know it's been said,' Henry assured him through gritted teeth. He glanced at Katherine. 'The fault lies not with me.'

Thomas followed his gaze and noted the worried frown that formed on Katherine's face as she wondered why she was being so scrutinised.

'I have made arrangements for the child to have

his own household, as you instructed if it turned out to be a boy. But do you mean to officially acknowledge the child as yours?' Thomas asked, returning his gaze to Henry.

Brow creased, head down, hands on hips, Henry considered. 'I do not wish to upset the queen,' he said carefully, 'but I fear it cannot be helped. It must be known that I have sired a male child. Do you not think so, Thomas?'

Thomas thought it would make little difference; acknowledging the boy would not alter the fact that Henry's only legitimate heir was a baby girl. But Thomas knew Henry wanted to be able to boast of a son and he readily agreed. 'Do you mean by proclamation?'

Henry shook his head. 'No, nothing like that. Just around the court, you know. That will be enough.'

'As you wish, Your Majesty. I shall return to York Place to see to it, if I have your leave.'

'Yes, yes, go,' Henry said happily and hurried back to his game.

Thomas made his way back to the palace. As he passed onto a path between enormous hedges, he heard the scatter of gravel and turned to see Katherine, her skirts hitched up, hurrying towards him.

'Madam?' he queried as she came to a stop. 'Forgive me. Had I known you wished to see me, I would have come to you.'

Katherine was out of breath and she put her hand to her heaving bosom as if she could still it. 'The king seems very happy.'

'Yes,' he said awkwardly. 'I had some good news for him.'

'What was it?'

Thomas cleared his throat and shuffled his feet.

'You do not want to tell me,' Katherine said, nodding. 'You think it will cause me pain.'

'I think it might.'

'It is not your place to decide what I can and cannot hear, Your Eminence.'

Oh, but it is, Thomas thought, but said nothing.

'It is of no matter.' Katherine shook her head. 'I can guess what your news was. I can count, you see, Your Eminence. I know it is near six months since Mistress Blount left court, and nine since she was in my lord's company.'

'Indeed, madam,' Thomas nodded, keeping his eyes on her shoes.

'Was it a boy?'

'It was.' He looked up. There was only the tightening of the throat, the pinching of the nostrils to suggest that Katherine was experiencing any deep emotion.

'I see,' she said quietly, nodding. 'Yes, that would explain the king's happiness. I am happy for him.'

'That is very good of you.'

'Is Mistress Blount well?' she asked, looking somewhere over his shoulder.

Henry hadn't enquired after the health of his mistress, the mother of his new son, but the wronged wife did. How little time it had taken for Henry to forget the beautiful Bessie. Had he always intended

242

her to be a vessel for his seed or had he actually loved her a little? *What does it matter?* Thomas chastised himself. *The king must have his dalliances. If the queen can turn a blind eye, who am I to criticise?*

'Mistress Blount was well when I left her.'

'I am pleased for that. Childbirth is a fearful time for a woman, and she is so young.'

Katherine seemed to have run out of things to say. Either that or she wanted to be away from him. She nodded curtly and turned back the way she had come.

Thomas stood there for a moment, staring at the gravel that bore the traces of Katherine's feet. She must have been hurt by the news of a boy for Bessie, but she had hidden it well. Despite all their differences, despite Thomas often wishing Katherine would keep her opinions to herself and stop influencing Henry contrary to Thomas's wishes, he couldn't help but be impressed with her. *She is a true queen*, he told himself as he began to walk.

CHAPTER NINETEEN

Thomas quickly scribbled his name on the piece of paper and hurried out into the antechamber, waving away the appeals of his secretaries as they tried to get his attention and make him stop.

'Everything will have to wait,' he called. 'I have to greet the king.'

He hurried through the courtyard of Hampton Court, his scarlet skirts hitched up above his ankles. He was aware he probably looked ridiculous, a fat old man running through the courtyard, but he couldn't be late to meet Henry.

Thomas had only just been told the king's barge had been sighted about four hundred yards away on the river, the king's colours flying from the stern and music coming from a smaller boat carrying his musicians that floated a little behind. He knew Henry and Katherine were nearby at Richmond Palace, but he had had no warning that Henry was thinking of paying a visit. If he had, he would have ensured a banquet was prepared or at the very least some entertainment.

He neared the river steps, slowing down now there was a chance of him slipping in the mud. The king's barge had already docked and Thomas slid to a halt, holding the large cross against his belly as he tried to catch his breath.

'Thomas,' Henry called as he stepped over the gunwale, raising his hand in greeting.

'Your Majesty,' Thomas panted, forcing a smile. 'Forgive me, I had no notion you were visiting me today.'

'I had to come,' Henry said grimly, drawing near. 'My secretary has returned with news.' He took a deep breath and shook his head, the news obviously terrible. 'Charles of Spain has been elected Holy Roman Emperor.'

Was that all? Thomas was greatly relieved it was not worse. The election was not news to him, for Pace had kept him fully informed while in Germany. Thomas heard laughter and looked behind Henry to see Compton and Bryan climbing out of the barge. When Thomas had purged the privy chamber of Henry's friends a few months previously, he had been convinced the king meant to abide by his advice and keep his quarters free of such parasites. It had been disappointing, therefore, to learn that Henry had invited a few of his closest friends back to serve him, namely Carew, Bryan, Compton, and one or two others. Thomas had meant to remonstrate with Henry over the matter, but he had not yet got around to it.

'Why don't we retire to my office, Your Majesty,' he said, gesturing back to the house, 'and we can discuss the matter in more comfort?'

Henry grunted and began walking. Thomas had to take two steps for every one of Henry's and he was panting again by the time they reached his study. Bryan and Compton had followed, but Henry had told them to wait outside in the courtyard.

'I sent Pace to further my cause as a candidate,' Henry said before Thomas had closed the door. 'And yet he comes back saying there was nothing to be done. How is that possible?'

Thomas gestured with a jug. Henry nodded and Thomas poured two glasses of wine. He handed one to Henry. 'If you'll forgive me for saying so, Your Majesty, it was always likely that the Electors would choose Charles. Even King Francis knew he would likely lose when he put his name forward.'

'But Pope Leo wanted me to stand,' Henry cried, taking the wine cup and taking a large swig. 'He said so in his letter.'

Oh Lord, how do I tell the king the truth without hurting his feelings? Thomas cleared his throat, putting his head on one side. 'I think Pope Leo was more optimistic about a third candidate being considered than he had any right to be. He was more concerned about either Spain or France gaining more territory than he was about having you become emperor.'

'Do you mean to say the pope didn't care whether

I became emperor or not?' Henry's expression was really rather fierce, and Thomas felt his heart beat a little faster.

He decided to try a different tack. 'Is it not consoling to know that King Francis was not made emperor but that your nephew was, Your Majesty?'

Henry frowned. 'My nephew?'

'Charles of Spain is the queen's sister's child,' Thomas pointed out. 'Just consider, if Francis had been made emperor, England would have been able to have little influence upon him. But with Charles as emperor, he can be sure that England will be available to him whenever he needs advice from a sovereign of more mature years. And he will need advice,' Thomas assured him as Henry opened his mouth to speak. 'Charles is very young and has only his Flemish ministers to advise him at present. He is now in possession of a very large empire and bears the duty of being Holy Roman Emperor. I expect he will find ruling all of it rather overwhelming. Who should he turn to when he does but his uncle?'

Henry rubbed his chin and glanced out of the window where his friends loitered. 'Bryan said I should have won the election.'

Thomas's jaw tightened. 'If you will forgive me, Your Majesty, Sir Francis does not understand such matters.'

'He's not an idiot, Thomas,' Henry protested with a little laugh. 'None of my friends are, and they all thought I had a chance of winning.'

Thomas could imagine the conversations; words

exchanged over rather too many jugs of wine, each one encouraging the others on. If only these friends of his would stop giving Henry stupid ideas, Thomas's life would be a great deal easier. 'It is done now, Your Majesty, and cannot be undone,' he said with a smile, determined to end the topic. 'On a different note, I do have some good news.'

'Oh, yes,' Henry said with less interest than Thomas would have liked. 'What's that?'

Thomas hurried over to his desk and snatched up the letter he had received that morning. 'This is from King Francis's secretary of the Council. I had feared that with the death of Maximilian, our peace treaty would not be honoured, but King Francis has put that fear to rest. The first contingent of hostages, in exchange for the return of Tournai, are ready to sail, and the king is sending a new ambassador who is to take up residence in London, so as to be permanently on hand should we need to send word to France. The ambassador,' he consulted the letter, 'an Olivier de la Vernade, will be sailing with the hostages.'

'So, Francis is still keen, is he?' Henry said.

Thomas struggled to hide his disappointment at the king's tone. Henry had obviously wanted to be Holy Roman Emperor far more than he had let on. 'Very keen, Your Majesty.'

Henry sighed and took a seat by the window. His eyes took in the large courtyard, his gaze moving upwards and along. 'This house of yours is coming along very well, Thomas.'

'Thank you, Your Majesty. I should hope it is by

now. It is more than a year since you last graced Hampton Court with a visit.'

'Is it really as long as that? Astonishing. Yes, it really is coming along. You have a very fine prospect too. I thought so as we came up the river. You know, I shall be quite jealous when it is finished.'

'I am sure nothing could rival Your Majesty's palaces,' Thomas said hurriedly.

'Mmm,' Henry murmured, tapping his fingers upon his knee, 'perhaps.'

'To return to European matters for a moment, if I may,' Thomas said. Henry dragged his gaze from the window back to Thomas. 'You may remember last year when the French were in London to sign the treaty?'

Henry nodded, his eyes narrowing.

'I had a private meeting with High Admiral Bonnivet just before the French left for home, and he expressed the hopes of his king that you and he might meet one day. Well, with Charles now emperor, the French could be considered to be in a vulnerable position. After all, the Spanish Empire now includes lands that border France, which means that France is effectively surrounded by the Spanish. She will be looking for allies against Charles.'

'But you just said I should consider Charles family,' Henry cried. 'Now you're suggesting I form an alliance with France against him.'

Thomas groaned inwardly. That wasn't what he was suggesting at all. 'France, England and Spain are already allied, Your Majesty,' he reminded him. 'The Treaty of London assured it.'

This was an exaggeration, he knew. With Charles now emperor, the treaty he had worked so hard to achieve was only a minor consideration for both of the foreign monarchs. Boundaries had shifted, new lines had been drawn. What was an agreement to preserve and defend the rights of brother countries when empires were being enlarged?

He continued. 'What I am suggesting is merely that France and England reaffirm their friendship.'

What he didn't want to say to Henry was that England needed to make a show of being friends with France, otherwise she would end up being seen as what she had long been considered during Henry VII's reign: a small island of no consequence.

Henry considered for a long moment. 'I give you leave to pursue such a meeting, Thomas. Though I cannot think where we can meet without an advantage being given to one over the other.'

'Oh, I'm sure we can settle on some neutral spot, Your Majesty. It will take some time to arrange but you can leave it all to me.'

There were shouts from outside and both he and Henry turned to the window. Bryan and Compton were in the court and accosting four women who were passing through. The men seemed to think it great fun but Thomas knew the women to be the wives of friends he was entertaining from Italy, and he could tell from their expressions that they were mightily offended.

Henry laughed. 'They're at it again,' he said, grinning at Thomas.

Thomas drew himself up. 'Do you think it right, Your Majesty, for gentlemen to act so to women? Surely, it is discourteous in the extreme? See, the women do not like it.'

Henry pressed his nose to the glass to look harder at the women. 'My friends are only having a little fun,' he protested, 'but I see what you mean, Thomas.'

'Your Majesty would never be so ungallant,' Thomas said pointedly.

Henry straightened and nodded. 'You're quite right, Thomas. I shall put a stop to it at once.'

He turned and left the small chamber. Thomas followed after him, hands clasped over his belly, allowing the gold cross to bob against his knuckles. He watched as Henry called out to Compton and Bryan to cease, then took the hands of the ladies and kissed each one with gentleness. They simpered and curtsied, mollified by his apologies, then hurried out of the court as the king told them to get on.

'You rogues,' Henry scolded his friends gently. 'What am I going to do with you?'

I could make a few suggestions, Thomas thought wryly, as he watched the three men leave.

❧

Must I always be shuttling back and forth at the whim of a woman? Thomas cursed as he climbed out of his barge at the river steps of Greenwich Palace, waving away the boy posted to greet him with impatience.

Henry had summoned him because it seemed Katherine had been told of the intended meeting between her husband and King Francis, and she wasn't happy about it. When Thomas had read the king's note stating this, he had had to stop himself from rolling his eyes and cursing the queen out loud. It wouldn't be good for any subordinates to hear him criticise the queen. It could so easily be reported back to her ears, and though he had no doubt he could deny he had spoken so, it would be foolish to put himself in such a position where he had to deny anything. So, he had to content himself with thinking unkind thoughts about Katherine.

Thomas hurried through the corridors of the palace, greeting only in passing those courtiers who bowed and bid him good day. The guards allowed him through to the privy apartments, and Thomas found Henry and Katherine in one of the smaller rooms, where the sun shone bright through the windows.

'Your Majesty,' Thomas bowed, trying to catch his breath. 'I came as soon as I received your summons.'

Henry nodded, his eyes flitting between Thomas and Katherine. 'We have a… a disagreement, I suppose you would call it. The queen and I.'

'So I understand,' Thomas said, his hands sliding over his belly to clasp one another. 'I hope I can be of some help in resolving the matter.'

'Let us hope so, Thomas,' Henry said fervently.

Thomas found the king's manner reassuring. Henry wasn't pleased with Katherine, that much was evident, and so Thomas needed to support him, not the queen.

'Well,' Henry said impatiently to Katherine, 'tell him what you think.'

Katherine didn't like being spoken to so. She was hurt by Henry but not enough that she would be silenced. She drew in a long breath through her nose then turned her glare on Thomas.

'This meeting you propose between my lord and King Francis. What purpose will it serve?' she asked.

'It will cement the treaty signed in October,' Thomas said, a little perplexed. Was not the answer obvious?

'Why does it need to be so cemented?' Katherine asked. 'Did you not do your job well enough that the treaty must be propped up?'

Her scorn was infuriating. Thomas's jaw clenched, and he had to take a deep breath before he trusted himself to speak. 'The treaty was well drafted. But, madam, you must realise the events of this year have made international relations more difficult than usual.'

'No, I don't realise that.'

Then you are a fool, he wanted to say. He knew what Katherine thought, what she felt. She hated the French, it was in her blood. She had long opposed any attempt Thomas made to ally England with France, and she had sometimes been successful. But Thomas knew, even if Katherine wasn't prepared to admit it, that Henry wasn't as persuadable as he once was. Katherine was losing her power over Henry, and Thomas was glad.

'King Francis has personally requested a meeting,' Thomas said. 'Such a request doesn't come every day.'

'So, if one of the other kings who signed your treaty asked to meet with my lord, you would arrange it?'

Where are you going with this? he wondered. 'I would certainly consider it.'

Katherine turned her face up to Henry victoriously. He met her gaze reluctantly.

'The queen thinks I should meet with Charles of Spain,' he said to Thomas.

So, this is what you're up to. 'King Charles has not expressed a desire to meet,' Thomas said.

'Only because you have not offered a meeting,' Katherine said.

'Kate,' Henry chided.

'Forgive me, Your Majesty,' Thomas said, not caring now if he showed his annoyance, 'but what do you want me to do? Extend an invitation to Charles? I'm not sure how the French would respond to that.' It was a lie. He knew exactly how. They would be very annoyed.

Katherine tsked impatiently. 'What does that matter?'

'Kate, will you be quiet?' Henry snapped before turning back to Thomas. 'Contact has already been made with Charles.'

'How?'

Henry glanced at Katherine, and Thomas suddenly knew how. Katherine had, somehow, got a message to her nephew. Thomas had thought he had eliminated all of Katherine's unofficial message bearers, but it seemed she had acquired at least one new channel of communication.

'Madam,' he began in a severe tone, 'I cannot stress strongly enough how inadvisable it is for you to conduct such conversations without my knowledge.'

'Oh ho, so I must consult with you, must I?' Katherine said, attempting levity, looking to Henry. The smile vanished quickly when it was not joined by her husband's. 'My lord, whose servant is this man? Or are we his?'

'Your Majesty,' Thomas said quickly, 'I serve you always in the only way I know how. By seeking to make you stand head and shoulders above your brother kings.'

Henry held out his hand. 'I know, Thomas. But it does seem to me my lady has made a point. Why should I only meet with Francis? He is not the only king in Europe. Perhaps he is not even the greatest.'

'Perhaps we could take one step at a time, Your Majesty. We are on very good terms with France. It has not been thus for many a year, and we should make good use of it. Meet with Francis, then we can meet with Charles of Spain.'

'But what if matters are agreed with France that are detrimental to Spain?' Katherine asked.

'Madam,' Thomas said too sharply, and put two

fingers to his lips, 'madam, you do not understand how alliances work. These are matters for men, not women.'

He had hoped to put Katherine in her place, and he looked to Henry to see if he had succeeded. Henry was musing, his brow furrowed, his teeth gnawing on his bottom lip.

'Perhaps it would not hurt to meet with Charles,' he said after a long moment. 'In fact, would it not be a good idea, Thomas? It would give me the upper hand to know what is on offer from Spain before I meet with Francis and agree with his terms.'

Thomas groaned inwardly. This was not the way to achieve the universal peace he had envisioned. 'This meeting with Francis is not about terms, it is about friendship. And, as such, we should not consider pitching one power against the other, Your Majesty. That is not how alliances function.'

'An alliance with France,' Katherine scoffed. 'Whoever heard of such a thing? The French cannot be trusted. Have not centuries of conflict taught the English that?'

'We live in different times, madam,' Thomas said. 'It is right that we seek for peace rather than war.' He appealed to Henry. 'Is that not true, Your Majesty?'

'I know what you think is right for England, Thomas.' Henry nodded. 'And I agree with you, I do. I will meet with Francis, as we planned, although the months pass and I fear it is too late to meet this year. As for Charles, well, I shall continue to think on it.' He ignored Katherine's tut of disapproval. 'To prove my intent to King Francis, Thomas,' he said, a new idea occurring to him, 'I shall grow my beard. I shall not shave until we meet.'

Thomas did his best not to frown, not to snigger. Was a beard really the best symbol of fidelity to his cause that Henry could come up with? 'I shall write to King Francis and tell him of your great sacrifice, Your Majesty.'

'Do,' Henry said, his face breaking into a grin. He rubbed his smooth chin. 'What say you, Kate?'

Katherine glared at Thomas. 'I say I do not like beards, my lord.'

CHAPTER TWENTY

'Months have passed and still no date is yet confirmed for my meeting with King Henry.' King Francis shook his head at his Council. 'Does Henry still desire to meet with me? What of these rumours that King Henry is corresponding with Charles of Spain about meeting him? Are they true?'

His chief minister spoke. 'It does appear to be true that Queen Katherine has been corresponding with Charles through his aunt, Margaret of Austria, and that she has expressed a desire to meet with him. But there is no evidence King Henry has been privy to these letters, and nothing more is asked for than the queen to meet with her nephew. We think these requests a mere family matter, nothing more serious.'

'No subterfuge?' Francis asked doubtfully. 'No double-dealing with Spain against us?'

'Not that we can discover, Your Majesty.'

Francis drummed his fingers on the table. 'And

yet, Cardinal Wolsey allows these letters to pass. If there is nothing in them—'

'Perhaps the cardinal knows nothing of these letters,' another counsellor suggested.

'Is that even possible?' Francis scoffed. 'You keep telling me Wolsey is the *alter rex* in England. Nothing passes his notice.'

'It is likely he cannot prevent the queen from corresponding with Margaret, there being a family connection,' the minister said. 'All the letters we have from the cardinal indicate he is fully in favour of the meeting with King Henry going ahead. King Henry himself had made good show of his intention.'

'His beard, you mean?' Francis's eyebrows rose doubtfully. 'Can we call that proof of his desire to meet?'

'Without evidence that King Henry is secretly dealing with Charles of Spain, we must take the king's beard as proof, Your Majesty,' his chief minister insisted.

Francis's gaze wandered to the window. Outside in the garden he could see a gaggle of girls. 'I suppose we must,' he said, rising and smoothing his hands over his doublet. 'Very good, sirs. Keep me informed,' and he strode out of the chamber, intent on sweeter pleasures.

∾

Thomas walked into the privy chamber and came to an abrupt halt. 'Your Majesty! Your beard!'

Henry stroked his smooth chin, embarrassment curving the small pink lips. 'Chastise me not, Thomas. I know I said I would keep the beard until I met with Francis, but I could not do it. It didn't suit me. It made me look ancient, I'm sure of it.'

'But you expressly said you would keep it,' Thomas protested. 'King Francis is expecting to see you with a beard.'

'We are more than half a year away from meeting,' Henry said. 'It would be down to my toes by the time we stand before one another. Would you have me look like Methuselah before him, Thomas?'

'It could have been trimmed,' Thomas said, a little desperately.

'''Twas but a beard, Thomas.'

'It was more than that, Your Majesty. It was a symbol of intent.' Thomas gripped his cross tightly. 'How King Francis will take this, I do not know.'

Katherine entered the room briskly, causing Thomas to step out of her way. 'If King Francis takes offence at the loss of a beard, then he is a child, not a king.'

'I speak not of the personal, madam,' Thomas said, 'but of the diplomatic. Of course, King Francis will not object personally, but it may be viewed by the French as an intentional insult, and an indication that we are planning to break the treaty.'

'There is no such intention,' Henry said.

'Even so, Your Majesty,' Thomas said in a voice that did not disguise his disappointment.

'Then blame me, Your Eminence,' Katherine said

angrily. 'In your letters to the French, say I could not bear the king with a beard. It is not a lie. I despised my lord's beard.'

'Aye, Thomas,' Henry nodded. 'Francis is a gentleman. He will understand the queen's dislike.'

Thomas wasn't at all sure Francis would understand, but he could not argue with Henry. Thomas had to stop himself from cursing the king aloud for his inconstancy. All he had to do was endure a beard. Was that really too much to ask?

He saw Henry raise his eyebrows at Katherine. She met her husband's gaze and nodded. Thomas wondered what was coming next. He waited.

Katherine drew herself up. 'Margaret of Austria has informed me that my dear nephew Charles has expressed a desire to meet me, Your Eminence.'

Thomas looked from her to Henry and back again. 'To meet *you*, madam?'

'Aye, to meet me, his aunt.'

'But presumably he means to meet with the king?' Thomas gestured at Henry.

'He makes no mention of that,' Katherine said, looking away. 'Why should he not want to meet me?'

'You mean to travel to Spain, then?'

Henry laughed. 'Kate to leave England? Not a bit of it, Thomas. Charles wants to come here.'

'To England?' Thomas was appalled.

'Yes, to England,' Katherine cried. 'And why not? Would you refuse my nephew, Your Eminence?'

Thomas counted to five before answering. 'I would not dare to suggest refusal, madam. It is the king who must give his consent. Or not give his consent, as the case may be,' he added carefully, looking up at Henry out of the corner of his eye. 'I need not remind you, Your Majesty, that the arrangements for your meeting with Francis continue apace. Unless,' he sighed and looked Henry straight in the eye, 'unless your cutting of your beard is a sign that you do not wish to meet with him any longer?'

'Not at all, Thomas,' Henry said, his face showing that he knew he had offended him. 'It is my greatest wish to meet with Francis.'

Mollified, Thomas smiled. 'Then what of Charles of Spain?'

'Could we not do both?' he suggested sheepishly.

Thomas took a moment before answering. He wasn't a fool, he knew his treaty was fragile and the smallest thing could break it. And if his treaty did come to nothing, then what did he have left? What would he have to show for all the effort he had made? It made sense to cultivate Charles as a backup, he had to admit. But how to do it without making Francis fear England's lack of commitment to the treaty? He glanced at Katherine. She was the key. Thomas made a decision. He would not broadcast the Spanish king's visit. If the French found out – and he knew they would find out – and demanded to know what was going on, he would tell them that it was a family visit, a nephew visiting his aunt, nothing more. He would just have to play it very carefully.

'I believe it would be possible to meet with Charles as well as with Francis,' Thomas said. 'But we must stage it as a family affair, not an official state visit.'

'My nephew does not want your pomp,' Katherine said scornfully. 'He leaves such displays of magnificence to you and the French.'

'Then that is fortunate,' he bit back. 'When does Charles want to come to England?'

'We thought it would be best before I meet with Francis,' Henry said, proving to Thomas that, despite his off-hand manner, he had thought long and hard about the matter. 'Charles is planning to visit his lands in the Netherlands in May. He will pass by England on his way. What better time than that?'

It was a good excuse, Thomas had to admit. It could be made to look coincidental, though the French would know it was not. But Katherine was not going to have it all her own way.

'Very good, Your Majesty,' he said to Henry. 'But from this point on, it would be better if all communications with the king of Spain go through me rather than through the queen.'

'I do not see why—' Katherine began.

'To avoid confusion, madam,' Thomas cut her off. 'To facilitate the smooth management of details.' *And to stop you making any secret arrangements of your own, you interfering bitch*, he thought savagely. Katherine, he felt, was determined to undo him.

Henry agreed and told Katherine she was not to correspond with either Charles or Margaret from this point on. Katherine scowled at Thomas but told her husband she would obey him in this as in all things.

CHAPTER TWENTY-ONE
1520

Thomas brought the Council meeting to an end. As the counsellors rose and gathered their papers, he asked Sir Richard Wingfield to remain behind.

'Is something wrong, Your Eminence?' Wingfield asked anxiously as he hovered by the table.

'Not at all, Sir Richard.' Thomas pointed to the chair by him. 'Please sit down. I shall get a crick in my neck if I have to look up at you. Now,' he said when Wingfield had seated himself, 'the king has a new commission for you. He has appointed you ambassador to the court of France.'

Wingfield frowned. 'But Sir Thomas Boleyn holds that post, does he not?'

'He does, and Sir Thomas has performed admirably in France. But I feel – that is, the king feels – in view of the treaty we have with France and the meeting that is being arranged, it would be beneficial to both England and France to have an ambassador who knows the king better. In your role of Knight of the King's Body, you have come to know the king very well. He trusts you implicitly and feels you will be an admirable communicator of his wishes to the French king.'

Wingfield positively swelled with pride at this praise. 'I cannot thank you enough, Your Eminence.'

'Thank the king. These are his instructions.'

It wasn't the entire truth. Henry had agreed that they needed a more familiar and personable ambassador to act as intermediary between himself and Francis than Sir Thomas Boleyn but had come up with several names as to who that person should be. A couple of them had been his friends. Henry had suggested Francis Bryan, a suggestion Thomas had immediately knocked back. Bryan as ambassador! It was a ridiculous notion. There would be a diplomatic incident within days of him arriving in France, Thomas was sure.

After much back and forth, Henry and Thomas had settled upon Sir Richard Wingfield. There was much to recommend him. He was intelligent and tactful. He had no ego to make himself appear more important than he was, so he wouldn't puff himself up at the French court and provide answers to questions he had no knowledge of or make elaborate promises England had no possibility or intention of keeping. But Thomas had spoken the truth when he said he and Henry had wanted an ambassador with a personal connection. Thomas understood how Henry felt about Francis. He was a brother king. More, Henry could almost see Francis as a younger brother.

They were alike in some ways. Both men were athletic and amorous, though Francis was certainly more predatory than Henry in that respect if all the accounts Thomas received were to be believed. Both men believed in the chivalric ideal and enjoyed martial displays of their prowess. And, like most brothers, there was rivalry between them. Anything that could be done to diminish that rivalry and strengthen the brotherly bond was worth pursuing.

And so Thomas and Henry had settled upon Wingfield, a man Henry had spoken and laughed with, who had been privy to all his private functions, his moods and his joy. In fact, Thomas reflected ruefully, Wingfield probably knew Henry better than Thomas did.

Thomas nodded to Tuke, who passed Wingfield a large parchment. Hanging from it was a ribbon and large, heavy red seal bearing the king's arms. 'That is your commission. We are looking for you to take over from Sir Thomas Boleyn no later than February. We want you to make it clear to King Francis, and to his mother, that you have been a close personal attendant to the king and that King Henry does King Francis great honour by sending an ambassador he values so highly. Can you do that, Sir Richard?'

Wingfield paused, but only for a moment. 'Yes, I believe I can, Your Eminence.'

'You are to communicate with me every week when you take up your post.' Wingfield nodded, but Thomas wasn't sure he had made himself clear. 'By that I do not mean your diplomatic reports only, Sir

Richard.' Yes, he was right, Wingfield had not understood. The frown on his forehead deepened. There was a need to explain. 'I will require letters from you each week telling me everything you have not thought worthy to include in the diplomatic dispatches. The gossip, the rumours, the scandals, the whispered conversations you overhear. Do you understand?'

'Yes, Your Eminence,' Wingfield said after consideration. 'I understand completely.'

'Then I think we are done here. You can begin making the necessary arrangements for yourself and your family. Apply to me if you need anything.'

Wingfield folded up his commission and left.

'He didn't like that last bit,' Tuke said. 'Probably thought it sounded seedy.'

'Then he will have a rude awakening when he gets to France,' Thomas said. 'Politics is a seedy business. And I cannot work without information, you know that.'

'I do know that, Your Eminence,' Tuke nodded. 'Now, Wingfield does too.'

This was the worst possible time to be ill. Thomas would have kicked something if only he had the energy.

He was getting used to feeling ill. These instances of fever or stomach cramps, pain in his kidneys or his head, had been with him ever since he had the sweating sickness three years earlier. He supposed the

267

sweat had weakened him in some way and he thought longingly of the good health he had enjoyed in his youth, when the worst he had experienced was a common cold or an upset stomach from bad meat. Back then, he thought, his face screwing up as a needle seemed to prick through his left temple, he could wake up at four in the morning, work until eight at night and not need to move from his desk once. How ironic that he had not appreciated his stamina then when his workload had been so much less than it was now.

He thought of all he had been planning to work on the following day when he had closed his office door the previous night and tried to sit up. He got no more than six inches off the mattress before giving up and falling back down.

'Will you lie still?' Joan's voice came to him, loud and irritated. 'I know you're worrying about your work, but there's no point. You know if you get up you'll make it worse. Rest and let this pass.'

Joan didn't need him to respond; indeed, the only response she wanted from him was acquiescence. She was right, of course, she always was. But of all the times…

'Have Tuke come here,' he said, noting how feeble his voice sounded.

'I'm already here, Your Eminence.'

Thomas turned his head as a shadow fell over him. Tuke stood by the bed, looking worried. Thomas didn't like his looming stance and flicked his fingers at a stool nearby. Tuke dragged it over, its legs screeching on the floor. Thomas wished he had picked it up but was too tired to complain.

For the next fifteen minutes, Thomas told Tuke what he needed to do, letters he needed to write, purchases to be made, men to be hired. He was sure he hadn't remembered everything, but his brain was foggy. The talking had wearied him immensely. He wanted to sleep and he said Tuke had best get on with his tasks.

Tuke rose from the stool. 'Before I go, I wanted to tell you that we had a letter from King Francis,' he said, waving a small scroll at Thomas.

'Oh, what does he want?' Thomas groaned.

Tuke smiled. 'Nothing. He's heard you're not well, that's all.'

'How did he hear?' Thomas said, as angrily as he could manage. If King Francis thought him frail, he might doubt the wisdom of leaving him to arrange the meeting with Henry.

'Now, Tom, don't go working yourself up,' Joan insisted, shoving Tuke out of the way and holding Thomas down in the bed.

'It's fine, Your Eminence,' Tuke assured him over Joan's shoulder. 'Sir Richard Wingfield told him of your illness. He thought it best to inform the French king lest there was some delay in our replies to his letters and he got the idea he was being ignored.'

'That was sensible of Sir Richard,' Thomas allowed. 'How is he doing over there?'

'Exceptionally well,' Tuke said with great emphasis. 'Sir Richard has been told he can approach the king at any time, no appointment needed. King Francis has even said he is free to enter the royal privy apartments. Sir Richard wasn't sure about this at first, and didn't dare go in there without being invited, but one of the king's men had a quiet word and told him the king was perfectly serious. Sir Richard has completely unfettered access to the king. We couldn't hope for more.'

'Never mind about the ambassador,' Joan said testily. 'Tell him what the king said, Brian.'

'King Francis wrote to say that if you need them, his finest physicians are ready to sail to England to attend you.'

'There, you hear that?' Joan cried. 'The king of France worried about you!'

Thomas relaxed. 'That is very kind of him. Brian, write and thank him but assure him his doctors will not be needed, that I am already on the mend.'

'But you are nothing of the sort, Tom,' Joan protested.

But Tuke understood and hurried away to write the letter. Thomas hoped that by the time King Francis received it, his lie would have become truth.

CHAPTER TWENTY-TWO

Sir Richard Wingfield smiled nervously as he walked through the corridors of the palace to reach the French king's private apartments. He still hadn't got used to this freedom to enter this most holy of holies whenever he liked. It was so unusual for a courtier to be given this kind of access and Wingfield felt sure he would be publicly rebuked and humiliated at any moment for daring to venture so far. But that hadn't happened yet, although, Wingfield thought uneasily, today might be the day.

He had had no sense of unease when he had awoken that morning. He had been feeling rather good, in fact, and had sat down to his breakfast thinking of his plans for the day: a spot of hunting with the king, perhaps a game or two of cards in the afternoon, and a fine dinner before bed. That pleasant plan had been dashed when he had gone to his office and began reading the letters his secretary had laid ready for his perusal upon his desk. Topmost was a letter from the cardinal. His heart sank as he began to read.

Wingfield put off the meeting with the king the cardinal had instructed him to have as soon as possible for at least an hour. He took that hour to gather his thoughts, assemble his arguments, try to anticipate what the French king's objections would be. Only when he thought he had an answer for every question did Wingfield make his way to the king's privy apartments.

The king was getting ready to go on the hunt and he greeted Wingfield with a generous smile and an instruction to hurry up and get ready. Wingfield wasn't sure he would be invited to ride with the king once he had delivered his news, so made no reply to this. He begged the king's complete attention for a few minutes and Francis, frowning, agreed.

How do I begin? Wingfield wondered, as all the inhabitants of the chamber, the *gentilshommes* as well as the king, stared at him, waiting for him to speak.

'Your Majesty,' he began, 'I have this morning received a letter from my lord cardinal.'

'How is my dear Wolsey?' Francis cried. 'Is he well again?'

'I understand he is,' Wingfield said. 'He writes to request a postponement to your meeting with King Henry.' There, he had said it. He fell silent and lowered his head a little, looking up from beneath his eyelids to see what the king did next.

Francis was frowning again, a much deeper frown than before. 'Why, Sir Richard?' he said at last.

Wingfield thought back to the letter and the excuse Wolsey had given. 'The preparations for your meeting are proving to be far greater than originally thought.' He spread his hands and smiled apologetically. 'We need more time.'

Francis seemed to grow taller as he moved towards Wingfield. 'I think this is not true, Sir Richard,' he said, wagging a long finger. 'I think your king requests a postponement because he intends to meet with King Charles of Spain.'

There was a gasp, feigned, Wingfield felt, from the spectators. Of course Francis would know of the proposed meeting with Charles, and of course he would not wish it to take place. But Wingfield had been ordered by Wolsey not to admit to it.

'Not at all, Your Majesty,' he protested. 'As you know, Charles of Spain will be returning to Flanders before going on to Germany. His route will take him through the Narrow Sea, and that stretch of water being what it is, it is thought possible that bad weather may force King Charles's ships onto English shores. It has happened to other ships in the past, I assure you.' *Stop*, he told himself, *you're protesting too much, you will not be believed*. He cleared his throat. 'And should that happen, should Charles be forced to make harbour in England, it is necessary for King Henry to greet him. I am sure you understand,' he ended hopefully, but he knew he had fooled no one. The excuse was pitiful;

even he had thought so as he read Wolsey's instructions.

'I imagine the chances of Charles's ships being blown towards England very great,' Francis said, his eyes narrowing. He raised his chin. 'I have many fine ships, Sir Richard, as you know. There is the greatest of them all, *La Grande-Françoise*. Fifteen hundred tonnes. I think she is as large as your king's finest ship, the *Henry Grace à Dieu*.'

Wingfield knew nothing about the tonnage of ships and had even less interest in them, but he knew what Francis was getting at. The French fleet was as big as England's, possibly bigger, and as Francis added while Wingfield's brain ticked over, they were all ready to sail, should he decide to set out. Was this a veiled threat against France's readiness for war should England disappoint her?

'All Europe knows Your Majesty's fleet is amongst the greatest to be found,' he said, hoping to pacify Francis.

'There can be no delay to our meeting, unless King Henry wants to cancel the whole thing?' Francis cried, flinging his arm wide, and Wingfield could sense the anger rising in the king.

Wingfield took a deep breath. 'King Henry wants nothing more than to meet with you. But he cannot, in all good conscience, fail to meet with King Charles should he come upon England's shores. It would be a courtesy, nothing more.'

He had no idea if that were true, but he had to

say so. Francis seemed to consider his last words and Wingfield waited, not daring to add anything. At last, Francis nodded.

'Very well, a brief postponement. But I will not countenance any date for our meeting later than the fourth of June. My queen will be accompanying me to our meeting, and she is big with child already. I will not risk her health nor the health of our child by forcing her to endure a later date.'

Wingfield, who knew how greatly Queen Claude was suffering with her latest pregnancy, did not doubt that the king spoke true when he spoke of her comfort being his primary concern.

Francis stepped forward, coming close to Wingfield. 'And you will remind the cardinal that I have given way on many points regarding this meeting. If England were not to agree to meet by the date I have stated, I would take it very amiss indeed. I might think that the English are not serious about this alliance between us, and I might also believe that King Henry will jump at Charles's bidding. I know the Spanish do not want us to meet. Let us not give them that chance, eh, Sir Richard?' Francis winked at Wingfield.

I have to promise him this, Wingfield thought, his heart swelling with resentment that he had had to deliver this message to a man, to a king, for whom he had a genuine liking. He gave his promise and begged permission to leave the king's presence and write to the cardinal and tell him what the king had said. Francis waved him away and Wingfield hurried out, wondering if he would still be welcome to join the king's hunting party.

~

Charles of Spain had arrived for his visit with his aunt and was even now anchored a mile off Dover, waiting for Thomas to board his ship and take him back to the shore.

Thomas almost wished the sea had been so bad that the Spanish ships had not been able to anchor but had instead been forced to sail on to Flanders, missing England altogether. But Charles was here now, and there was no getting out of the visit.

He, Henry and Katherine had left London a few days earlier and travelled to Canterbury to stay at the Old Palace. Warham was in residence and he had welcomed the king and queen effusively, Thomas noticeably less so. It seemed the old man still resented Thomas for taking his position as Lord Chancellor, even after almost five years. And yet, to Thomas's eyes, the old man looked a great deal better for not having that particular burden. *He should be thanking me*, Thomas thought, as he saw the king and queen settled into their rooms.

Thomas only had time for a hasty supper, for the king had asked him to greet Charles in person. And so Thomas had left the relative comfort of the Old Palace in a coach with only Tuke as a companion and headed for Dover Castle, where he and Charles would stay overnight before heading back to Canterbury.

At Dover, he had a brief rest of no more than half an hour, during which he took refreshment and attended to his clothing. Thomas was determined that he would look his best when he greeted the Holy Roman Emperor. He stepped down into the small boat at the dockside that would row him out to the big Spanish ship, and felt it wobble beneath him. It had been some years since he had so much as set foot on a seagoing vessel, and that had not been a pleasant experience. He had still not forgotten the seasickness he had experienced when he had taken up his secretarial post to the Deputy Lieutenant in Calais. Thomas kept his eyes closed as the boatman pushed away from the dockside.

It seemed an age, though it was probably no longer than ten minutes later, when the boat bumped against the side of the Spanish ship. Thomas opened his eyes and his hands sought eagerly for the rope ladder. He had to hitch up his red robes and make what he thought was a rather undignified entrance onto the deck.

'Your Eminence.'

Thomas looked around. The speaker was a young man with a long face and a wide, jutting chin. Thomas had seen a portrait of Charles of Spain and knew this to be the same man. 'Your Imperial Majesty, it is a great pleasure to greet you on behalf of King Henry and to invite you to return with me to stay at Dover Castle as the king's most honoured guest.'

Charles kissed Thomas's ring and they exchanged

pleasantries. The sky was beginning to darken, and Thomas said they should be getting back to Dover Castle. Charles readily assented, and Thomas made his way back down the rope ladder and waited while Charles and his entourage joined him. When they landed back at Dover, Thomas showed Charles immediately to his rooms, and offered to leave him to rest.

'No, no,' Charles said, halting Thomas at the door. 'I would like to talk with you, Your Eminence. Please stay.'

Thomas hesitated, wondering what Charles wanted to talk to him about. If it was the French, Thomas was disinclined to speak and so risk revealing his plans. But he could not easily refuse the Spanish king and so nodded and took the proffered seat.

'I would like to thank you for arranging this meeting with my aunt and the king,' Charles said. 'I know it could not have been easy. You are so very busy arranging the meeting with France. Your meeting with the French is still going ahead?'

No point in denying it, Thomas told himself. 'It is. In only a few weeks' time, in fact.'

'So I understand. And what is this meeting meant to achieve, if I may ask?'

'To demonstrate friendship. King Francis was very keen to meet his brother, King Henry.'

'As I am to meet my uncle, King Henry,' Charles laughed. 'Perhaps our kinship is the stronger, eh?'

'Your aunt is eager to make your acquaintance,' Thomas said evasively. 'It is very good of you to make the effort to come to England to see her.' He knew

Charles hadn't come to England merely to see Katherine.

'Let us talk like men,' Charles said, growing serious. 'I am pleased at the prospect of meeting my aunt, it is true, but we both know that is not why I am here. You agree?'

Thomas inclined his head.

'I would be very disappointed if you and King Henry were to tie yourself to France without considering the benefits of an alliance with Spain.'

'Your Imperial Majesty,' Thomas said, 'I assure you, I consider everything.'

'Of course, of course, the great Cardinal Wolsey, eh?' Charles nodded as he chuckled. 'Tell me, is there anything I can do to make you look more favourably on Spain?'

'I cannot cancel the meeting with France,' Thomas said carefully.

'I am not asking you to. No, by all means, have your meeting. I hear it will be very grand. All I ask is that you agree to nothing that will be detrimental to my country.' Charles clicked his fingers at the secretary who had so far stood quiet and unmoving in a corner of the room. The secretary stepped forward and put a roll of parchment into Charles's outstretched hand.

Charles handed the parchment to Thomas. 'Please, read.'

Thomas unrolled the parchment and read. The content made his heart beat a little faster.

'You are bestowing the bishopric of Pace upon

me,' he said, his eyebrows raising, impressed. His gaze dropped further down the page. 'And a pension of seven thousand ducats from Your Imperial Majesty. You are indeed most generous.'

'It is no more than you deserve,' Charles assured him. 'I like to reward those who have done their best for me.'

Thomas rolled the parchment back up. The smile on his face was genuine, unfeigned. 'Thank you.'

'You accept?' Charles asked.

Thomas considered for the shortest of moments. Officially, this bishopric and the pension were a reward for services already rendered, not promised. Charles as yet had asked nothing more of him, and so he was not compromising the meeting with France by accepting.

'Yes, I do,' he said. 'I accept most gladly.'

❧

Thomas had to stop himself from yawning. He had stayed up late talking with Charles and had risen early to ensure the coach and horses were ready to take them both back to Canterbury. He had had hopes of dozing while on the road, but Charles, who was young and therefore indefatigable, insisted on talking some more, and sleeping was out of the question. Thomas's replies had grown increasingly monosyllabic; he didn't want to say anything in his tiredness that he would come to regret.

They had arrived at the Old Palace and Thomas

had introduced Charles to his aunt and Henry. Katherine had been in tears as she embraced her nephew, while Thomas had observed Henry looking his nephew by marriage up and down. He readily interpreted his expression. Henry was decidedly unimpressed by the young man, and Thomas was not surprised. In comparing the two men, Charles certainly came out wanting, and Thomas found himself feeling almost ridiculously proud of his king. The truth was, if anyone wanted an image of the perfect king, they need only look at Henry.

Although the court was at Canterbury, the royal party was to dine in private. Charles's visit was not an official one and to parade him before the court would have been counter to purpose. They retired to a small chamber off the main hall where a few of the highest nobles had been chosen to serve them.

Thomas could have done without the dinner. He had spent most of the past three days on the road and the constant jolting of the coach had played havoc with his stomach and bowels. The thought of several hours of eating and drinking did not appeal, but he knew he must endure it for form's sake.

He watched as Henry, Katherine and Charles washed their hands in the rose-scented water held in a bowl for them by the duke of Buckingham, then moved to do the same. His mind was on other matters and he had not even looked up to acknowledge the duke as he dipped his fingers into the warm water. Had he looked up he would have noticed the duke's face turn furious. All he did notice, however, was the bowl tipping towards him, and the water sloshing down over his robes and soaking his silk slippers.

'Forgive me, Your Majesty,' the duke said to Henry, who, along with the others, had ceased their chatter to see what had happened. 'My hand slipped.'

'You fool, see what you've done,' Thomas hissed, snatching a linen cloth one of the stewards quickly thrust at him, and dabbing at his robes. The steward was on his knees, doing the same to his slippers.

'I don't serve the likes of you,' Buckingham snarled. 'Call me fool again and I'll have your head.'

Thomas's eyes blazed. Buckingham had spoken low but it was possible his words had been heard by the others. How dare he humiliate him in this way? But what could Thomas say? Henry would, no doubt, defend the duke's position, for he was always mindful of rank and protocol, and Thomas couldn't bear another humiliation before Charles, especially not at the hands of the king. He swallowed down his anger and turned to the two kings and the queen.

'No matter, accidents happen. I can bear a little water.'

'As long as you don't try to walk on it,' Henry said and laughed loudly.

Charles and Katherine smiled tightly at his blasphemy before taking their seats.

As dry as he could hope to be, Thomas took his. He barely paid attention to what was said during the meal. His mind was entirely occupied on the duke of Buckingham and how he would pay him back for daring to make him look a fool.

'It was good to have this opportunity to meet, Your Eminence,' Charles said to Thomas as they were rowed back to his Spanish ship, now anchored off Sandwich.

Charles had said goodbye to Henry and Katherine at the dockside, his aunt clinging onto him so strongly Henry had to practically disengage her, mouthing an apology to Charles over her head. Charles had been polite, but it had been clear to Thomas that he was finding Katherine's sentimentality a little trying and was glad to be leaving. The visit had been useful and profitable for Thomas, and he was now glad he had agreed to Charles coming to England, despite the diplomatic difficulties it had presented.

'I hope you have enjoyed meeting your aunt, Your Imperial Majesty,' Thomas replied.

'She is a very great lady,' Charles said, 'though different from what I imagined. I had heard that her marriage was a love match, yet my aunt is much older than her husband, and he so handsome and lusty, I think.'

'The queen is six years older than the king. And I think King Henry takes after his mother and her father, King Edward IV. Queen Elizabeth was considered extremely beautiful and he very handsome.'

Charles nodded. 'I see.' After a moment, he said, 'From something my aunt said, I feel she is not pleased about my uncle meeting with the French. Is that fair?'

Thomas groaned inwardly. Just what had Katherine said to her nephew? 'I'm afraid the queen harbours a deep resentment of the French, it is part of her heritage. And,' he sighed and spread his hands, 'she is a woman.'

'Of course,' Charles nodded. 'I understand these matters. I know you must entertain the alliance with the French, but I hope I have convinced you that you also have a friend in Spain.'

'You have made that very clear, Your Imperial Majesty, and I thank you. It is my greatest wish that there should be peace between the European empires. Wars are costly affairs. They inhibit the flow of trade that makes all our countries wealthy. I'm sure a man such as yourself, educated, intelligent, would agree that war should be avoided whenever possible.'

'If only all men were like us, Your Eminence,' Charles said. 'But Francis and Henry, they love war, do they not?'

Thomas hesitated, careful of his reply. 'They both love feats of arms. It is not the same thing.' He hurried on, eager to stop Charles asking any further questions. 'And both kings have already demonstrated their desire for peace. You yourself were party to such an intent with the Treaty of Cambrai. The only problem you had, Your Imperial Majesty,' he laughed a little self-consciously, 'was that you did not include England.'

'That was remiss of us,' Charles agreed. 'But my grandfather, well, no one could tell him what to do.'

'Yes,' Thomas agreed ruefully, thinking of how often Emperor Maximilian had lied to him and to many others. 'I know that from bitter experience to be true.'

'I do not wish to prevent this meeting with King Francis,' Charles said, 'but I would like to get a first-hand account of how it went when it is all over. From you, or from my Uncle Henry. I shall be at Gravelines, I think, when it is over. I propose that we all meet again then. What say you, Your Eminence?'

'Have you mentioned this to the king, Your Imperial Majesty?' Thomas asked carefully.

Charles leaned a little closer. 'Why should I ask my uncle when I can ask you and get a definite answer?'

Thomas knew he was being flattered but it did feel good. *Why not meet again after?* he asked himself. *It can do no harm, and if, as I think, Henry is already wondering if an alliance with the French is a good idea, then it would make sense politically.* 'I'm sure a second meeting can be arranged,' he said smoothly.

'Excellent,' Charles said happily as the small boat bumped against the larger ship's sides. 'That pleases me greatly. And, now we are friends, Your Eminence, rest assured that when the papal chair becomes vacant, you will have my support.'

'What do you mean?' Thomas called as Charles began ascending the rope ladder.

Charles climbed on deck and leant over the rail.

'Why, I shall support you when you want to become pope!'

Thomas hardly noticed the swelling sea on the way back to Sandwich. His mind was full of the brand-new idea Charles of Spain had just put in his head.

CHAPTER TWENTY-THREE

After more than a year of planning, the time had come for Henry to meet Francis.

The location was in France on neutral ground, in a valley called the Val d'Or, and it had been a monumental feat to transport everything that was needed for the meeting from England to France. It had taken a week just to load the transport ships with all the timber, canvas and bricks needed to build the temporary structures which the king and queen, and indeed Thomas himself, would call home for the three weeks of the meeting, as well as the various halls and entertainment spaces. Some of these spaces would be large tents, which would all need erecting, but the royal apartments and the banqueting hall had been designed to resemble solid structures and would take many days to build.

Then there had been the provisions to send over, vast quantities of meat and wine, and the transport of animals, including horses for the tilts, cows to provide milk, hens to provide eggs, and oxen to pull all the carts.

And these transports didn't include getting the king and queen and all the courtiers over the Narrow Sea. Thomas had been insistent that every noble in the realm, save the duke of Norfolk, who had been left to head the skeleton Council in the king's and Thomas's absence, attend the meeting. There had been much grumbling about this, dukes and earls complaining about the cost it would entail, the inconvenience it would put them to, but their presence was required to show the French the quality of the English court. Thomas had even told humble knights to make themselves available, feeling keenly that quantity as well as quality mattered for this meeting. Though King Francis had originally suggested to Thomas that this meeting be a quiet affair, a suggestion Thomas had pooh-poohed immediately, he knew that the French were bringing a large contingent, and it was necessary that England match, if not exceed, their number.

Upon his return to shore after seeing Charles off, Thomas had ensured the king knew all he needed regarding leaving England and arriving in Calais, and then made his way to Deal, where a ship was waiting to carry him to Calais. Worry mounting within him as the date of the meeting drew ever closer, Thomas had wanted to go on ahead of the royal party to make sure all his preparations were being carried out to the letter. He trusted the men he had deputised to oversee the work in his stead, knowing he couldn't be everywhere at once, but he needed to check. He dashed off a letter of farewell to Joan, asking her to pray for him, firstly and not a little jokingly, that he would survive the sea crossing, and that everything would work out well. He knew she would pray every morning and every night that it would be so, and he found this reassuring.

As he hunkered down in his cabin in the belly of the ship, not daring to go on deck in case his seasickness returned, he decided he would make more time for Joan when all this was over. He had been so preoccupied for so long now, he knew he had neglected her, and was keen to remedy that. *When I get back, we will go to Hampton Court and stay there for at least a month. I will need the rest after all this, and Joan will enjoy the gardens and the fresh air.*

Thomas arrived in Calais, memories coming back to him of his days there as secretary, and went immediately to the Val d'Or. His heart was beating fast as he set out on his mule accompanied by his retinue, dreading what he might see. What if everything wasn't as it should be? What if the work was behind schedule? What if some of the ships had sunk in the Narrow Sea and now there was no time to arrange replacement supplies?

He crested the hill and looked down. He breathed a sigh of relief. The valley was abuzz with workmen, and he quickly scanned the scene before him. He had ordered that two hillocks be built up at the separate entrances to the valley to allow each king to make a grand entrance, and he saw that those had already been created. Excellent.

Thomas turned his gaze to the centre of the valley where a huge fabric pavilion was being erected. The pavilion was where most of the public feasting and events were to take place and the sight of it quite took Thomas's breath away. He had seen the original plans, of course, knew how it would be constructed and from what materials, but it was still something to behold. From where he was, he could believe the pavilion was solid, the fabric exterior having been so fashioned as to look like wood and stone.

Looking further, Thomas saw that the private apartments for the king and queen were already erected, as was his own, sited next door to Henry's. He could even make out his coat of arms painted on the side.

His anxiety beginning to lessen as he realised everything appeared to be on schedule, Thomas nudged his mule's sides and the docile animal began to canter down the hillside towards the valley.

～

Thomas was feeling more nervous than he had in many a year. *How many heads of state have you met over the years, that you feel sick to your stomach at meeting King Francis? You've just left Charles of Spain, who could be said to be much greater than Francis, and yet here you are, stomach turning over like a schoolboy. Pull yourself together.*

And yet, despite knowing this, Thomas could not

help his nervousness, for he knew that he was embarking on the most important three weeks of his life. Not even his elevation to cardinal came close to competing in importance. All of Europe would be watching and reading the reports of this event to discover how it went, to see if it was a success or a failure, and Thomas knew its success or otherwise would be attributed solely to him. He simply couldn't afford to fail.

Thomas had prepared well for this first meeting with Francis, a meeting needed to finalise all the details: the payments for Tournai, the betrothal of the dauphin to Princess Mary, as well as the smoothing of feathers ruffled by Henry's meeting with Charles of Spain. He had bought new robes especially for this day, determined not to wear garments that were faded or had fraying sleeves. Brand-new scarlet silk caressed his thighs as he rode out on his caparisoned mule, a velvet mantle flowed down his back and his clerical hat sat squarely and firmly upon his head. His body servant had expected him to wear his cardinal's hat and had brought it forth to put it on Thomas's head. Thomas had waved him away irritably. The broad-brimmed hat with its long and heavy tassels was intended to be more of a symbol than a wearable item, and he had ordered the body servant to give the hat to one of the pages to carry on a cushion as he walked before him.

Ahead of the hat rode six bishops, and before them two huge gold crosses, one symbolising Thomas's position as archbishop of York and the other his position as papal legate. No one, he had decided, would be in any doubt of who he was or the power he represented.

Once he had inspected the Val d'Or and been satisfied that all the work was being carried out as per his orders, he prepared himself to receive Admiral Bonnivet and the dukes of Alencon, Bourbon and Vendome, who would act as his escort to King Francis waiting for him in Ardres. They had all bowed low to him and kissed his ring, and it had all been very satisfactory.

The French party escorted him to the castle, and as the cavalcade approached, cannon were fired from the battlements to welcome him. Thomas had expected to ride through the gateway into the courtyard beyond and, from there, be taken to see the king. But Admiral Bonnivet held up his hand to halt the procession and Thomas, pressing his heels down in his stirrups to rise from the saddle, tried to see what was happening.

He heard the sound of hooves and, a moment later, six or more horses emerged from the gateway. At the head was a horse and rider more richly dressed than the others and Thomas realised with a shock that this rider coming towards him was Francis himself.

The king rode right up to him, his horse sniffing the nose of Thomas's mule. The horse being much taller than the mule, Thomas felt as if the king were towering over him and indeed, Francis had to bend low to be able to put his arms around Thomas.

Thomas wasn't sure whether he should reciprocate, but as Francis held him, he decided to return the embrace. As his hands pressed against Francis's back, he felt Francis's own fall away. Had he done wrong? he wondered in a panic. He quickly snatched the hat from off his head and greeted the French king. His first instinct was to dismount and bow but he stopped himself, remembering that he was here not only as archbishop of York, as Lord Chancellor of England and as cardinal but also as papal legate and, as such, held as much authority as the pope himself. The pope would not bow to a king and so Thomas must not either.

'Come, come,' Francis beckoned him, gesturing back towards the town. Francis's Swiss Guard, a product of his successes in Italy, hurried up to flank them.

Thomas nodded and he kicked his heels into his mule's side and his entire cavalcade followed the king's smaller party beneath the gatehouse and into the town. Only then did the king dismount and Thomas, his legs shaking a little, did the same. Another embrace, another greeting and Thomas had finally, officially, met the French king. It had all been a little unreal, but it had been, he felt, a very good start.

～

Thomas couldn't fault Francis's hospitality. He had been given a sumptuous suite of rooms in the castle, just down the corridor from the king's. But as comfortable as his rooms were, he knew he wasn't here purely to enjoy himself. There was plenty of work still to be done before Henry and Francis met in the Val d'Or.

Before he had left Henry in Calais, Thomas had wrung from the king the power to act in his name. If any decisions needed to be made that would ordinarily have been passed to the king to make, Thomas now had the authority to make those decisions all by himself. It was quite something, he reflected, to have the unquestioning authority of a king. Henry had not even had to think twice about it.

'Yes, of course, Thomas,' Henry had cried, flinging his arm around Thomas's shoulder. 'You must speak for me. I know I can trust you to always think of me first.'

It had been as simple as that. But would it be as simple to get Francis's consent? Henry had known Thomas for years but Francis only knew him through letters and ambassadors' reports, and might not feel he could trust an Englishman to act for him. But he knew he must try for Francis's consent to act in his name. To have only one king's consent was not enough.

Thomas made his way to the small chamber set aside for the negotiations. Tuke was with him but none other. Waiting for them was a French clerk, sitting by the window, pen already in his hand, waiting to make a record of the first words spoken. Thomas acknowledged him with a nod and headed to a seat along one side of the table. It had taken quite an effort of will not to occupy the head of the table as he was wont to do in Council, but he would not presume on the prerogative of a king to take that seat. And yet when Francis entered with six of his aides, he didn't take that seat but the one opposite Thomas. *He's doing everything right*, Thomas thought, impressed. *All kindness and hospitality towards me, respect for my office. He really wants this meeting with Henry to mean something.*

They got the effusive greetings out of the way quickly. It seemed Francis wanted to get down to business as much as Thomas. Now was the time to ask.

'Your Majesty,' he began, 'before I left King Henry to come here, I obtained from him the authority to act as plenipotentiary. To put it simply, I speak to you as if I were the king of England, and you can speak to me knowing that I speak for him. I request that you grant me the same power.'

Francis frowned, his long finger tracing patterns on the Turkey carpet covering the table. 'You wish me to give you the authority to speak on my behalf?'

'That is correct.'

'You? An Englishman?'

Thomas laid both his hands flat on the table. 'If it would help, Your Majesty, you could think of me in my role of papal legate rather than as Lord Chancellor of England. I am, after all, here to serve both King Henry and Your Majesty to the best of my abilities.'

Francis leaned back in his chair and grinned at his aides. 'So many titles you have, Your Eminence, it is difficult to keep up.' There was a ripple of laughter around the chamber.

'Are you agreeable, Your Majesty?' Thomas pressed.

Francis considered a moment, caught the eye of his minister beside him, then nodded. 'I trust you, Your Eminence, and I will do as my brother Henry has done. I give you permission to act in my name.'

Thomas thanked him, lowering to hide the smile he knew would be thought of as smug. Now he needed to give Francis something in return.

'I am aware you were concerned over King Henry meeting with Charles of Spain.'

'I saw no need for it,' Francis said, a little irritation appearing in his expression. 'Henry has an accord with *me*, does he not?'

'Of course. But Charles is the nephew of Katherine the queen. Family obligations apply in such cases. King Henry would have been dishonoured if he ignored Charles. His reputation as a man of honour would have suffered greatly.'

Francis shrugged one shoulder. 'That I understand.'

'And I can assure you that the meeting was a family matter only. No politics were discussed. In fact,' Thomas gave a little laugh, 'I believe the king barely got a word in. Queen Katherine was so pleased to have finally met her nephew, she rather monopolised his company.'

'So, there is no truth in the rumour that Charles proposed himself as a husband for Princess Mary?'

Francis asked sceptically. 'Because, if you remember, your princess is betrothed to the dauphin, my son.'

'I do remember that very great day,' Thomas assured him smoothly. The two-year-old Mary had been formally betrothed to the dauphin during a ceremony when the French had come to England to celebrate the signing of the Treaty of London. 'How do these rumours start?' he asked the room laughingly.

But it was true. The eighteen-year-old Charles had indeed proposed himself as a husband to his cousin Mary, and Katherine had desperately wanted Henry to agree. Henry had had to quietly remind Katherine of Mary's betrothal to the dauphin and suggest that the disparity in Charles and Mary's ages was a great barrier. Charles had shrugged and said he was prepared to wait for her to grow up, a blatant lie if ever Thomas had heard one. It would be at least a decade before Mary was of marriageable age and Charles would be needing an heir long before then.

'So, it is not true?' Francis pressed, and Thomas saw he was seriously annoyed at the possibility of it being so.

'Absolutely not,' Thomas said with vehemence. *It isn't a lie*, he reminded himself. *Mary will never marry Charles, whatever Katherine thinks or wants*. 'The princess is betrothed to your son, Your Majesty.'

Francis studied Thomas's face for a long moment. Thomas kept the same expression, determined not to be outfaced and found wanting by the king.

'Very well, I shall take your word, Your

Eminence,' Francis said. 'Now, let us move on to the first day of the meeting.'

❧

Thomas had parted from Francis to return to the Val d'Or. He was a little sorry that he had not met with Queen Claude or Louise de Savoie, as they were still making their way to Ardres, but it could not be helped. He had to leave the French king in good time to ensure all would be ready to receive him and Henry.

If possible, the valley was even busier than when Thomas had left it a few days earlier. He knew that ships had arrived in Calais during his time at Ardres, not least the *Katherine Pleasaunce*, carrying Henry and Katherine, and that all the supplies had made their way to the valley.

It was really quite astonishing; the entire valley had become a building site. Foundations for temporary structures were being laid, wood sawn and planed – Thomas had had to cover his mouth when he had visited the carpenters' lodge to avoid choking on the sawdust and shavings – painters running their brushes over wood and canvas, and men hammering all the different parts of the structures together.

I've done all this, Thomas mused. *This is all because of me. None of this would exist if I hadn't imagined such a day as this was possible.*

He moved on, listening to Tuke as he rattled on, explaining about the work Thomas was inspecting.

The bread ovens were built and already producing. That was excellent; men couldn't work without bread in their bellies. But more wood was needed here, Tuke said, extra men needed there... still so much to do. Would it all be finished in time?

Thomas headed for the centre of the field where the biggest structure of all was being put together, the temporary palace where most of the feasting would take place.

It was huge, three hundred and twenty-eight feet square and made up of four blocks. When he had seen the plans of the palace, he had doubted whether such a building could ever be made in so short a time. More, could such a building, only ever designed to be temporary, support all the people who would live, sleep and eat inside it? But the architect had assured Thomas it would be built inside a week and that it would withstand all that God and Man could hurl at it.

Seeing it now, with brick foundations up to eight feet high and a timber frame on top of that of thirty feet, Thomas could believe it. But what astounded him more than the construction was the appearance of the structure. Though the roof was not yet on, Thomas knew that it would sit atop a frieze created in the Italian style with scroll work and leaves that would demonstrate his interest in the latest architectural fashions, and the roof would be merely oiled canvas painted to look like slates. The architect had told Thomas that a proper roof was not possible, for the foundations were insufficient to support one. It didn't matter. It would look splendid, Thomas knew, and he told himself not to worry how much it would cost.

He looked around the valley, a little uneasy at how much still had to be done but reassured that it would look magnificent. In less than a week, both kings would arrive for their meeting. They would look down on the valley from their vantage points and they would see what had been achieved. Henry and Francis would be mightily impressed, and they would know it was all down to him.

CHAPTER TWENTY-FOUR

They had been waiting for the sound of cannon.

Thomas and Henry had left behind the four thousand or so Englishmen and women who had come to France to accompany the king at this historic meeting, and they now stood, mounted, on the little artificial hill Thomas had ordered constructed. Sir Thomas Grey, Marquess of Dorset, Sir Henry Guildford, the Master of the Horse, and Sir Richard Wingfield waited with them.

At exactly five o'clock, Thomas turned round in his saddle and looked back towards Guines, knowing the air would be rent with three explosions, the gunners following his orders to fire three cannon shots on the hour. Horses whinnied as the explosions burst, and Thomas patted his mule to calm him. A moment later, there were another three explosions, further away and a little quieter, these three having been shot from Ardres in answer.

Thomas tried to swallow down the lump in his

throat, but it seemed immovable. It was time. All the work of the past few years had come down to this moment.

'Ready, Your Majesty?' he asked Henry who was mounted on his fine horse to his right.

'I am, Thomas,' Henry replied. 'Are you?'

'Yes, Your Majesty. Shall we begin? The French are making ready. See.'

Thomas jerked his chin at the mound on the opposite side of the valley and saw Henry look. 'What is he like?' Henry asked, his eyes narrowing.

'He is a most amiable gentleman, Your Majesty.'

'You know what I mean, Thomas,' Henry said impatiently. 'In looks. Does his portrait do him justice?'

Thomas considered. Francis was said to be handsome, but Thomas thought his eyes too narrow and his jaw too long to be truly so. Henry, he believed, was certainly the more attractive of the two men, but Francis had a confidence that Henry, surprisingly, seemed to lack, and it was that confidence, Thomas reasoned, that made him so attractive, especially to women. But that was not what Henry wanted to hear.

'I think it does, and yet the portrait does not convey his charm.' He knew it was dangerous to praise the French king too much, but he wanted Henry to be on his best behaviour and felt that saying Francis had charm would make Henry work his own. He glanced at Henry's profile and saw the bottom lip starting to pout. 'But you are the taller, and your calves are bigger.'

Henry turned to him and grinned. 'Those will help me in the tournaments, then, won't they, Thomas?'

Thomas nodded. 'Shall we?' he said and raised his arm and gestured to the musicians behind them to begin playing.

Henry nudged his horse's sides and the animal began to step down the slope. Thomas followed, trusting Grey, Guildford and Wingfield to do the same. As he steered his mule, his knees digging in to keep himself upright, his eyes switched from the slope before him to the mound opposite. The French had begun their descent.

Both parties were headed for the pavilion in the centre of the valley. It almost shone in the daylight, the sun's rays catching the cloth of gold that hung down from the frame. Thomas could see the tapestries hanging inside swaying a little in the breeze. It took several minutes for both parties to reach the pavilion, each drawing rein at either end.

'What now, Thomas?' Henry said quietly, his lips hardly moving.

'You now ride forward alone,' Thomas said. 'You see that spear sticking out of the ground. That is where you should stop. Francis will meet you there.'

'You're sure, Thomas? I do not want to look like a fool, waiting for him to come to me.'

'He will meet you there,' Thomas insisted.

Henry nudged his horse on, and to his relief, Thomas saw Francis do the same. They came to a stop by the spear, and both men, in the same moment, raised their hands to their bonnets and swept them from their heads in greeting. Another moment, and their arms were around one another, their horses sniffing each other's backside. Henry and Francis dismounted, put their arms around each other's shoulders and entered the pavilion.

Thomas gave a huge sigh of relief. The first trial had been made, and it had gone well.

'Let us join the kings, gentlemen,' he said to his companions. They all dismounted and entered the pavilion.

~

How is it possible not to tire of so much fun? Thomas wondered as he applauded King Francis back to the lists to have another charge. The next would be the fifth tilt of the day, and the seventh consecutive day of tilting. Thomas had always agreed with Henry that it was an enjoyable sport, but he had always been an observer, never a combatant, and he had come swiftly to the conclusion that five tilts were quite enough for one day, enough, in fact, for a lifetime. Why, he wondered despairingly, had he thought he could bear the endless parade of horse and man when he had been back in England deciding what entertainments to put on each day?

Thomas looked sideways to where the two queens sat. He examined their faces. Both Claude and Katherine were smiling, but Thomas did not think their smiles reached their eyes. He believed he detected weariness, not enjoyment in their expressions. Katherine had never been particularly interested in tilting, he knew, and Claude was heavily pregnant. He had noticed how her attendants had been trying to make her comfortable by stuffing cushions behind her back and setting a footstool at her feet. No doubt they were wishing they could retire to their private apartments and leave their husbands to continue their entertainments unwatched by their wives.

Francis lined his horse up for another charge. Henry was standing at the other end, far back from the central pole, watching his brother king. Francis was tilting against an English knight this time. Thomas checked his list, running his finger down the names of the tilters, found the knight but didn't recognise the name. He would be just one of the many knights brought over to make up the numbers, no doubt. He looked up as Francis and the knight made their charge, the hooves thundering and reverberating in his ears. He felt a headache coming on and suddenly wished Joan was with him. She would have given him one of her simples; they always did the trick and eased his aching head.

He closed his eyes as pain stabbed his brain. He did not, therefore, see the crash of the two men. But he heard it, and it was loud and fierce: the splitting of wood as the lance broke, the cry of pain or surprise as the man hit the ground, the screams of the crowd.

Thomas gasped, opened his eyes and got to his feet, headache forgotten. Francis was down, unseated by the knight. *Good God*, Thomas panicked, *if he's dead, it's the end of everything. It might be the end of me.* He clutched the wooden railing and leant over.

'Is the king hurt?' he cried to one of the many guards who had rushed to Francis.

But Francis was getting up, waving his gauntleted hand and shouting in French that he was unharmed. He got to his feet with the aid of his Swiss Guard, two of whom had taken hold of the English knight and were forcing him to his knees.

Thomas saw Henry running towards Francis, and for a horrible moment thought he was going to protest at his subject's treatment. But Francis was yelling at his guards to release the knight. The next moment, Henry was asking Francis how he fared, and Francis was patting the air, insisting no harm done.

Thomas breathed a sigh of relief. Francis was unhurt, he assigned no blame to the English knight, and he and Henry were even now walking away, arm in arm, laughing about the incident. He fell back into his chair, the throbbing in his head returning with a vengeance. He heard fussing to his left and turned to see Queen Claude's ladies fanning her and dabbing her brow with handkerchiefs. Katherine was looking pained and leaning over towards her, assuring her counterpart that her husband was quite safe and well. Claude seemed to calm down, and Katherine shifted back in her chair, her job done. She must have felt Thomas's eyes upon her, for she turned swiftly to face him, her expression stony.

'I hope you think all this worth it, Your

Eminence,' she said, leaning towards him. 'The French king could have died, and then where would we all be?'

'There is always a risk with the tilt, madam,' he said, trying not to be annoyed by the truth of her words. 'The kings know that.'

''Tis a stupid sport,' she said, turning her face back to the yard. 'I should not let my lord take part.'

'I doubt if you could stop him, madam,' Thomas said, a little more harshly than he knew he should. 'Indeed, he would not welcome such an attempt to restrain him.'

'And you know that, do you?'

'I know the king.'

'You think you know him, but you don't. You see what he wants you to see, Your Eminence. You think you can control him, don't you? Well, let me tell you, no one controls Henry. And, one day, you will discover that for yourself.'

Katherine twisted her body away from him, a sign she wished to converse with him no longer. Thomas's top lip curled as he continued to watch her. He wanted to tell her that she spoke nonsense, that he had no desire nor intent to control Henry, only to help him become the king God had destined him to be.

Her words had made a chill run through his veins, and he felt tears prick at his eyes. Thomas turned his attention back to the tilt – the herald was announcing the next rider, Henry – and rubbed his temples. He tried to focus on the charge but all he could think of was that, despite the work he had put into this event, all he wanted now was for it to be over so he could go home.

~

The event was coming to an end and Thomas was glad. He was tired of tilts and jousts, tired of smiling all day long and watching courtiers vomit up the wine that he had made flow too freely.

And he was tired of eating. Every day, every meal, was a feast, and his stomach and bowels were punishing him. He had no appetite for the food before him, no thirst for the wine. He chastised himself for his lack of enthusiasm but had not the energy to cheer up.

He tried to concentrate on the lady beside him. Queen Claude was talking to him about her son, the dauphin, when the table they were seated at suddenly rocked and drew their attention.

'Oh, what are they about now?' Claude said indulgently as Francis and Henry rose and walked around the table to the space in the centre of the tent.

Oh no, Thomas thought, horrified, as they began to untie their doublets. *They're not. They can't be.*

But they were. The two kings were going to wrestle one another.

Katherine, sitting on Thomas's other side, clutched his arm. 'Stop them,' she said through gritted teeth.

Thomas rose and called to Henry. 'Your Majesty, are you sure this is a good idea?'

Henry waved at him dismissively, and threw his doublet to Brandon, who was standing nearby, grinning like an idiot, clearly enjoying the show. The kings both proceeded to remove their shirts, and the courtiers, English and French alike, were cheering them on as they began to circle one another.

Thomas could hardly bear to watch. He could see all his hard work going up in the dust that Henry and Francis were kicking up as they lunged at one another. He wanted to grab both of the kings and scream at them that they were about to spoil everything, but instead slid his hands beneath his thighs and ordered himself to be still. He glanced at Katherine, then at Claude. *Say something*, he urged them. But they both remained resolutely silent.

Francis suddenly lunged and grabbed Henry around the waist. Henry's back arched at the assault but Francis wasn't able to lift him off his feet. Henry bent over Francis and grabbed him around the waist. It would have been a good move, but Francis realised his danger and released Henry, forcing Henry to relinquish his hold. They drew together again, their hands making loud slapping noises against each other's skin.

Francis bent his body and got in beneath Henry's chest. He put one arm around Henry's now sweat-slickened back and leant into him. Henry was a huge man, but Francis was no slight boy and he managed to tip Henry backwards. Henry's reddened face screwed up in anger as he fell. When his back hit the ground, he let out an enraged cry.

Both Katherine and Thomas leapt to their feet,

alarmed that Henry had been hurt. Francis raised both his arms above his head and roared triumphantly at his French courtiers, who were cheering and clapping their king with enthusiasm.

Henry pushed aside those few Englishmen who had rushed to his side to help him to his feet. 'Again!' he yelled at Francis.

Francis, who had his back to Henry, turned. He was smiling as he looked Henry up and down, then glanced at the floor and looked back at Henry. He grinned. 'One defeat is enough for you, brother Henry.'

'I insist on a rematch,' Henry cried, his fingers curling into a fist.

'My lord,' Katherine pleaded, finding her voice at last. Henry ignored her.

Queen Claude, unable to hide her pleasure at her husband's triumph, nonetheless saw the anguish on her sister queen's face, and held out her hand to Francis. Ever the gentleman, he took it, and Thomas saw the gentle tug she gave him to encourage him to resume his seat.

With Francis seated and accepting a cup of wine, Henry had no choice but to do the same. He snatched his shirt from a man who held it out gingerly to him and stomped around the table to his chair. Katherine muttered soothing words to him, but Thomas could tell Henry wasn't listening.

The dinner continued, but there was no missing Henry's fury. He scowled as he stuffed food in his mouth and ignored anyone who tried to talk to him.

What made it worse was that Francis refused to acknowledge Henry's ill humour. He continued to accept the congratulations of his courtiers and listened to a blow-by-blow account of their match with avidity. If only Francis had kept quiet or made light of their encounter, Thomas felt the evening could be saved. But as soon as the food was removed, Henry rose, took Katherine's hand, and bid Francis and Claude a very curt goodnight.

Thomas hurried after Henry, after doing his best to smooth over the abrupt departure of his king with Francis and Claude. He knew they hadn't been fooled by his assurance that Katherine had asked her husband if they could retire due to her being weary. The looks they had given him told Thomas they knew exactly why their counterparts had left: King Henry was sulking.

∾

Thomas clasped his hands before him, the large cross that hung from his neck resting on his thumbs. He believed Henry's temper would be soothed by more feminine entreaties than his, and so waited for Katherine to speak.

Katherine was watching Henry pace up and down with a pained expression. For once, Katherine didn't seem to mind Thomas's presence; in fact, he saw with some amusement he knew was entirely out of place that she was grateful for it. *I am not going to take the blame for this*, he mentally warned her.

311

'My lord, please,' Katherine begged as Henry began thumping the wall, making them shudder. She looked worriedly around the room as if frightened the wooden palace would come crashing in on them. Thomas hoped the carpenters had used good joints to hold the walls together.

'Henry,' Katherine said sharply when he continued to rage, 'you're frightening me.'

This sentence pierced Henry's rage and touched his chivalric heart. He stopped pacing and stood in the middle of the room, a tall tower of fury trying to be contained. 'Forgive me.'

'All is forgiven if you will but be calm,' Katherine sighed.

'He threw me, Kate,' Henry cried.

'I know, I know.'

'Humiliated me, in front of everyone. Is that a show of brotherly love?'

Thomas decided not to point out that Henry would have done the same to Francis if he could. He had no desire to pour oil on the flame of Henry's rage.

'It was a sport, my lord,' Kate said, reaching for Henry's hand but not managing to grab it. 'You have proved yourself the better man in so many other ways. Has he not, Your Eminence?'

Thomas stepped forward, taking his cue. 'Indeed, Your Majesty. You are a much finer dancer than King Francis, your tilts were performed with greater skill, and the French king has no ear or ability in music, unlike your songs which have entertained us all these past weeks.' Fulsome praise and not all of it an exaggeration, Thomas could honestly claim.

Thomas's words seemed to mollify Henry. His breathing began to slow and he allowed Katherine to take his hand and encourage him to sit beside her. It was a relief. Henry in a rage was not a pleasant sight to behold.

'How much longer do we have to stay here?' Henry asked sulkily.

'A few days only,' Thomas replied. 'I will perform a high mass tomorrow and then all is done.'

'And then we can meet with Charles again,' Katherine said, patting Henry's arm happily.

'Aye, Charles,' Henry nodded. 'Now there is a man who knows how to treat his fellow king.'

Thomas cringed. No doubt Henry would continue to compare Charles with Francis, and Francis, after this little fracas, would come off the worst. He did his best to hide his disappointment. All his hard work, all the months, even years of planning, and it had probably all been undone because his king's pride had been hurt.

'You may leave us, Your Eminence,' Katherine said curtly, a gleam of triumph in her eyes. 'My lord needs to rest.'

Aye, and you need to whisper in his ear how he should never have agreed to meet with Francis in the first place, not when he had Charles of Spain begging to be his friend. Thomas bowed out of the room and the doors closed after him.

The sun was high in the sky when Thomas climbed the wooden steps onto the platform and took his seat beneath the canopy alongside the high altar. He recalled Henry's question of the previous day, when the king had asked how much longer they had to be in the Val d'Or. *Nearly over*, he told himself with pleasure. *Come tomorrow, we will all be packing up to go home.*

It was quite hard to imagine the valley being returned to nothing. All the temporary buildings would be taken down and anything salvageable would be shipped back to England. Thomas was already working out how the wooden posts that had held up tents or been part of the building structures could be used by shipbuilders, how the ornamentation could be sold to builders or perhaps used at Hampton Court. He would depute Tuke to oversee the storage and shipping of all the hangings and tapestries, he told himself, making a mental note. Such exquisite and expensive pieces would need special care.

Stop getting ahead of yourself, he chided himself as the French papal legate, Cardinal de Boisy, nodded to him and took his seat on the other side of the altar. Thomas peered over the altar to make sure de Boisy was seated a step lower than he. Satisfied that he was, Thomas sank back into his chair.

He had had a very late night after leaving Henry and Katherine in their private apartments and had to rise early, he having so much business still to do. In order to hold this mass, the tilt-yard that had seen so much action over the past few weeks had been turned overnight into a temporary open-air chapel. Thomas had supervised the rebuilding, instructing the workmen to keep their voices down to avoid waking the nobles sleeping in their tents in the field beyond. The tilt-yard galleries had been kept as they had been, and it was there that the royal parties, the most senior nobles and all the various ambassadors were taking their seats as Thomas watched. He scrutinised their faces looking for signs that they were just as tired as he. But no, apart from Katherine and Claude, all the men seemed happy and eager. Most were young, of course, and had the energy for all the fun and games of this remarkable event.

Thomas was starting to feel hot in his vestments, and he was glad for the shade of his canopy. He wriggled his toes in his jewelled slippers, taking pleasure in their glinting in the sunlight. It was some time before everyone was seated, and he used the time well, half closing his eyes and letting the hubbub carry on around him.

But then there came a quiet, only the hiss of murmured conversations and the occasional shout of the men working in the camp beyond to be heard. Thomas rose to begin the mass, a ceremony he had performed so often he could do it without even needing to think about his words or his actions.

And so, the mass for him passed in something of a blur. It was only when he returned to his seat and the choirs of both France and England began to sing that Thomas came to himself once more. He took pleasure in the sound of their clear voices and was sorry when the songs came to an end and it was time for the elevation of the Host. He rose from his seat once more and moved to the altar.

Thomas raised the Host above his head. There was a gasp. Thomas dropped his gaze to his audience, wondering what on earth had happened. Everyone seemed to be staring into the sky and Thomas looked up, squinting against the sunlight.

The dragon kite was flying!

He cursed beneath his breath. It was too early; the kite shouldn't have been flown until the mass was over. Oh, someone was going to pay for this mistake.

Thomas had thought the kite a very clever idea when it had first been proposed to him. The dragon was a symbol for Henry, the Welsh dragon from which the Tudor line descended, but the animal of the kite could also be viewed as a salamander, the symbol for France, and so honour Francis at the same time.

His audience so distracted, there was no point in continuing with the mass. He, like everyone else, kept his gaze on the flight of the dragon. Its eyes blazed with fire and a tongue flicked in and out of its mouth as the wind took it one way and the other. It even roared as it flew. It remained over the camp for a few minutes, but then the wind changed and drew it away inland until it was no longer visible.

His audience chattered amongst themselves about the dragon kite, and Thomas had to wait for them to remember where they were and what he was supposed to be doing. They all fell silent, shamefaced for talking, and he was able to conclude the mass. He sat back down when it was over with a sigh. *It comes to something when I'm upstaged by a kite*, he thought miserably.

~

The farewells had been said. Francis and Claude had already departed back to Ardres, and Henry and Katherine were preparing for their own journey to meet with Charles at Gravelines. The historic meeting between Henry and Francis was over, and Thomas couldn't have been more glad.

He was straining on his close stool. He closed his eyes and pushed, feeling sweat prickling on his forehead and upper lip at the exertion. He would need to be purged, he reasoned, if he wasn't able to evacuate his bowels soon. He felt bloated and fat, *even fatter than usual*, he mentally corrected. When he got back to England, he would go on a fast. Take a break from rich food for a while. Take a break from the court too, he promised himself, remembering his intention to take Joan to Hampton Court.

'Shall I read you your letters, Your Eminence?' Tuke called through the screen that separated Thomas and the close stool from the rest of the room.

'You may as well,' Thomas said through a groan, and Tuke began to read aloud. After another ten minutes, Thomas gave up the effort and emerged from behind the screen, shaking his head at Tuke in defeat.

'You'll be better when we get back to England,' Tuke promised.

'Aye, when,' Thomas nodded grimly. 'But I cannot hope for that just yet. We must meet with Charles of Spain before I entertain hopes of seeing Dover again. Is there any news from Charles?'

'There is,' Tuke nodded, 'but you're not going to like it.'

'Why should today be any different? What is the news?'

'Well, his secretary has written to say King Charles is looking forward to his meeting with King Henry but that he needs to ask for a change of meeting place. He wants it to take place at Bruges rather than Gravelines.'

'Does he say why?'

'His business in the Netherlands is taking longer than he expected. The secretary says it would be more convenient if King Henry could come to Bruges rather than making King Charles return to Gravelines.'

'What he is actually saying is that his business is more important than meeting with King Henry,' Thomas said with annoyance. 'Well, I'm not having that. How dare he? The king and I have just hosted the most important international event of the past twenty years and Charles thinks he can have us wait on his convenience. You write back to that secretary, Brian, and tell him absolutely not. Charles must meet us at Gravelines or I shall cancel the whole thing.'

'The queen won't like that.'

'I don't care what the queen will like or not like,' he snapped. 'Write that letter.'

'Do you actually want me to threaten to cancel?' Tuke asked doubtfully.

'Yes, I do,' Thomas said emphatically. 'I'm in no mood to humour Charles. It's he who wants to meet with us, not the other way around.'

'But I thought we were interested in meeting with him?' Tuke ventured. 'Did you not talk of a potential alliance between us, France and Spain?'

'I did once, but after the events of this week, I think that might be wishful thinking, don't you?'

Tuke made a face of agreement.

'But still, perhaps I am being too brusque.' Thomas considered. 'Very well, write that a meeting in Bruges is not possible due to the arrangements that have already been made to meet Charles at Gravelines, but that we are prepared to delay that date until the third of July, but not beyond. King Henry must sail for England on the fourth. There,' he raised an eyebrow at Tuke, 'does that meet with your approval, Brian?'

Tuke grinned and sat down to write the letter.

❧

Charles agreed to meet at Gravelines as arranged.

The journey to Gravelines gave Thomas a chance to reflect on the meeting in the Val d'Or. Had it really gone as badly as he feared? He was beginning to think not. True, Henry being beaten at wrestling by Francis had been a low point, but there had been no lasting damage done. By the end, Henry and Francis had parted in amity. Thomas had already received letters of congratulations from the French Council and more were coming in from other countries who had been keeping a close eye on the affair and felt they should congratulate the cardinal on the success of his spectacle.

No, he thought with pleasure, he had been too critical of himself, putting too high an expectation on the whole event. It had been stress that had made him think it had all been a disaster. The event had had two objectives: to celebrate the Anglo-French alliance and to show the world what Thomas Wolsey was capable of achieving. Both those objectives had been met and met magnificently. The meeting could be classed as nothing less than a great success.

Katherine, as Thomas had expected, had been joyful at meeting her nephew again, but he sensed that Charles had done his loving nephew routine in England, and now all he wanted to do was find out how the meeting with Francis had gone. And so, Thomas had tactfully, yet forcefully, suggested to Henry that Katherine was wearied by the journey and that she should retire for the sake of her health. Protesting, and shooting angry glances at Thomas, Katherine had been shooed from the room, leaving the three men to talk business together without her tiresome sentimentality getting in the way.

As soon as she had gone, Charles had begun with his questions. Had Henry and Francis got along well?

Had there been any upsets? Had Francis talked about Spain? Did he have any plans to threaten Spanish interests?

Henry and Thomas answered him in all honesty, saying that Spain had not been mentioned and that Francis had made no boasts about his triumphs in Europe or any intention to act against Spain. Thomas noted, however, that Henry omitted the wrestling match he had lost against Francis. That wound was still too raw.

Charles was satisfied that he was in no present danger from France and content that England would not support France if she did decide to threaten Spain. He tried once again to propose himself as a husband for Princess Mary but did not press the matter when Thomas shook his head and said it was not possible.

They parted, Katherine once again resorting to tears at her nephew's leave-taking. Henry was now eager to return to England, and Thomas along with him. It had been more than a month since he sailed from England to Calais, and he was missing his home. He boarded the ship at Calais, for once not dreading the voyage across the Narrow Sea.

CHAPTER TWENTY-FIVE

Upon his return to London, Thomas stayed only briefly at York Place, just long enough to ensure all matters were in order. When he arrived, he was told that Joan had left for Hampton Court the previous week and awaited him there. *That was just like her to have anticipated my wishes*, he thought fondly, and sent a note on ahead that he was leaving at once to join her. He left Tuke in charge, trusting him above all others to take care of his affairs in his absence, and took one of his other secretaries with him to Hampton Court.

Thomas slept for most of the journey down the Thames, the curtains of his barge pulled to protect him against river breezes and curious eyes. But he stirred suddenly, sensing he was drawing near to his destination, and leaning forward, pinched the curtains open.

There she was, the brand-new red brick edifice standing proud against the cloudless sky. She looked beautiful. Her gatehouse stood five storeys high, the red of the brick contrasting pleasingly with the cream of the stone windows and gateway jamb. The clock at the top chimed the hour. Thomas felt that he had never seen a more lovely sight nor heard a more lovely sound.

The barge passed on, down to the river steps. Thomas was standing and ready to disembark even before the barge had been tied up, so eager was he to enter Hampton Court. He hurried over the caked mud that should really have been grass but which suffered from constant foot traffic from the river, round to the front and crossed over the bridge across the moat. He paused a moment as he stood below the gatehouse and looked up. *I'm home*, he thought with a deep breath of pleasure, and ordered the gate to be opened for him.

He took his time as he entered Base Court, turning around and around, looking everywhere, not wanting to miss a thing. He hadn't seen the court since he had left the previous year. Then it had been filled with workmen's wheelbarrows, bricks, flagstones, poles of timber and flapping canvas. Now it was empty of such workaday items and he was free to view it in its full splendour.

Conscious that his secretary was watching him with a bemused eye, Thomas decided he would leave his inspection – *my exploration*, he thought with plea-sure – until later. He made his way to his private apartments. Dismissing the secretary, telling him to go to the kitchens and get himself a meal and ordering one to be brought to him, Thomas opened the door of his bedchamber.

He stared down at the two trunks sitting in the middle of the room.

'Joan?' he called.

He heard footsteps from the smaller inner chamber, and a moment later Joan appeared. She smiled sadly. 'There you are.'

'Yes, here I am,' he said a little confused by her manner. She seemed strangely subdued. 'What? No kiss for me?'

She stepped forward and kissed his cheek though he had offered her his lips.

'Have you not unpacked yet?' he said, pointing at the trunks and trying to laugh. Something was wrong. Joan hadn't kissed him properly and she was trying not to meet his eyes.

'They are not for unpacking. I packed them when I got here,' she said, stepping away.

Thomas took off his gloves and cap and threw them on the bed. 'Are you going to tell me what's wrong or do I have to guess?' He couldn't keep the irritation out of his voice. This was not the welcome he had anticipated.

Joan took a deep breath and, at last, looked up at him. 'I'm going home, Tom. I'm going back to Norwich.'

'For a visit?' he asked, his throat tightening as he waited on her answer.

She bit her lip. 'For good. I've… I've had enough.'

'Of what?'

'Of all this,' she gestured at the room, her eyes resting on the expensive hangings. 'Of you never being with me—'

'I'm with you now.'

'For the moment only,' she said helplessly, her hands falling to her skirts. 'I'll have you to myself for this night, but tomorrow you'll be back in your office, working away, or entertaining guests, guests I'm not allowed to meet.'

'I told you it would be like this.'

'I know.' She nodded. 'I know you did and I'm not blaming you. But I can't bear it any more. I'm lonely, Tom, and I don't want to be lonely in a house with four hundred other people in it.' She laughed humourlessly. 'You don't understand.'

Thomas sighed loudly. 'Of course I understand.' He stared down at the trunks. 'Where will you stay?'

'Your sister has invited me to stay with her for a week or two.'

'She knows about this?'

'She knows I've been lonely, yes. I had to have someone to talk to, Tom, and Elizabeth understands loneliness.'

'And after that?'

'I'll go back to my family. Father could do with my help in the business.'

'Aye, he will be glad of you, and I suppose it will please you to be useful in that way again.'

He had the sense that he was not dealing with this matter correctly, that perhaps Joan wanted him to protest that she could not leave him, that things would change, that he would do all he could to make her happy. But he couldn't say those things. He would always need to work and she would always need to be kept out of sight. He had taken her for granted, he saw that now, always expecting her to be there when he needed her. He had not given a thought to how she might need him, and he was sorry for it.

'You're not going to stop me?' she asked with a shy smile.

'I want you to be happy, Joan,' he said, 'and it's clear you're not happy with me. I never meant to make you unhappy, 'tis just the way of things.'

'I know,' she said, 'and I don't blame you, really I don't. I'd like for us to remain friends. We can do that, can we not?'

Thomas reached for her hand and she slid her fingers into his. There was a familiarity to the gesture that he knew he would miss. 'Of course we can,' he said with more enthusiasm than he felt. 'And you will never want for anything, Joan—'

'No, Tom,' she said, snatching her hand away. 'You've already given me so much.'

'Nevertheless, I mean it. I will not see you struggle. You need only write to me should you need anything, and I shall send you money every month, at least until you are married.'

She looked at him, surprised. 'Why talk you of a husband? I have none in mind.'

'But you deserve one,' he said, 'and I shall find one for you. You're still young enough to have another child.'

'One I can keep,' she said sadly.

'Aye,' he nodded, 'one you can keep. You need not worry about ours, Joan. They will always be looked after.'

'I know, and you will let me visit them from time to time?'

'Of course, but not—'

'But not as their mother.' She nodded. 'I know.'

'I'm sorry,' he said, knowing how inadequate his apology was.

Joan reached up and stroked his face. 'You're a good man, Thomas. I shall always love you.'

'Just not enough to put up with all this,' he laughed and gestured at the hangings as she had done.

She didn't answer. 'I'm going now,' she said. 'I'll send the men up for the trunks.'

'But I was going to tell you about France,' he protested even as she walked past him to the door.

'Oh, I know it was marvellous,' she said carelessly. 'Brian wrote to me, told me all about it. I hope the king appreciates all you did. I should say you've earned a rest. I'll write from Elizabeth's. Goodbye, Tom.'

'Goodbye, Joan,' he said.

And then she was gone.

He stood staring at the closed door for a long moment, until it opened again and four servants entered to take away the trunks. He nodded at them to get on with it, then went into the inner chamber to disrobe, not wanting to call his body servant to help him, wanting to be alone, if only for a moment. A few minutes later, he heard the food he had ordered being laid out for him in the bedchamber. Clad in his dressing gown, he went into the other room, sat down at the table and began to eat.

He chewed the pork without really tasting it, drank the wine without savouring the bouquet. He couldn't blame Joan for leaving him. Now he thought about it, he could see that his way of life hadn't been much fun for her. He should be grateful that she had stayed with him as long as she had. His bed would feel cold and empty, he knew, but he was no longer a young man and thoughts of the flesh rarely troubled him. He could get another woman, he supposed, but he found he lacked the desire to do so. *I'm really too busy to waste time dallying with women*, he mused. *Maybe it's for the best that I'm on my own. Joan has done me a favour. I can truly concentrate on my work now.*

The door opened and one of his secretaries strode in. 'Forgive me for disturbing you, Your Eminence, but a letter has just arrived from the king. I thought you would want to read it without delay.'

Thomas sighed. He hadn't been at Hampton Court for an hour and already the king was claiming him. He dabbed his lips with his napkin and held out his hand for the king's letter.

'No rest for the wicked, eh?'

COMING SOON

Thomas Wolsey's story will conclude in

'Forsaken'

AUTHOR'S NOTE

This novel has attempted to cover the personal and professional life of Thomas Wolsey during the years 1515 to 1520, from the beginning of his true reign of power as cardinal to the pinnacle of his international achievements, the Field of Cloth of Gold.

Wolsey was such a busy churchman, administrator, politician, diplomat and courtier that it would have been impossible to cover everything he was involved in during these years. To say that I have cherry-picked when writing this novel is an understatement.

So, the reader will not have found all the treaties and alliances, achieved and attempted, within these pages. There were many of these in this period, some between Continental powers, and others in which England played a minor role. I have chosen to portray only those that had a significant meaning or impact on Wolsey.

Events in Scotland, apart from a very brief

mention, have had no place in this novel. Margaret Tudor's troubles in Scotland had very little bearing upon Wolsey personally, and as the matter of her deposition and return to Scotland dragged on for over a year and involved many negotiations, I felt it would be tedious for myself and for the reader to include it.

Then there are the smaller matters that I have decided to omit. For instance, I have not included Wolsey being made godfather to Charles Brandon's son. The reader might think this important in terms of relationships between characters, but in reality such an event meant little personally, and I felt it did not warrant inclusion.

The reader may have expected Thomas Cromwell to put in an appearance. While Cromwell was almost certainly in Wolsey's service at this point, he would have been only one secretary amongst very many, and I felt that to include him was not only unnecessary but would have taken something away from Wolsey himself.

In regards to secretaries, to avoid burdening the reader with too many names, I chose to merge all the clerical staff who would have been employed by Wolsey into the person of Brian Tuke, a real historical figure who did serve Wolsey as secretary.

As for Joan Larke, Wolsey's mistress, I was unable to discover exactly when she and he decided to part, but I felt that the ending of their relationship provided a fittingly anticlimactic coda to the novel, coming as it does after Wolsey has had his greatest professional triumph.

If you have enjoyed this book, it would be wonderful if you could spare the time to post an honest review on whichever retailer platforms you use.

Reviews are incredibly important to authors. Your review will help bring my books to the attention of other readers who may enjoy them.

Thank you so much.

∼

Join my mailing list to stay up-to-date with my writing news, new releases and more.

Join at my website here:
www.lauradowers.com

Made in the USA
Las Vegas, NV
09 September 2023